MURDER RUNS IN THE FAMILY

THE BEELER LARGE PRINT MYSTERY SERIES

Edited by Audrey A. Lesko

Also Available in Beeler Large Print by Anne George

**Murder on a Girls' Night Out
Murder on a Bad Hair Day**

MURDER RUNS IN THE FAMILY

ANNE GEORGE

BEELER LARGE PRINT

Hampton Falls, New Hampshire, 2000

Library of Congress Cataloging-in-Publication Data

George, Anne
    Murder runs in the family / Anne George
        p.   cm—(The Beeler Large Print mystery series)
    ISBN 1-57490-258-X (acid-free paper)
        1. Patricia Anne (Fictitious character)—Fiction. 2. Mary
    Alice (Fictitious character)—Fiction 3. Women detectives—
    Alabama—Fiction. 5. Genealogists—6. Alabama—Fiction.
    7. .Large type books.
    PS3557.E469 M874 2000
    813'.54—dc21   99-05883

Published in Large Print by arrangement with
Avon Books, Inc., a unit of The Hearst Corporation.

BEELER LARGE PRINT
is published by
Thomas T. Beeler, *Publisher*
Post Office Box 659
Hampton Falls, New Hampshire 03844

Typeset in 16 point Adobe Garamond type.
Printed on acid-free paper, sewn and bound by
Sheridan Books in Chelsea, Michigan.

For all the Freds, especially mine.

ACKNOWLEDGEMENTS

My thanks to the librarians at the Birmingham Public Library and Samford University for their help. The special genealogical collections at both institutions are truly remarkable and were made available for my use. I would also like to thank Doris Temple, Virginia Martin, and Mary Fondren, whose love of genealogy was contagious and who were always patient when I would call and ask, "Look, what if—".

CHAPTER 1

"PUKEY LUKEY IS HERE," MY SISTER MARY ALICE murmured as she was ushered into the front pew beside me. She turned and gave the groomsman a little wave.

"Did she say Pukey Lukey's here?" my husband Fred whispered into my left ear.

I nodded. Luke is our cousin from Columbus, Mississippi, who always went to the beach with us when we were children. His car sickness was so epic, it has become a family legend.

Handel's Water Music soared to the vaulted ceiling of Birmingham's St. Mark's Episcopal Church.

"You look great," I whispered to Mary Alice. And she did. She actually looked rather regal with her usually pink hair calmed down to an ash blonde, and the tunic top of her lavender dress knocking off about thirty pounds. Which still left her at well over two hundred. "Five twelve and pleasingly plump," she describes herself.

"Hmmm," Mary Alice said, checking me out. "You look good, too, Patricia Anne." Rare praise. I smoothed the blue chiffon skirt I had bought at The Petite Shoppe, size six. Mary Alice and I are asked all the time if we are really sisters. Mary Alice sometimes asks what they mean by "really," which confuses the questioner. I tell her that's tacky, that God knows, after sixty years, she should be used to the question and just answer yes.

"What's on your hair?" she asked.

"Roux Spun Sand. It'll wash out."

"That's a shame."

"Tell her I like your gray hair," Fred whispered.

I thought about this a moment. Then, "Fred likes my

1

gray hair," I relayed to Sister.

"Hah."

Handel's Water Music fortunately blanketed my answer.

Mary Alice looked around. "Do you think the flowers are too dark a pink?" she whispered.

"Absolutely not. They're beautiful."

"I cannot believe Debbie is having a wedding like this."

I couldn't either. Mary Alice's daughter, my niece Debbie Nachman, is a successful thirty-six-year-old lawyer, the single mother of two-year-old twin daughters. When she and her fiancé, Henry Lamont, announced at Christmas that they were being married in March, none of us had expected Pomp and Circumstance. But they fooled us. Which was how we ended up in the first row of St. Mark's with at least three hundred people in the pews behind us.

"That stained-glass window doesn't look much like Jesus," Sister muttered.

"What did she say?" Fred asked.

"She said that stained-glass window doesn't look like Jesus."

"She should know. Probably knew him."

"What did he say?" Mary Alice asked.

"Nothing." I raised my eyebrows at Fred. At sixty-five, Mary Alice is only five years older than I am: Two years older than Mr. Smart Alec on my left.

"Yes, he did. He said something about how old I am."

"Ignore him."

"What did she say?" Fred whispered.

The organ segued into "Ode to Joy," and the crowd rustled expectantly. The side door opened and Henry, the groom, and our son Freddie, the best man, followed the minister out. They looked so handsome, I opened my

2

purse and started looking for a Kleenex.

"Oh, God. They're both chewing gum," Mary Alice hissed.

"What did she say?" Fred asked.

"They're chewing gum, Fred!"

The men turned to face the audience. Freddie smiled at us, and all three of us made chewing motions madly. For a second he looked surprised, and then we saw his Adam's apple disappear as he swallowed. He poked Henry with his elbow, and in a minute Henry's gum went down, too.

"Good," Mary Alice nodded.

Our daughter, Haley, was the first down the aisle. The rose-colored bridesmaid dress, while not practical, was very becoming. Its Basque bodice made her waist look incredibly tiny, and the color gave her olive skin a pink glow.

Mary Alice's daughter, Marilyn, was her sister's matron of honor. Almost six feet tall and brunette, she was so much like her mother had been at that age, it was eerie. To see her standing by my five-one, reddish blond Haley was to see Sister and me thirty years before.

The organ crashed into a fanfare that brought everyone to their feet, and the bride swept down the aisle on her cousin Philip Nachman's arm. Really swept. Her dress would have put Princess Di's to shame.

"My God," Fred said. "That much virginal white could damage your retina."

"Shut up." I punched him with my elbow as we sat back down.

"Dearly beloved," the minister began. Mary Alice and I both got out Kleenex.

It was a traditional ceremony. Debbie, this most independent of women in her thirties, who had been making it on her own for years and doing a fine job of it, thank-you-ma'am, and who, when she decided she wanted children, had been inseminated at the University sperm bank, was "given" by her cousin to Henry Lamont, who was seven years her junior. A wonderful man, granted, but without the proverbial pot to pee in. A temporary condition. Henry was going to be one of the great American chefs. We, all knew it.

After the vows were exchanged, Debbie and Henry knelt for a prayer, and then the organist blasted out the recessional. They stopped to kiss Mary Alice and an elderly cousin of Henry's who had sat in the mother's place on his side. The wedding party rushed by, grinning, and then Philip Nachman escorted his Aunt Sister out while Freddie collected Henry's cousin.

"Well, that's it," Fred said.

People were getting up, talking, laughing. I wiped my eyes one last time.

"That was a sticking wedding," I said.

"A what?"

"You know. You can just tell some couples are going to stick together."

We worked our way out into the aisle.

"Didn't you tell me Mary Alice promised old Philip to raise Debbie as a Jew?" Fred asked. "I wouldn't exactly call this place a temple. Maybe a cathedral."

The "old" Philip that Fred was referring to was Debbie's father, Mary Alice's second husband. He was also the uncle of "young" Philip Nachman, his namesake, who had given the bride away. "She said she forgot to," I explained.

"She forgot to?" Fred laughed, really laughed, was still laughing as we went out the church door. And I realized I hadn't heard that deep chuckling laugh of his in quite some time. A pinprick of worry tingled for a second. But

4

only for a second, as we were caught up in the crowd of friends and relatives that milled around the front of the church.

"Patricia Anne!" Pukey Lukey hugged me. He is a distinguished-looking multi-millionaire insurance executive in his sixties. He is married to a lovely woman and is the father of a member of the House of Representatives. In short, he has led an exemplary life, been a shining star in the family pantheon. Mary Alice still hates him.

"There was puke in his eyelashes!" she says. "It's one thing to be car sick, but he just exploded. Ruined every vacation we ever went on."

Sister remembers these early excursions to the beach better than I do. I like Luke, though I tend to keep my distance—just in case.

"Luke," I said, moving back, "how nice to see you. I know Sister will be thrilled you're here."

He looked pleased. I think he still harbors the hope that Mary Alice will forgive him some day. After all, it has been sixty years.

Luke shook hands with Fred, and I hugged his wife Virginia.

"Such a beautiful wedding," she said. "Minnie says it's the prettiest one he's ever seen."

Minnie is Virginia's nickname for Luke. She confessed to Sister and me at another family celebration where she had singularly downed a bottle of Gallo Rhine that it was short for "Minute Man." A confession that brought pure joy to Sister's heart. Poor Luke.

"It was beautiful," I agreed.

"And Haley looked like a doll. And Freddie and Alan were so handsome."

I beamed. My children might not be in the House of Representatives, but they are, indeed, very nice, beautiful

5

people.

"And the flowers were gorgeous. That pink! And Debbie's dress was fantastic. And the groom is so cute I could eat him with a spoon."

I cast an appraising eye at Virginia, who kept on babbling. She had started her celebrating early, I realized.

"Patricia Anne!" My friend Bonnie Blue Butler had worked her way through the crowd. "Wasn't that some wedding?"

I agreed that it was and introduced her to Luke and Virginia.

"You're from Columbus, aren't you?" she said, shaking Luke's hand. "Mary Alice talks about you all the time."

Luke looked pleased. "That's nice to hear."

"Does anybody need a ride to the reception?" Virginia asked.

"No!" we chorused.

"We need to go on ahead because we can't stay long."

"We'll see you there," I said.

"Pukey Lukey is a fine-looking fellow." Bonnie Blue watched them walking away.

"He's nice, too. I'm just glad he doesn't live closer to Sister. She'll never forgive him." We thought about that a minute. "She still hasn't forgiven me for losing her Shirley Temple doll." We thought about that a minute, too. "Fifty-five years."

"You want to ride with us to the reception, Bonnie Blue?" Fred asked. "We'll bring you back here."

"Sure."

"I'll go get the car. You ladies have on heels."

"That's a fine-looking gentleman, too," Bonnie Blue said as Fred left. I couldn't have agreed more. At sixty-three, Fred still has a young man's walk. I pushed my bifocals down and watched him. Nice!

6

The crowd was in no hurry to disperse. A warm March sun made it pleasant to stand in front of the church and chat. No doubt about it, Debbie had lucked out on the weather for her wedding day. In March, anything can happen weatherwise in Alabama. And usually does. Birmingham's only recorded blizzard roared through several years ago on March 13, leaving eighteen inches of snow and 500,000 traumatized people, most of whom had never seen more than a dusting of snow in their whole lives. But today was glorious. Happy the bride the sun shines on.

"You look mighty festive," I told Bonnie Blue.

"Big, Bold, and Beautiful Shoppe," she said. "Look at this." She turned so I could see the back of the cream-colored suit. The jacket was cut in a modified "V" in the back, and the skirt had a long kick pleat that mirrored the "V" of the jacket.

"Snazzy," I said.

"Slimming."

"Good-looking."

"Thanks." Bonnie Blue grinned at me. "I like your outfit, too. I trust they didn't charge you full price for something that little."

"A bundle," I admitted.

Several people called hello or stopped to speak. Traffic was inching by, but the sun felt warm and I was in no burry to leave. Bonnie Blue yawned.

"My feelings exactly," I said. "I didn't sleep much last night. We didn't get back from the rehearsal party until after twelve and then I couldn't go to sleep."

"But we got them married.

"We sure did."

Bonnie Blue Butler is one of my favorite people. I first met her at the Skoot 'n Boot, a country-western bar that

7

Sister bought, swearing it was a wise investment, since line dancing was the hottest thing since the jitterbug. Bonnie Blue was working there, running the place actually. The first time I saw her, I remember thinking she and Mary Alice looked like each other's negative. The same size, the same way of walking, the same mannerisms. They even carried identical purses. But Bonnie Blue was about fifteen years younger and her skin was a beautiful coppery chocolate.

But it was our shared love of Henry Lamont, today's groom, that really made us fast friends. Bonnie Blue had worked with him and I had taught him, and I think he was as dear to each of us as a son.

Now we stood together waiting for the car that was moving about a foot a minute. The car in which we could see Fred tapping his palms on the steering wheel.

"Debbie better make that Henry happy," Bonnie Blue said. "That's all I got to say about it."

"Amen," I agreed. Then I remembered Debbie was my niece and that I loved her. "I hope they make each other happy."

"Amen. You and Fred have been married how long?"

"Forty years. Forty happy years."

The car pulled up in front of us and Fred leaned over and opened the car door. "Dammit! Next time you walk."

The reception was held at The Club. This is a beautiful private club on the crest of Red Mountain. Not much imagination went into naming it, but a lot went into the design of the building. Every room has walls of windows that afford spectacular views of the city of Birmingham on one side, and on the other Shades Valley and Shades Mountain.

There are two things that always startle people who are visiting Birmingham for the first time. The first is that the terrain is mountainous, the rolling last gasp of the Appalachian chain, rich in ore. The second is the statue of Vulcan, the god of the forge. The largest iron statue in the world, it stands on the crest of Red Mountain close to The Club where the reception was being held. Visible from anywhere in downtown Birmingham, it makes getting lost almost impossible. Head toward it, you're going south. If it's on your left, you're heading west. So it does serve a navigational purpose as well as being a symbol of the iron industry that the city was built upon.

And it's a nice tourist attraction. There's a pleasant park at the base of the statue for picnics, and the people who climb the steps to the top of the statue are rewarded with a spectacular view of downtown Birmingham and distant mountains. There is also a neat little gift shop with T-shirts and beer huggers emblazoned with the back view of Vulcan and the words, "Buns of Iron." That's because the picnickers are being mooned by the largest iron butt in the world. So are all the residents on the south side of Red Mountain. Vulcan, the god of the forge, wears an apron that comes only halfway around.

Every few years, a halfhearted attempt will be made to cover Vulcan's derriere. But nothing comes of it. The truth is that most of us are rather fond of old Vulcan, bare-assed though he is.

From The Club, the view of Vulcan is from the side, so he looks fairly majestic. Many of the guests had already moved onto the terrace and, like Vulcan, were looking over the city. The wedding party was in the ballroom, though. Debbie and Henry had decided not to have a receiving line, but we could see the white dress surrounded by well-wishers. Mary Alice was nowhere in sight.

"I wonder where Sister is," I said.

9

"Here," she hissed in my ear, making me jump. "Come help me do something with these pantyhose. They keep working their way down to my knees."

"Are those the pantyhose I sold you? I told you to get the extra-long queen. What did you do? Just get queen?" Bonnie Blue, who works at the Big, Bold, and Beautiful Shoppe, was taking Sister's plight personally.

"I think I'll go get some champagne or something," Fred said.

Bonnie Blue frowned. "Cause if you just got queen you're gonna be walking like a duck all day and not a thing we can do about it."

"I bought what you put on the counter."

"Then you got the extra long. Let's go see what's wrong, cause that's bound to be what I sold you. I don't believe that's what you put on, though. Extra long you got no trouble. Look at this." She held up her leg for our appraisal.

I watched the two of them walk away. Mary Alice was, indeed, walking like a penguin.

"Hey, Mama." My daughter Haley came by, holding the arm of Dr. Philip Nachman, who had stood in as the father of the bride for his late uncle. Uncle Philip is buried with Sister's other two husbands at Elmwood. Together.

"Have you heard them complain?" Sister asks.

"Where's Papa?" Haley asked.

"Gone to get some champagne."

"Go look at the cakes. They're incredible." Haley gave a little wave, and they headed toward the terrace. Philip leaned down and said something to Haley, and she smiled at him.

"Hmm," I said to myself, watching them.

I looked around for Fred, but he had disappeared. I decided to take Haley's advice and go see the cakes.

"Mrs. Hollowell?"

I turned to see Henry's cousin, who had filled in as the mother of the groom. A lot of substitutes at this wedding.

"Mrs. Bryan, how are you? Wasn't it a beautiful wedding?" I had met her the night before at the after-rehearsal party. Sister had introduced me to "Meg Ryan."

"Bryan," she had corrected gently.

"I'm sorry," Sister said. "I can't imagine why I keep saying that."

I couldn't either. Meg Bryan was nobody's gorgeous young movie star. More the Jessica Tandy type. Frail-looking with wispy gray hair, she had an intelligent face with strong echoes of youthful beauty. Our grandmother would have labeled her immediately "Southern Lady."

"I don't think I've ever seen a lovelier wedding," she said. "Henry's mother and aunt, God rest their souls, would have been so proud of him today up at that altar. They would have been pleased that he swallowed his gum, too."

Meg Bryan and I smiled at each other. "Would you like some champagne?" I asked.

"That would be lovely. And to tell you the truth, I'd love to have a go at the buffet. Have you seen it yet?"

I shook my head. "We just got here."

"It's unbelievable."

"Henry planned it," I said.

"That's what he told me. I think he's found his niche, don't you?"

I agreed. "You know he's going to be a chef at the Brookwood Country Club, don't you? He'll start as soon as he gets back from his honeymoon."

"And your sister is talking about buying a restaurant and making Henry a partner. Wouldn't that be nice?"

I thought about sweet, imaginative Henry in business

11

with his formidable mother-in-law. "Yes, indeed," I lied through my teeth. "'Come on, let's see if we can get to the buffet. I want to see the wedding cakes, too."

Most of the guests were still clustered in the center of the ballroom, so Meg Bryan and I had an unobstructed view out of the window as we walked by, I spotted Fred on the terrace talking to Lukey (the Minute Man) and Virginia. All of them held out empty champagne glasses for refills as a waiter walked by. I tried to remember if I had ad put any aspirin in my purse. He'd be looking for some soon.

"Meg Bryan!" a voice hissed loudly. Meg and I both jumped and turned to see a very blond, very elegant-looking middle-aged woman in a yellow suit advancing on us. She was gripping a stick of celery, and from the look on her face, had it been a knife, Meg Bryan would have been in trouble.

"Hello, Camille," Meg said.

"You bitch." The woman thrust the celery at Meg, who automatically reached out and took it. "Stick it!" With that, she turned and stalked toward the door.

"What in the world?" I was so startled, it took me a moment to speak.

"A dissatisfied client. It happens." Meg's face was pink, but she calmly opened her purse and dropped the celery into it. "I always forget that Birmingham is beautiful," she said, looking down at the city and deliberately changing the subject.

"I do, too," I admitted, looking around to see if any more dissatisfied clients were approaching us wielding vegetables.

"It's just so different from South Alabama. The vegetation. Everything."

"'You're from Fairhope?" I watched the woman Meg

had addressed as Camille disappear through the door.

Meg nodded. "Right on Mobile Bay. Lived there all my life."

"That's beautiful, too."

"Yes, it is. Sometimes I think it's too beautiful. Makes me not want to leave. And I do have to leave to do research. I'm a genealogist."

"That's interesting. You know all about your family tree, then."

"Sometimes I think I know about everybody's family tree." Meg Bryan smiled. "Which is what caused the little scene a moment ago. I'm a professional genealogist, and Camille Atchison had me doing some research for her. Obviously, she didn't like my findings."

"Obviously." I thought of the anger on the woman's face.

Meg continued, "While I'm here, I'm going to Samford University and the Birmingham Public Library to do some work. Both of them are excellent research centers. Are you familiar with the Southern History Department at the library?"

"My first job was there," I said. "You're going to be rambling through some of the stuff I filed forty years ago."

"Oh, most of it is on computer now. You can just pull it right up."

"Un huh," I said, suddenly feeling a hundred years old.

"And my last computer is so small it's no problem to carry. Fits in my briefcase. The genealogy program I use is pretty good, too. DOS based, which is fine. I'm writing a new Windows one that's better, though."

"Un huh." I looked at Meg Bryan, who seemed to have sloughed about twenty years. Her eyes were bright and her cheeks were still flushed from the Camille incident.

"I tell you, Mrs. Hollowell, the world of genealogy is a

13

dog-eat-dog world. You know?"

"I never thought about it before," I admitted. "But I think you may be right."

"Well, it is. Dog-eat-dog."

"But you enjoy it?"

"I'm a big dog."

And I believed her. This frail old lady had suddenly become Jessica Tandy with an overlay of pit bull, eyes narrowed and lips curled. I had been about to ask her what, specifically, had made Camille Atchison so angry, but decided it was none of my business and that she would tell me so, politely, but in no uncertain terms.

"For instance," she continued as we worked our way to the buffet table, "suppose you find Henry Hudson's maternal great grandfather. Absolutely perfect documentation. You better guard it like a setting hen or somebody'll steal the nest egg. You know what I mean?"

I had no idea what she meant. Why would anybody be looking for Henry Hudson's maternal great grandfather? I nodded politely, though.

"Not just amateurs, either. Professionals. Are you a DAR, Mrs. Hollowell?"

"I don't think so."

"The Daughters of the American Revolution. Are you a member?"

"No."

"Oh, you should be. Your maiden name was Tate, wasn't it?"

I nodded.

"Incredible!"

"It's a fairly common name around here."

"I meant the cake." Meg Bryan stopped. "Would you look at that!"

In sixty years of attending weddings, I had never seen

14

such a cake. It rose in many tiers of white icing decorated with marzipan flowers the same pink as the bridesmaids' dresses. On the top were rubric lilies that matched the bouquets the bridesmaids had carried.

"Good Lord," I said, wondering if "baroque" could describe a wedding cake. "How are they ever going to cut it?"

"Very carefully." The groom had come up behind us. We both hugged him and wished him every happiness.

"A beautiful wife and two daughters. How could I miss?"

He had also just added on Sister as a mother-in-law. But I smiled and agreed that he would be sublimely happy from this moment on.

Henry kissed each of us on the cheek. "Aunt Pat. Cousin Meg. Y'all get you some lunch now."

We assured him that we would, and watched him greeting other guests as he walked away.

"Yes, indeed," Meg Bryan said. "Henry's going to be fine."

It wasn't crowded at the buffet table yet because most of the guests were still concentrating on champagne. It's at parties like this that I most regret being allergic to alcohol. It would have been nice to let the bubbly add to the celebration. On the other hand, I enjoy the food more.

I was piling my plate with fruit, sliced turkey, little quiches, and various salads when Sister came up.

"I know you're anorexic, but would you please make an effort. This stuff cost me a fortune."

I just grinned. "Thanks, I will." I took another quiche. "Did you get your problem solved?"

"Bonnie Blue had another pair in her purse. They're a little dark, but God knows you shouldn't look a gift horse in the mouth. I told Bonnie Blue, I said, 'Bonnie Blue, I

15

can't believe you're this organized.' Can you, Patricia Anne? Believe Bonnie Blue's that organized?"

"She's organized."

Mary Alice turned to Meg Bryan. "Are you getting some of everything? How about the tortellini salad?"

"I'm fine. Thanks."

"Fruit? How about a peach? God only knows where they came from in March, but I'm supporting some third-world country this month."

"No, thank-you," Meg smiled.

"Go mingle," I told Sister, "and count not the cost."

"Count not the cost? Are you crazy? I may have to get married again."

"There's no one here old enough."

Mary Alice frowned. "I cannot believe you said that, Patricia Anne." She started to walk away and turned. "Oh, by the way, Fred's out on the terrace tête-a-têting with some blonde."

"There's no such verb, Sister."

"Well, whatever you call it, he's doing it." This time she kept going.

Meg Bryan laughed. "You two sound like me and my sisters."

"How many do you have?"

"Four. I'm the oldest. Our family name was March, so there's Jo, Amy, Beth—" She noticed the look on my face and smiled. "Beth lives in Hawaii with her husband and three children. The rest of us are still in Fairhope."

I grinned. "You scared me for a minute.

"How do you think Beth's always felt? The third daughter is Trinity, though. Papa named her. I think he thought that would be the end of it, but Mama got right back to her plan."

"They're fine names."

16

"Yes, they are. Trinity and I are both widowed now and live in the old family home."

Both our plates were full. "Tell you what," I said, "why don't we just take our food and mosey out to the terrace? It's so nice out there." Also no one out there was wearing a yellow suit.

"Fine," Meg agreed.

CHAPTER 2

MARY ALICE HAD BEEN TELLING THE TRUTH; FRED WAS in deep conversation with a cute young blonde. Since my hands were full, I nudged him gently in the leg with the toe of my shoe. There was no reason for him to say, "Ow," and jump like he had been shot. I suggested later that maybe the champagne had lowered his pain threshold, but he said that wasn't it, that I had kicked him hard as a son-of-a-bitch.

Be that as it may, and it's my word against his, Meg Bryan and I were introduced to Kelly Stuart, a manufacturer's rep who called on Fred and who—big smile with Nancy Kerrigan teeth—just loved doing business with him.

"Oh, my, what wonderful-looking food, Mrs. Hollowell," Kelly said. "I think I'll have to go get some before I faint dead away. I'm famished. You want me to bring you a plate, Fred?"

"No thanks," Fred smirked, remembering to move his leg just in time. "I'll get something after a while."

"I'll see you later, then." She gave us a little wave.

"What does she sell?" I asked. Fred owns a small metal fabricating plant, not the kind of place where you would picture a pretty and flirty Kelly.

17

"Nuts and bolts. You know." At least he had the decency to look sheepish.

"You want some food?" I asked, taking pity.

He reached over and took a quiche from my plate. "That's good."

"Why, don't we go sit on the wall? We can share."

"Do you mind if we sit at one of the tables?" Meg asked. "Heights bother me."

"Sure." Several of the wrought iron tables were empty, since most of the guests were still milling about. We settled at one of them and relaxed in the sun.

"This is some fancy reception," Fred said.

"Sister says she may have to get married again to pay for it."

Fred and I laughed comfortably, but I realized that Meg Bryan didn't know why.

"She's had three husbands," I explained. "All of them were at least twenty-eight years older than she was and rich as Croesus. She has to worry about money like she does a hole in her head."

"And Debbie's father?"

"He was the middle one, Philip Nachman. She had a child by each one. Marilyn, the oldest, is Will Alec Sullivan's child. And Ray belongs to Roger Crane. Ray's not here today. He's in Bora Bora or Pago Pago, one of those double-named places. He just bought a dive ship. That's why Philip Nachman gave Debbie away. Not the daddy Philip, but the nephew. Cousin. Am I confusing you?"

"No."

"You're confusing me," Fred said.

"Meg keeps up with names professionally," I said. "She's a genealogist."

"Is that right? I'd like to look up my family tree

18

someday," Fred said, surprising me. I'd never heard him mention it before. He reached over and helped himself to a cantaloupe cube from my plate.

"Birmingham is a good place to do it." Meg looked animated. "There's a special collection at both Samford and the public library."

"I might do that," Fred declared.

"Mary Alice has been kind enough to invite me to stay over for a few days while I do some research. I'd be happy to show you how to get started."

"I know the names as far back as my great great grandfather on my father's side," Fred said.

"Then you're well on your way. Some people who come to me don't even know who their grandparents were."

The plate that was on the table between Fred and me was almost empty. I got up and announced I was going for a refill and asked if I could bring them anything.

"My great grandmother was born in Madison, Georgia. I know that much," Fred said.

I don't even think they knew when I left.

Inside the ballroom, the crowd was standing in a circle around the dance floor. The =66=combo was playing "Wind Beneath My Wings," and Debbie and Henry were dancing. I scooted back out and got Fred and Meg. "You don't want to miss this," I said.

The looks on the newlyweds' faces said it all. Henry held Debbie lightly as they moved around the dance floor, and neither took their eyes off the other. It was possible, I thought, that this was the real moment of marriage. And then Richardena Tucker, the twins' nanny, stepped onto the floor holding a toddler with each hand. Debbie took one little girl and Henry the other. And they danced, first separately, each holding a child, and then together with Fay and May held between them. It was, as Sister said later, a Kleenex moment.

And then the whole wedding party moved onto the dance floor. Haley was dancing with Dr. Nachman and seemed to be enjoying herself immensely. I tried to remember what Sister had told me about him. Widowed. Mid-fifties.

"What kind of doctor is Philip Nachman?" I asked Fred.

"Philip Nachman?"

"The nephew. Dancing with Haley."

"Don't know anything about him, honey."

"Look at them. I think we're going to find out."

"Then let him be a sinus doctor. Please, God, let my daughter bring home a sinus doctor."

I laughed, but only at his tone of voice. Knock on any door in Birmingham, Alabama, and a sinus sufferer will answer. Maybe it's the warmth, the humidity, the lush foliage. Who knows? But a good ENT (Ears, Nose, and Throat) is worth his weight in gold here. Literally after a few years' practice. People in other parts of the country say we talk through our noses. Well, yes.

The dance ended, everyone clapped, and there was a general rush to the food.

"This would be a good time to speak to Debbie and Henry," I said. I looked around and saw Meg Bryan talking to Mary Alice. I caught her eye and motioned that we were going over to see the bride and groom. She nodded fine.

Debbie and Henry still stood holding the two-year-old twins, Fay and May. Neither Sister nor I can tell the girls apart, though Sister swears she can. She also is sure Henry is their father, because he was a donor at the sperm bank when he was in college. Today I wasn't sure she was wrong. Henry's face was bent toward the twin he was holding and she was looking up at him, and the resemblance was eerie.

"Aunt Pat! Uncle Fred!" Debbie greeted us. "I wondered where you were."

We hugged her, admired her dress, and wished for her, with all our hearts, supreme joy.

"We'll have you over for dinner soon as we get back," Henry promised, shaking Fred's hand.

"We'll hold you to that."

A final hug and we moved to make room for some other well-wishers. As we started off, Fred said, "Wait a minute," and ran back and whispered something in Debbie's ear. As he came back toward me, he was beaming. "ENT!"

The next hour passed quickly. The cake was cut, the top tier saved for the wedding couple's first anniversary. At one point we saw Mary Alice in animated conversation with a man who looked like Father Time with a brunette rug. Ninety, at least, he wasn't doing much of the animated conversing, but he did look interested in what Sister was saying.

"By George," Fred said, "I think she's done it."

"Could be," I agreed. "I think Bill better hurry back from Florida." Bill Adams has been Sister's "boyfriend" for several months. A nice, handsome man of seventy-two, strong enough to dip Sister when they dance, he was spending the winter months, as he always did, in St. Petersburg. Absence was not making Sister's heart grow fonder. Even the Valentine roses and the card, "Come on down. With love, Your Snowbird," had not appeased her. "Whoever heard of a snowbird from Alabama!" she snorted. His absence from Debbie's wedding was probably the death knell for that romance.

Our son, Alan, and his wife, Lisa, stopped to chat for a

21

moment. They were staying with us, so we would have a good visit later. Right now, Lisa was bubbling about the cake and Debbie's dress and had we noticed how well Haley and Philip Nachman seemed to be getting along.

"He's an ENT." Fred said. "Pray, children. Pray."

"He's at least twenty years older than she is," Alan said.

"At the pinnacle of his profession. Pray, children."

They left, laughing, and Bonnie Blue took their place with the announcement that her feet no longer had feeling in them and she would be on the terrace with her shoes off when we got ready to go.

A loud noise outside made the combo's ineffective drumroll even more ineffective.

"What on God's earth?" Fred asked.

I knew the surprise Sister had planned. I grabbed Fred's hand and started toward the terrace. "Come on, Bonnie Blue."

We rushed outside to see a helicopter hovering over The Club. As we watched, it settled on the helipad on the roof.

"Is that the LifeSaver from Carraway Hospital?" Bonnie Blue asked.

"Of course not," I said. But her question was also answered by the bride and groom, who came from the ballroom followed by the members of the wedding as well as most of the guests. Debbie had changed into a short, pale-blue suit, but Henry was still in his formal wear.

"Good-bye!" everybody shouted as the newlyweds climbed the spiral stairs to the helicopter. "Good luck! Happy honeymoon!"

Debbie turned, looked, and threw her bouquet directly to Haley. Then they disappeared over the rooftop, and in a moment the helicopter rose into the air. We watched as it headed toward the airport across the valley.

22

"Wow," was all Bonnie Blue could say.

"Haley caught the bouquet," Fred said happily.

But I didn't say anything. I was too busy wiping the tears from my eyes so I could see the helicopter becoming smaller and smaller in the distance. Be happy, children. Be happy.

We dropped Bonnie Blue off at the church and headed home. I was tired, but pleasantly so. I reached over and patted Fred's leg. "You're a handsome man."

"Thank-you, ma'am. What brings this on?"

"Just thinking. And you're supposed to say, 'You're pretty good-looking yourself.' "

Fred covered my hand with his. "You are. You know I think so."

"I don't want any bottled blonde named Kelly bringing you food." I moved my hand farther up his leg and squeezed harder.

"Absolutely not. Scout's honor."

"Or selling you nuts and bolts." Farther and harder.

"Nuts and bolts are scratched."

"Or even smiling at you."

"No smiles! No smiles!" Fred was laughing and pushing against my hand, which had hit pay dirt. "For God's sake, Patricia Anne, you're going to make me have a wreck."

"Just remember," I said, giving him a good squeeze.

"I promise!"

"Cross your heart."

"Move your hand, woman. The guy in that pickup can see right in here."

"We're so old, he'll just think his eyes are deceiving him." I gave him another tweak. "Don't be so self-conscious, Fred."

"Self-conscious? My God, Patricia Anne, you're groping

23

me on the Red Mountain Expressway!"

"When you think about this later, and you will, be kind." I removed my hand, slowly. "Now, what is this about you wanting to look up your family history?"

"What?" Fred looked confused.

"You told Meg Bryan you wanted to look up your family history."

"Oh, that." Fred turned on the right turn signal for our exit. "I think it would be nice to know something about my family. Wouldn't you like to know where you came from?"

"I came from Mama and Daddy and Nanna and Granddaddy. And Grandmama Alice. That's enough."

"But think of all the people whose genes we carry. For instance, where did Haley get her olive skin? Strawberry-blond hair and olive complexion. Not your usual combination."

"But beautiful."

"Of course it is. But where did it come from?"

"The hair came from me. And Sister has olive skin. I'm sure you're in there somewhere, though."

"She was having a great time, wasn't she?"

The conversation had taken another ninety degree turn. After forty years, it's no problem following. "Great."

Haley is our youngest child and has been widowed for over two years. She and her husband, Tom, had married right out of college, but put off having a family while they established careers. Haley is a nurse and works in cardiac surgery; Tom was heading up the corporate ladder at one of Birmingham's largest engineering firms. At thirty-two, they were just beginning to think about a baby when a drunk driver put an end to everything. For a long time Haley was so immersed in grief, we wondered if we would ever see our laughing, happy daughter again. But in the past few months, she had been more like her old self. When we saw her enjoying herself like she had been today at the wedding, it did our hearts good.

We turned onto our street, a nice old neighborhood with sidewalks and porches. Leaves on the trees, just emerging, cast a green glow.

"Alan and Lisa aren't back, yet," Fred said. "They probably won't be back until late." He reached over and patted my leg.

"Then you've got time to go to the grocery for me," I said. "I've already got the list made out."

Fred tightened his hold on my leg and squeezed. "I don't want that produce man saving you those special grapefruits." Farther up my leg and a good squeeze.

We went into the house laughing.

Later, when I took our old dog Woofer for his afternoon walk, I thought about Debbie and Henry, how much they would learn about each other. How much they would never know about each other. But maybe that's the secret of a happy marriage, depths still there to plumb. Surprises. And a whole lot of luck. I shared this with Mitzi Phizer, a neighbor and old friend, who was out in her yard picking a bouquet of tulips.

"Nope," she said. "I plumbed all Arthur's depths at least thirty years ago and I'm still fond of the old fellow. The luck part I agree with, though." She handed me three red tulips. "Here. For your kitchen table. Now tell me about the wedding. I can't believe Barbara chose today to move, and I had to keep the baby." She pointed to the monitor beside her on the walk and smiled. "Listen to him snoring. He's so precious."

Mitzi is like a lot of people in our generation whose children have postponed parenthood. By the time you get grandchildren, you are overcome with the miracle of it.

Our Alan and Lisa have two boys that we adore, but they came at the usual grandparent age, and I was still much involved in my teaching career. I'm beginning to see that there's something akin to awe, though, in these older grandparents. I also realize that's probably how I'll feel when Haley has a baby.

I told Mitzi about the wedding. She listened to me with one ear and to the monitor with the other. The dress, the music, flowers, cake. The helicopter.

"Oh, my. Debbie went whole hog, didn't she? I wish I'd been there."

"It was quite a wedding," I agreed.

A tiny chirp from the monitor sent Mitzi scurrying. "Got to go. When Mary Alice gets the pictures, I want to see them," she called.

"Save a whole day!" I unwrapped Woofer's leash from my legs and woke him up. "Come on, lazy."

A car pulled up beside me. "Hey," Sister said. "Get in."

"What are you doing here? I thought you might still be at The Club."

"I just came from there. Everybody left at one time. One minute there was a big party going and next minute it was just me and the waiters. I started home and then decided I wanted to do a postmortem."

"Who died?"

"What do you mean 'who died?' "

"A postmortem?"

"On the wedding. You know." Sister looked a little down. Tired.

"I'll meet you back at the house," I said. "I'll be there in a minute."

Mary Alice nodded and drove off. I don't know why I was surprised to see her looking sad. After each of my children's weddings, I've had to go to bed for a couple of

26

days. All the excitement and planning and then it's over. An emotional roller coaster. And things are never the same again.

Mary Alice was sitting at the kitchen table and Fred was getting each of them a beer when I walked in.

"You want a Coke?" he asked. I nodded that I did.

"Gatlinburg?" he said, handing Sister her beer. "They flew to Gatlinburg?"

"They went to Gatlinburg?" I asked. I was surprised. Read Sunday's Birmingham News and you'll see that fifty percent of the newlyweds go to Gatlinburg for their honeymoon; forty-nine percent go to Panama City, Florida. Occasionally a couple, either very imaginative or moneyed, will opt for someplace exotic like the Virgin Islands. Somehow the helicopter had hinted strongly at this one percent.

"Debbie's car was at the airport," Sister admitted. "And Gatlinburg's fine."

"Of course it is," I agreed.

Sister sighed and took a long swig of her beer. "It's where Philip and I went on our wedding trip." She frowned. "Or maybe it was Will Alec." Another swig. "Anyway, it's a nice place for a honeymoon. Where did ya'll go? I can't remember."

"We didn't," I said. "No money. Two dollars for the license and ten dollars for the preacher did us in."

"Y'all should go on a honeymoon. A cruise. I know a wonderful travel agent I could fix you up with."

Fred changed the subject. "Where's Meg Bryan?"

"Haley and Philip took her home. Richardena and the twins, too. The babies were getting tired and Meg said she had some work to do."

"She told me she wanted to do some research while she was here," I said.

"She's a sweet lady," Mary Alice said. "I think it would be interesting being a professional genealogist."

"It's a dog-eat-dog world."

Sister and Fred both looked at me, surprised. I explained to them about Camille Atchison's anger, what Meg had said about people stealing information, about Henry Hudson's great grandfather, about Meg's pitbull look and being a big dog. "And how do you get to be a professional genealogist, anyway?" I wanted to know.

"You do it for a living?" Fred surmised.

"No, that's not it," Mary Alice said. "She told me she went to school at Samford and earned a professional certificate. It's a complicated business."

"Dog-eat-dog," I said.

"A degree in looking up ancestors?" Fred finished his beer and stood up. "Whoever heard of such."

"Something like that," Mary Alice said. "Get her to tell you."

"I will. I told her I might do some research into my family history, and she said she would show me how to get started."

"You want to find out about your family?" Mary Alice looked innocent, but Fred was suspicious.

"Why not?" he asked.

"Sometimes it's best to let sleeping dogs lie."

"What dogs?"

"The dogs that eat dogs." I couldn't resist.

Fred raised his eyebrows at me, got another beer from the refrigerator, and went out the back door.

"Now," Mary Alice said. "Let's get down to the postmortem."

The dresses, the flowers, the gum-chewing. Haley and Philip Nachman. Yes, indeed, Sister had noticed, and twenty years was not much of an age difference at all. The food, the cake, the dance with the twins, and no, I didn't think Mama would have thought that was tacky or the white dress either (we both knew I was lying through my teeth).

We hashed it all out. I even found out that the elderly man Sister had been dancing with was the CEO of the biggest bank in Birmingham.

"Buddy Johnson," she said. "Didn't you think he was handsome?"

"Maybe fifty years ago." The remark went unnoticed.

The sun was getting low in the sky. Alan and Lisa must have joined Freddie and Haley for an afternoon of partying.

"Seventeen yards in the train," Sister was saying. I looked out of the kitchen window and saw Fred sitting under the peach tree with Woofer beside him. He wasn't doing anything, maybe talking to Woofer. But just sitting on the ground is not like Fred. The slight alarm I had felt at the church became a clang. Something was not right with my husband.

CHAPTER 3

"I FEEL FINE, FRED INSISTED WHEN I CONFRONTED him. I had all but pushed Sister out of the door promising to call her later. "I'm just sitting here enjoying the weather."

"You've never just sat and enjoyed the weather in your life."

"Sure I have. Look how that peach tree is fixing to bloom. I hope we've had our last frost."

"Don't hand me that. What's wrong?"

"Nothing. I promise. I'm just a little worried about the

business."

The business. My heart slowed its racing. This I could handle.

"No pains in your chest? Shortness of breath? Nothing hurts?"

"Just my pride." Fred smiled. "Calm down, Patricia Anne. You're going to have me around for a while."

I sank down beside him. Woofer came and put his head in my lap. "Tell me," I said.

"It's nothing. Really. At least I hope not. Universal Satellite has quit sending us any of their business. I called, and they said we'd been taken off their approved supplier list."

"Why? They've always been your best customer."

"Damned if I know. I'm trying to get some answers."

"It'll be okay," I assured him. "I'm sure it's just a mistake."

"I hope so. I don't think we can get along without their business."

"Hey," I said. "We'll eat, and the house is paid for. Metal Fab isn't a vital organ." The last statement I wasn't sure about. The company Fred started and has nurtured for thirty years *is* vital to him. "It'll be okay," I said again.

"Sure it will. I'd like to hang onto it for a few more years, though, and sell it so we can retire with nothing to worry about." He got up and reached for my hand to pull me up. "Come on. It's too pretty a day to sit here moping."

"But why didn't you tell me?"

"There's not a thing you can do."

"I can worry with you."

"That's why I didn't tell you. I don't want you worrying."

Alan's car pulled into the driveway.

30

"This is between us. Okay?"

"Okay," I agreed.

Lisa leaned over the fence. "Hey, you two lovebirds. We've brought the biggest pizza you've ever seen."

It was nice having the two of them for a quiet visit. They live in Atlanta, as does Freddie, our oldest, and when they come they usually bring the children. But this weekend their boys were on a camping trip with the Scouts in the Smokies.

"I cried," Lisa said, "when I put them on the bus. They're growing up too fast."

"You need to think about having another one," I said.

Lisa and Alan both laughed. "It's Freddie and Haley's turn, Mama," Alan said. "Speaking of which, we've been at Haley's apartment watching basketball, and the ENT was there, Pop."

"Ah. The power of prayer." Fred reached for another piece of pizza. Worry hadn't affected his appetite.

About two o'clock in the morning, though, he was up taking Maalox.

"You're sure you're okay?" I mumbled.

"I'm fine. I promise. Go back to sleep, sweetheart."

And I did.

The wedding was on Saturday. Sunday was a quiet day. Lisa and Alan left around three to go back to Atlanta. We rented a movie at Video Express, and I opened a can of chicken noodle soup for supper. Fred didn't want to talk about Metal Fab, and Mary Alice didn't make one of her usual pop-in visits. It wasn't until Monday that, as Mama always said, the fit hit the Shan.

It started peacefully. Mary Alice called and asked if I would like to have lunch with her and Meg Bryan at the Tutwiler, that Meg was going to the library and she,

Sister, thought it would be nice to take her out to lunch and the Tutwiler was so convenient and so elegant since it had been completely remodeled that Meg would be impressed, surely, since she, Meg, remembered the old Tutwiler, the one that hadn't even been at the same place and what had been where the Tutwiler was now had been the Ridgeley apartments. Did I remember when the only drugstore open at night in Birmingham was the one in the old Tutwiler? Right in the middle of town and nobody ever robbed it, did they?

"What time?" I asked.

"Quarter to twelve. I'll pick you up."

I spent the morning straightening the house, changing the sheets, and doing a couple of loads of wash. I skipped my usual peanut butter and toast mid-morning snack so I could splurge on an elegant lunch, and got out the beige spring suit I had bought last year. The weather was holding, and Vulcan was mooning Shades Valley when Woofer and I had our walk.

Sister blew the horn right on time, and when I got in the car, I saw that she and Meg had dressed up, too. Sister was in a navy suit with a navy polka-dot blouse. Meg Bryan looked frail and lost in a bluish-gray linen jacket over a pale flowered dress. Skin, hair, and material all seemed to blend together. It made me wonder if I had imagined the pit bull.

But, no. She had come prepared with two briefcases, one of which contained her computer. The other contained documents that the CIA would have had trouble getting their hands on. At lunch, these briefcases occupied the fourth chair at our table. Occasionally, Meg would reach over and pat them. Shades of Jimmy Stewart and Harvey.

All in all, it was a pleasant lunch, though. We had ust ordered a piece of strawberry cheesecake to be cut in thirds when a deep voice behind me made me jump.

"Meg!"

Meg jumped, too. Then, "Hello, Bobby," she said.

"What are you doing here?"

"I came to my cousin's wedding. I'm going to do some research while I'm here."

"Where's Trinity?"

"At home."

The man had moved up behind the chair on which the briefcases rested. I half expected Meg to grab them. Instead, she introduced us.

"Mrs. Hollowell, Mrs. Crane, I'd like you to meet Judge Robert Haskins."

The judge acknowledged the introductions, though he clearly wasn't interested. "What are you researching?" he asked Meg.

"Don't you wish you knew." A smile flitted across Meg's face. Or was it just a curl of the lips?

"It's the Fitzpatrick thing, isn't it?" The judge was a small man with a pinched face. His small glasses kept sliding down his nose and he kept pushing them up

"Nothing important," Meg said. "Just a Mobile family."

"Did you finish the Whitleys?"

"Yes."

"Ah hah!" The judge pounded the back of the chair. "I was hoping you'd say that."

"Why?"

"You just think you have." He was actually chortling now. "You just think you have, Meggie, my girl."

"What do you mean?" Meg's face was as pink as it could ever be. More pale purple.

"I've got something in my office you need to see, Meg."

"What?"

"It'll cost you."

"Cost me what?"

"A look at Vincent Fitzpatrick."

Meg thought for a moment.

"Excuse me," the waiter reached around the judge to put our cheesecake down. "More coffee?"

"Please," Mary Alice and I said.

"Hand me that front briefcase, Bobby." Meg said. She took it from the judge and riffled through it, drawing out a manila envelope. "You show me yours and I'll show you mine."

"My office is right over at the courthouse, Meg. Just across the park."

"Let's go." Meg Bryan pushed her chair back. "I'll be in the Southern Department at the library in a little while, girls. Probably by the time you finish your coffee. Would you mind meeting me up there with my briefcases?"

Mary Alice and I looked at each other.

"Fine." Meg Bryan and Judge Haskins exited the dining room.

"What the hell was that about?" Sister wondered.

"Who knows? Here," I cut Meg's cheesecake in half, "there's more for us."

"Your anorexia's better, isn't it?" Sister said. Sometimes I think she really believes I'm anorexic.

"I'm forcing myself."

Mary Alice had recovered from her slight bout with empty-nest syndrome and was in a good humor today. "What do you suppose is on that computer?" She pointed toward the chair.

"Nothing we would recognize if we saw it." I held the last bit of cheesecake on my tongue, savoring it. "Do you think this is Sara Lee?"

"Don't be silly. They make their own desserts here."

"Well, it could be. Sara Lee's great. Put your own topping on it and everybody thinks you made it yourself. Henry says a lot of restaurants do that."

Sister shrugged and looked thoughtful. "Maybe we ought to let Meg look up our family tree."

It was my turn to shrug. "You and Fred. And you know what you're going to find? Horse thieves. Murderers. You'd be as unhappy as that woman was at the wedding. That Camille Atchison. Who was she, anyway?"

"I have no idea. Somebody from Henry's list." She took her last bite of cheesecake. "It still might be fun. I'll bet we have all kinds of interesting ancestors. I wonder how much she charges."

I was chasing graham-cracker crumbs around my plate with my fork. "Meg? A lot. Probably by the hour."

"That's okay."

"Maybe for you, Miss Moneybags. Fred's going to do his own." I gave up on the last of the crumbs. "Come on. Let's go over to the library. See what's available."

We collected Meg Bryan's briefcases and headed for the Southern Department on the third floor of the research library. The downtown Birmingham Public Library should be added to the list of things that surprise people who come to the city for the first time. Actually two large buildings connected by a walkway over the street, it boasts the largest circulation of any library in the South. So much for stereotypes. Alabamians read.

The research library is housed in what was the main library. It has high vaulted ceilings, murals of mythological figures, and row after row of study tables and lamps that are well-used. And unlike the new, modern building across the street, it smells like a library, a combination of old books, ink, furniture polish, floor wax. It's as distinctive as the smell of a school.

I sniffed appreciatively as we crossed the main reading room to the elevators.

"You need a Kleenex?" Sister asked.

And then we were in the department where I had had my first job. A portrait of Miss Boxx, the lady who had been responsible for this impressive collection of Southern history, stared at me as sternly as she had when I was nineteen. The artist had captured her daring anyone to mess up what she had spent years amassing.

"The genealogy stuff is over here," I said, turning left.

"Good God!" Sister said as a dozen Megs looked up from the tables to see who had come in. They all frowned and then resumed their work.

"They all look alike," Sister whispered.

"I think it's the same bunch that was here forty years ago." We giggled and got the same frowns. "Come on, let's look at some Georgia stuff. Fred said his great grandmother or somebody was born in Madison."

"What was her name?"

"I don't know. Maybe we'll run up on some Tates. Everybody in Alabama came from Georgia or South Carolina. Or Virginia."

"That really narrows it down." Mary Alice folllowed me to the Georgia section. Bound records are arranged alphabetically by states.

"Land grants?" I asked, looking at the shelves. "Census records? Deaths?"

"Yuck." Mary Alice plunked the briefcases down on a table. Two Megs looked up and frowned. "Let's just wait on Meg."

But I had opened an 1842 census record and discovered a Tate listed in the index. "Look. Page ninety-four."

"Probably a horse thief like you said. I just want to know about the good ones."

"This is a good one. Joshua Tree Tate, landowner. Wife Maria Caldwell Tate. And five children. See?" I handed the book to Sister.

"What kind of a name is Joshua Tree? Isn't there a real tree named that?"

"I'll bet his mother was a Tree."

"Shhh," said the two old ladies at our table.

"You know what, Mouse?" Sister whispered, calling me by my childhood nickname. "These boys would all have been just the right age to serve in the Civil War."

"Those records are here, too," I said. "We could find out what regiment they were in and whether they were killed."

We were hooked.

It was at least a half hour later when Mary Alice wondered where Meg was. "She said she would be. here in a few minutes."

"She's fine," I said. "Look. Here's where one of the sons married his brother's widow."

Another half hour had passed when we began to hear an unusual amount of noise outside. Fire trucks, police cars, ambulances. All seemed to be coming to a screeching halt close to the library.

"Think someone needs to shout 'Fire'?" Sister asked.

"Something's going on. I wish these damn windows weren't so high."

The librarian was talking into her phone. She hung up and came over to our table. "Something's happened over at the courthouse. Nothing to concern us."

"A shooting?" one of the Megs asked eagerly.

"I don't think so," the librarian assured her.

"We better go find Meg," Sister said. "She may be

trying to cross the park and they have it blocked."

But the small park between the courthouse and the library wasn't blocked. We cut right across to the back of a crowd that had collected around a couple of police cars, a fire truck, and a rescue squad. From inside the library, it had sounded like a dozen sirens wailing at once.

"Someone must have had a heart attack," I said.

A man in front of us turned. "Somebody took a dive," he said.

"What?"

"Jumped from the eighth floor."

"Oh, my God!" Mary Alice pressed her hands to her mouth. "Let's go back to the library, Mouse."

I agreed. My stomach has never cooperated at the sight of blood.

We had neared the fountain in the center of the park when we heard footsteps rushing up behind us.

"Wait, wait!" Judge Haskin's said. Short of breath and redfaced, he staggered to the curb of the reflecting pool, sat down, and put his head between his knees. "I think I'm dying," he gasped.

I grabbed a Kleenex from my purse, dipped it in the pool, and held it against his forehead. "Just keep your head down."

"That water's filthy," Sister said. "Kids pee in it." I gave her a hard look. "You know. When they go wading."

But the judge wasn't worried about bacteria. He took the wet Kleenex and held it against his eyes. I reached in my purse for another one.

"Are you having a heart attack or something?" I asked, kneeling beside him. "The paramedics are right over yonder."

"She's dead," he mumbled.

"What did he say?" Sister asked.

38

"He said, 'She's dead.' "

"It was a woman who jumped?"

"Oh, God." The judge began to sob, loud gasping sobs. He still hadn't raised his head, and I could see the deep pink of scalp through thinning white hair.

And then I knew. "It's Meg," I said. "Meg's dead, isn't she?"

Mary Alice sank down on the curb beside Judge Haskins. "Don't be ridiculous. It couldn't be Meg."

But the judge's head was nodding up and down, affirming what I had said.

Mary Alice grabbed his shoulder and gave it a shake. "Are you telling us that Meg Bryan jumped from the eighth floor of the courthouse?"

His head moved sideways in a no.

I closed my eyes in relief. Mary Alice gave a small whistle, a "whew."

"The ninth."

Sister and I stared at each other. "What?" we said together.

He sobbed again. "She's dead."

Mary Alice reached into the reflecting pool with cupped hands and doused Judge Haskins's bowed head. "Sit up and talk like you've got sense!"

For a moment, I thought she'd killed him. The gasping breathing stopped. Then, with a long sigh, he raised his head. "Do you have another Kleenex?"

I handed him another, and he wiped his face. "Thanks."

"Well?" Mary Alice said. Behind us, the fire truck was leaving.

"Meg jumped from the ninth floor. Or the tenth. Anyway, I was sitting at my desk on the eighth and she came sailing by. Looked right in at me. I think she said good-bye. Like this. The judge mouthed, "Goood-byyeeeee" and hiccuped. Tears began to run down his face again. "It was awful." His hands were trembling against his pants legs. Old hands. Liver spots.

"Are you all right?" I asked.

"I don't know," he said truthfully.

"Meg's dead?" Mary Alice asked.

"That's what he said, Sister." I patted the judge's hand.

"Dear God. Why would she have done that?"

The judge said he had no idea, that they had compared their genealogical findings and Meg had left. The next thing he knew, she was sailing past his window looking right in, "Goood-byeeee." He mouthed it again.

"She sure didn't seem suicidal to me." Mary Alice said. "She ate a good lunch, didn't she, Mouse. Three of those veal medallions with orange sauce on them. Green beans with almonds."

"We finished her cheesecake," I offered.

The three of us were quiet for a few minutes, watching as the crowd parted for the rescue squad. Nothing more they could do here.

"Patricia Anne," Sister said. "You need to go tell them who the body is."

"She's your company. Your son-in-law's cousin."

The judge got up. His legs were still shaky, but his voice was steady. "I'll go tell them," he said.

"Where will they take her?" Mary Alice asked. "Ridout's?" Ridout's has always seemed an apropos name for a funeral home.

"The morgue, I guess." The judge started away and turned. "Will you call her family?"

"I don't know how," Sister said.

"Her sister, Trinity Buckalew, lives in Fairhope. She'll get the word around. Believe me."

40

"One of us will call," Sister promised.

"You'll call," I said. "She was your company." I watched the judge walking away and thought of what he was walking to, the broken body on the courthouse steps, the blue-gray jacket and flowered dress crumpled and bloody. The black purse with the contents scattered. Shoes flung onto the sidewalk. I shuddered.

"Wait a minute!" I yelled to Judge Haskins.

He turned. "What?"

I jumped up, ran to him, and snatched Meg Bryan's briefcase, the heavier one with the computer inside, from under his arm.

"Oh, I'm sorry," he said. "I'm so upset, I don't know what I'm doing."

"Tell me about it." I walked back to the reflecting pool. "Did you see that?" I asked Sister. "He was trying to get away with Meg Bryan's computer, and her lying over there dead as a doornail."

Sister shook her head. "I still can't believe it. She was so nice and quiet. So ladylike." She pointed toward the crowd. "Look at all that commotion. That's not ladylike at all."

CHAPTER 4

"YOU MEAN," FRED SAID THAT NIGHT, "THAT YOU AND Mary Alice had lunch with this lady, that she didn't seem at all upset or suicidal, and yet she went over to the courthouse and jumped out of the ninth-floor window?"

"Maybe the tenth. She passed Judge Haskins's window and he thinks she said, 'Goood-byyeee.' Really shook him up, her sailing by the window like that."

"Gooood-byeeeee?"

I nodded. "That's what he said."

"Where were you and Mary Alice?"

"At the library, Fred, and damn it, don't lay a guilt trip on me. She didn't say, 'I'm going to go jump out of a tenth-floor window. Splat.' She seemed fine. And if we'd been there, face it, it's not like we could have given her CPR."

"I'm not trying to lay a guilt trip on you, honey. I'm just having a hard time believing Meg Bryan would commit suicide that way. Remember how she wouldn't even sit on the wall at The Club on Saturday? Said she was scared of heights."

I shivered. "Damn, I'd forgotten about that." I got up from the table to pour some more tea. "Shook the hell out of the judge. That's for sure." I handed Fred a packet of Sweet'n Low. "I didn't tell you he tried to steal her computer."

"What?"

"He had it, under his arm and was hightailing it out of the park. I just happened to see it, and snatched it away from him. He said he was so upset he didn't know what he was doing. But he knew. I think it's got all kinds of genealogy research stuff in it that he wants."

"What did you say his name is?"

"Judge Robert Haskins. You ever heard of him? Looks sort of like a weasel."

"Nope." Fred stiffed his tea. "Where's the computer now?"

"Mary Alice has it. The other briefcase, too. She was going to call the family in Fairhope."

"I'm surprised she didn't make you do it."

"She tried." We smiled at each other. I hesitated, and then asked, "Did you hear anything from Universal Satellite today?"

Fred shook his head no. "They won't return my calls."

42

He pushed his chair back and stood up. "I'm going to go watch *Jeopardy*."

Well, so much for that conversation. I looked out into the lighted backyard. Several years ago, we had had a bay window put in the breakfast nook, and it immediately became our favorite place to sit. My sweet Fred placed some lights in the shrubbery, creating just the soft effect I wanted. The incentive for his doing it was the estimate a couple of landscape architects gave me. Fred hit the road to Wal-Mart running. But that was okay. Tonight I could see how pretty the forsythia and quince were.

Our dog Woofer's igloo doghouse is partly hidden by shrubbery. But only partly. I know it's big, and that a small family of Eskimos would fit right in, but Woofer's getting old. When it's snowing or raining, I like to think of him snuggled up in his igloo.

I sipped my tea and looked out at my peaceful yard. I thought about lunch, about Meg Bryan who had seemed to enjoy herself and then, an hour later, had been dead.

"Heights make me nervous." Wasn't that what she had said? "Heights make me nervous." Did they make her nervous because she felt the urge to jump? I'd heard of that.

Woofer came from his igloo, walked over to the peach tree, and hiked his leg. I tapped on the window, and he came to the door to be let in.

"Bernard Baruch!" Fred yelled at the television. "It's Bernard Baruch, you dummies."

I opened the door for Woofer, let him in, and gave him a dog biscuit.

Or someone could have pushed her. I scraped the dishes and began to stack them in the dishwasher.

Someone like Judge Haskins, who wanted what was on her computer. He knew she had left it with us. Probably knew she was writing. a new program. Maybe that was it. Push her out of the window, grab the computer, and make a mint. Like the guy who started Apple. Not that he had thrown anybody out of a window, but he sure had made a mint. And wasn't it ironic that Meg, who was working on Windows. had jumped out of one. I put the detergent in and started the dishwasher, and ground the scraps in the disposal with such a racket that Woofer loped into the den leaving a definite smell of dog behind him.

A knock at the back door startled me. I looked up and saw Mary Alice.

"Tell Fred I knocked," she said when I opened the door.

"Sister knocked, Fred," I called. He's always complaining that she barges in without knocking.

He came and stood in the den door holding his hands to his chest. "I'm not sure I can take I the shock."

"Smart-ass." Mary Alice came in carrying a large tote bag. She put it down on the kitchen table with a clunk. "Tapes," she said. "Of the wedding. I thought we'd watch them and cheer up some. This day has been hell, Fred, pure hell for Patricia Anne and I."

"Me," I said.

Mary Alice turned and looked at me, puzzled. "Didn't I say you?"

"You said 'for Patricia Anne and I.' But it's Patricia Anne and me. For me. Objective case."

Mary Alice's eyes narrowed. "Stick it up your textbook, English teacher."

And Fred laughed. The traitor. Mary Alice smiled at him appreciatively.

"Did Patricia Anne tell you everything that happened today?" she asked him.

"She told me enough to curl my hair."

Mary Alice looked at his head. "I assume you're being facetious."

It was my turn to laugh. Fred has a very nice, full head of hair that used to be ash blond and has gradually become gray blond. It's hair. What can I say? But every morning he stands before the mirror examining the width of his forehead. And every two weeks he goes to a barber named Edna who tells him all her female problems. He swears she is the only one who can cut his hair right, but after hearing the ordeal of the third miscarriage, he was shaken for days. Mary Alice, of course, knows all this.

Fred turned and walked back to the den. We followed him, Mary Alice carrying one of the tapes.

"Did you get in touch with Meg's family?" I asked.

"Her sister."

"Which one?"

"Trinity. She said she'd be here tomorrow to make arrangements and have Bobby Haskins arrested."

"The judge?" Fred stepped over Woofer.

"She says he killed her." Mary Alice knelt by the VCR. "How do you turn this thing on?"

"That button on the left. But wait a minute," I said as Sister put the tape in. "She said the judge killed her? Did she say why she thought so?"

Mary Alice shook her head no. "I'm staying out of it." She pushed the Play button and the wedding music from St. Mark's blared out, making us all jump. "Too loud!" Mary Alice adjusted the volume.

"Look, Fred," I said, pointing to us sitting in the front row. "There we are."

"And I'm fixing to come down the aisle." Mary Alice got up from her knees, groaning, and sank down on the sofa.

Fred reached over and pushed Stop. Both Sister and I

45

looked up in surprise.

"What's the matter?" I asked.

"A woman you had lunch with either committed suicide or was killed a few minutes after she left you. Her sister says it was the guy you met, the guy who tried to steal her computer."

Mary Alice and I looked at him and nodded yes.

"Well?" He looked from one to the other.

"Well, what?" Mary Alice asked.

"Don't you think you ought to talk about it?"

"Okay," she agreed.

The three of us sat and looked at each other.

"I know," Sister said finally. "You know that book, *The Tenth Good Thing About Barney,* or maybe it's thirteenth. Anyway, we could do that about Meg."

Fred looked at me like what the hell is she talking about. "It's a children's book," I explained. "About a cat that dies and they make a list of the good things about him. I cry every time I read it."

"I'll start," Sister said. She looked down at her hands. "Meg Bryan was clean. The whites of her fingenails were so white they didn't look real." She nodded to me.

"Meg Bryan was smart," I said. "She knew how to work a computer. Even how to write her own programs." I nodded to Fred.

He got up and turned the TV on. The wedding music soared forth.

"See," Sister said. "There I come down the aisle. That dress looks good, doesn't it? Those damn pantyhose are already making me walk funny, though. Can you tell it?" I assured her that you couldn't.

The camera panned across the aisle and there was Meg Bryan sitting by herself on the groom's side. She was clutching a navy-blue purse, and her legs were crossed neatly at the ankles. She was also smiling. At Henry? This time I reached over and pushed Stop.

"Did you call Henry?" I asked Sister.

"I haven't yet. I will in the morning."

"She's one of his few relatives."

"I told you I'd call him." Sister reached her hand toward the TV. "Can I turn this back on?"

I shook my head. "It makes me sad."

But Fred surprised me. "Let's see it," he said. "It's a celebration of life."

Celebration of life? This remark was so unlike him, Mary Alice cut her eyes around at me.

"Turn it on," I said.

And soon we were caught up in the celebration. There we were, madly chewing, and the camera moving to show the groom and best man swallowing. There were the bridesmaids, Marilyn, tall and dignified, and Haley, flushed, lovely, smiling at someone at the altar. And then the bride in the wonderful white dress.

"The ENT!" Fred exclaimed, pointing toward Philip Nachman. "Look, he and Haley are giving each other the eye."

And there we were exiting the church, talking to Bonnie Blue, entering The Club, watching Henry and Debbie dance with the twins. Watching Haley dance with Philip. "Look at that!" from Fred.

Once again we sat on the terrace with Meg Bryan and ate and talked and smiled at the camera. I found myself smiling back at the TV images. And when the helicopter lifted off, I clapped as I had at The Club.

"Thank-you," I told Fred as the helicopter faded in the distance and the screen went dark. "I'm glad we saw it."

He smiled.

Mary Alice blew her nose loudly into a Kleenex. "That

47

was very nice. Do you want to see it again?"

"No," Fred and I said together.

"Well, I brought you a copy. You can look at it anytime." She ejected the tape. "I've got some videos of the babies. You want to see them?"

Fred begged off with work to do; I claimed fatigue, utter exhaustion. Which was true. But I would watch them later, would look forward to watching them later, which was also true. I think I'm as crazy about those two-year-old twins as Sister is.

"Come over in the morning," Sister said as she was leaving. "Trinity Buckalew said she would be getting into town about eleven and asked if I would meet her somewhere and help her find her way around. I told her just to come to the house."

"What do you need me for?"

"Well, my Lord, Mouse. The woman's sister's dead. She may be falling apart. Probably is."

"Trinity Buckalew?"

"Yep."

"She sounds like a Quaker, doesn't she? Maybe a Shaker."

"Quaker or Shaker, she's going to be at my house in the morning. Probably falling apart."

"I'll be there," I promised.

After Sister left, I put Woofer out and went to see if Fred wanted a cup of hot chocolate. But he was asleep, lying on the bed with his clothes still on and his glasses hanging on the end of his nose. When I slipped the glasses off, he woke up and blinked.

"Mary Alice gone?"

"And everything's locked up."

He got up and went into the bathroom. When he came back, he had on his pajamas.

48

"You're a nice man," I said.

"Tell me about it." He lay down and closed his eyes.

"You're wise. You understand about celebrating life. You're pretty."

He snorted.

"Well, I think you are." I rubbed his shoulder. "You have nice hair, lots of it, and cute buns."

He snorted again. And again.

"Fred?" But he was snoring away. I fixed myself a cup of hot chocolate and watched the late news. The anchorwoman didn't mention a suicide at the courthouse.

"Trinity Buckalew," the formidable woman standing at the door said. If I hadn't just seen Julia Child on Good Morning America dumping mashed potatoes into a bowl of rutabagas and getting paid a fortune for it, I'd have sworn she was standing here at Mary Alice's house holding out her hand.

"Patricia Anne Hollowell." My hand was engulfed by Trinity's.

"This is the Crane residence, isn't it?"

"I'm her sister. Won't you come in? We're so sorry about Meg."

"Yes. Well," she stepped inside and looked around, "we all knew it was going to happen some day."

"She was depressed?"

"Of course not." Trinity Buckalew leaned forward and examined the hall tree. She was wearing a bright blue cape that swung forward like wings. "Interesting," she said. "Who made this?"

It was her husky, authoritative voice, I realized, as well as her size, that reminded me of Julia Child. "I have no idea," I admitted. "It belonged to our grandmother."

She pushed her bifocals up so she could look through

49

the bottom part. "Interesting."

"May I take your coat?" Somehow "cape" wouldn't come out. "My sister's on the phone, but she'll be here in a minute. There's coffee on the sunporch."

Trinity Buckalew straightened up and slipped her cape off. She also removed the matching blue felt hat that reminded me of the ones Daddy used to wear. "Thanks." She handed them to me and I immediately hung them on the hall tree, which she could have done herself, of course, but I was being polite.

"How tall are, you?" she asked.

"Five one. Why?"

"Just wondered." She stretched, reaching both hands toward the ceiling. "Stiff from the drive," she explained.

"Come have some coffee, then." I pointed toward the sunporch.

"Could I have a Coke and some aspirin instead?"

"Sure. I'll get it. Come on back."

We walked back to the sunporch, which is my favorite room in Sister's house. Filled with wicker furniture and plants, it overlooks the city from the crest of Red Mountain, just as Vulcan does. Mary Alice rattles around in this huge, elegant old house. The cost of heating and cooling it boggles my mind. But it would take a bulldozer to get her to move. And looking out over the valley, especially at sunset, it's easy to understand why.

"This is lovely," Trinity Buckalew said, walking to the window. "Look at that view."

In the bright light of the sunporch, I could see that she was not as old as I had first thought. Probably around my age, sixty, which would be about right, since she was Meg's second youngest sister. Gray hair that had been held down by the felt hat had sprung straight up, and the only makeup she wore was lipstick. But Trinity Buckalew, far from pretty, was an attractive woman with interesting, angular features. She looked nothing like Meg.

"I'll go get your Coke and aspirin," I said. "Make yourself at home."

She nodded and turned back to the view. "Look at the planes taking off."

I went into Sister's ultramodern kitchen, where she has never cooked a meal but where the caterers can move around comfortably; patted Bubba, her fat, lazy cat who spends his days sleeping on a heating pad on the Corian counter; and got a couple of Cokes from the refrigerator.

I was pouring them into glasses when Sister came in. "What's she like?" she whispered.

"Big. Not fat, just big. Looks like Julia Child. Sounds like her, too. Said they knew it was going to happen.

"What?"

"Meg dying."

"Really? She said that?"

"And she wears a blue cape and a blue felt hat like a man's."

"Really?" Sister reached for the Cokes. "I'll take these in."

"Wait a minute." I reached for my Coke. "What did Henry say?"

"He says he's madly in love with my daughter. I told him not to consider interrupting their honeymoon, that we would go to Meg's funeral."

"You told him what?"

"Well, Meg came up for the wedding. Lord, Mouse. Don't stand there looking like you've swallowed a bug. It's the least we can do. Tit for tat."

"Not exactly," I said, getting the aspirin from the cabinet and following her out of the kitchen.

"Trinity," I heard her say, "I'm Mary Alice I'm so

51

grieved about dear Meg."

As I rounded the corner of the sunporch, they were already hugging. Grateful that I was not caught be-tween them, I sat down on the wicker sofa, opened the aspirin bottle, and took two.

"How tall are you?" Trinity sniffled.

"Five twelve. Why?"

"Just wondered."

"How tall are you?"

"Six two."

Neither woman seemed to think this was unusual information to elicit during an introduction. Mary Alice produced a small package of Kleenex from her pocket and said, "Here," handing one to Trinity. "I know right where I'm going to take you this afternoon. The Big, Bold, and Beautiful Shoppe. They have the most wonderful things for tall women."

"I have a headache," Trinity said.

"I'm sure you do. You just sit right down and I'll go get you some aspirin."

I held up the bottle.

"Oh, good." Mary Alice reached for it.

"Four," Trinity said.

"Are you sure, dear? It's not good for your stomach, you know. I've got some Tylenol if you'd rather have that."

"Four aspirin." Julia Child's voice.

"Sure." Mary Alice handed her the bottle of aspirin.

"Here's your Coke," I said.

Trinity sat down on the sofa beside me. The wicker squealed. Mary Alice sat facing us in a chair with cushions covered in a bright material, a white back-ground splashed with big red poppies.

"Nice room," Trinity said. She took the aspirin one at a

time, throwing her head back like a chicken as each tablet went down.

"Thank-you." Mary Alice dabbed at her eyes one last time. "Now, tell us what we can do to help. Patricia Anne and I are at your beck and call. Just tell us."

Trinity Buckalew took a long drink of Coke, hiccuped, and put the glass on the coffee table. "I guess first I have to go identify the body. Where would it be?"

Mary Alice and I looked at each other blankly. The morgue? But Judge Haskins had said something about Ridout's, hadn't he?

"I'll call," Mary Alice said sweetly.

"And then I want to swear out a warrant for Bobby Haskins's arrest."

Mary Alice and I looked at each other again. "Trinity," she said. "I don't think it's that easy."

"Oh, I have proof. Right here." Trinity reached into her purse and pulled out a small manila envelope. "Right here," she repeated. She moved her Coke, dried the coffee table with her napkin, and pulled a sheet of paper from the envelope. "See?" she said, opening it.

Sister and I both got up and leaned over to look at it. It was a legal document of some kind that had xeroxed poorly.

"See?" she repeated. She pointed to the top of the page. "Look at that."

I pushed my bifocals up, but they were small help. "Does it say State of Georgia?" I asked.

"It says more than that. It says Bastard, State of Georgia. And you know who this was, girls?"

We both shook our heads. I pointed to the document. "Is that name Catherine?"

"You better believe it. Catherine Anne Taylor, mother of the bastard, Clifford Adams Taylor, who just happens

53

to be the great great grandfather of one Judge Robert Haskins. These are bastardy papers, ladies," Trinity announced proudly.

Sister and I looked at each other blankly.

"I don't understand," I said.

"Bastardy papers?" Sister asked. "You think Judge Haskins would kill somebody because they found out his great great grandfather was born out of wedlock?"

"Of course. One of the hazards of genealogy." Trinity Buckalew tapped her forefinger against the document. For once, neither Sister nor I could think of a word to say.

CHAPTER 5

"IS THIS WOMAN HITTING ON ALL CYLINDERS?" I whispered to Mary Alice. Trinity Buckalew had asked directions to the "little girls' room" and disappeared down the hall. The document proclaiming Clifford Adams Taylor a Georgia bastard still lay on the coffee table; I picked it up. "Would anybody really commit murder over something like this?"

Sister shrugged. "She seems to be sensible. So I assume they would."

"But why?"

"Lord, Patricia Anne, I don't know. Some people just set a store by having a nice family, I guess."

"You mean a legal one."

"Whatever." Sister got up, straightened her back, did a couple of loosening-up sideways stretches, and said she was going to locate the morgue in the yellow pages and reckon how it was listed.

"Dead Layaway?"

"Not a damn bit funny!"

54

I didn't think so, either. But the truth was that Meg's death had shaken me, and when I get upset my gut reaction is to joke about what's upset me. I figure it's as good a way as any of coping. Better than some. But it drives Sister nuts.

"Act like you've got sense!" she hissed, turning and heading for the kitchen.

Chastised, I sat and looked over the valley and drank my Coke. I heard the sound of a toilet being flushed, footsteps down the hall, and Mary Alice's voice as she talked to either Bubba Cat or to the morgue.

"Hard to believe, isn't it?" Trinity was standing beside me pointing to the bastardy document. "But people have killed for less."

Hard indeed. "It just seems so unimportant."

"Not to a person trying to establish his lineage."

"I guess so."

Trinity Buckalew sat down in the poppy-splashed chair. I noticed that she had combed her hair and put on some lipstick while she was in the bathroom. She sighed and looked out over the valley. "A whole world out there," she said.

I nodded.

"Meg will be cremated. It's her wish to have her ashes sprinkled on Mobile Bay."

I nodded again. There were no jokes in me now. Meg Bryan would go to no more weddings; she would enjoy no more lunches. I felt tears sting my eyes.

"There, there." Trinity reached across and handed me a Kleenex.

"What's the matter?" Mary Alice asked, standing in the door.

"Your sister is a remarkably empathetic woman," Trinity said.

Mary Alice looked at me suspiciously. I wiped my eyes.

"I called the morgue," Sister said.

"Well, we might as well get this over," Trinity started to get up, and the wicker screeched.

"No." Sister sat on the sofa and looked at us, and Trinity settled back down. "You don't have to identify the body, Trinity."

"Why not?"

"They said it wasn't necessary."

"Trinity says Meg wanted to be cremated," I said. "Sprinkled on Mobile Bay. I think that's nice, Sister, don't you? To be sprinkled on Mobile Bay?"

"Very nice," Sister agreed.

Trinity stood up. Huge against the windows. Huge looking down at Sister. "Why don't I have to identify the body?"

"It's already taken care of," Sister said.

"By whom?"

"Well, I think they gave me the wrong name."

Trinity sat down heavily in the poppy chair. "Bobby Haskins. That bastard Bobby Haskins. Right?"

Mary Alice nodded. "I'm sure they're wrong."

Trinity closed her eyes and leaned back in the chair. Sister and I looked at each other nervously.

"Is she all right?" I mouthed.

Mary Alice shrugged. We sat for what seemed like several minutes in silence.

"Trinity?" Mary Alice finally said. "You okay?"

"Of course I'm all right. I'm thinking."

"Well, while you're thinking, Patricia Anne and I are going to go fix some sandwiches. Chicken salad suit you? Low fat mayonnaise. Or cream cheese with olives. The cream cheese is low fat; I don't think they've done anything about olives yet, but there aren't many of them

56

in it. Or how about we fix some of each? How does that sound?"

"Peanut butter and banana," Trinity said, not opening her eyes.

"That's fine." Mary Alice headed for the kitchen. I followed and shut the door. "Peanut butter's loaded with fat," she mumbled.

I was right on her heels. "You said Judge Haskins identified the body? I can't believe that."

Mary Alice opened the cabinet and took out a jar of peanut butter. "God," she read the label. "Fifteen grams." She came back to the counter and reached in the bread box for a loaf of bread. "It gets weirder, Mouse. The woman I talked to said Meg's husband, Judge Robert Haskins, identified the body and claimed it. The body's been moved."

"Meg was married to Judge Haskins?" I pulled a stool over to the counter beside Bubba's heating pad and watched Sister slather peanut butter on Merita white. "Are you sure?"

"I'm not sure about anything except my new son-in-law has strange relatives." Mary Alice reached for a banana. "Get the cream cheese, Mouse."

I got down and went to the refrigerator. "Judge Haskins was Meg's husband? They sure didn't act married." I checked the date on the cream cheese. I've gotten some unfortunate culinary surprises out of Sister's refrigerator. "Besides," I said, coming back to the counter, "that man looks like a weasel. Remember I told you that? How much he looks like a weasel?"

"So did my darling Will Alec. I remember on our wedding day Grandmama Alice pulled me aside and said, 'Honey, that man's just downright feral-looking.' I didn't know what she was talking about, so I said, 'Thank-you.' I think it was the whiskers, though, don't you?"

"Well, he grew the whiskers because he didn't have a chin."

"That's true. But I loved him." Sister reached for a banana. "Lord, Lord, all that Coca-Cola stock."

"I guess so." I was rinsing my hands when the second part of Sister's announcement hit me. "The body's not there anymore?"

"Nope." Mary Alice put the top slice of bread on Trinity's sandwich and sliced it in half. "Here. Find out what she wants to drink."

"She's going to have a fit when you tell her."

"I know it. I thought we'd just work it into the conversation. Make it easier for her."

"You mean like 'Have another sandwich, Trinity. And by the way, your sister's husband, who obviously isn't on your party list, has claimed her body and taken it somewhere.' "

"It's at Roebuck Chapel. And, yes, something like that. We could just bring it up casually."

"Casually."

"Gently. We don't want it to be too much of a shock."

"God forbid." I snatched the peanut butter sandwich from Sister and marched into the sunroom. Trinity wasn't there.

"Trinity," I called down the hall, "here's your sandwich. What do you want to drink?"

There was no answer. I put the plate down and walked toward the front of the house. "Trinity?"

Her cape and hat were gone from the hall tree, her car was gone from the driveway.

"Trinity?" I opened the door and called. Dumb. I went back to the kitchen. "She's gone."

"Gone? Where?" Sister had a mouthful of chicken salad.

"How should I know? To swear out a warrant for Judge Haskins?"

Sister chewed thoughtfully. "Maybe." She pushed the plate of sandwiches toward me. "Here."

"It's really none of our business, you know." I reached over Bubba Cat and got a sandwich half.

"But I can't believe she was that impolite. She could at least have said good-bye. Here I am fixing her a perfectly good peanut butter and banana sandwich and she's taking off." Sister picked up the plate of sandwiches. "Come on. Let's go watch *One Life To Live*. I swear, I can't believe Nicki has come back after all these years, can you? Vicki was doing so good for so long. Sane as you or me. Never should have left Clint, if you ask me."

"She's probably not thinking right because of her grief."

"No. It's Vicki all right. The whole other evil personality."

"I meant Trinity. Trinity's not thinking right."

"True. I'd hate to be in Judge Haskins's shoes."

I thought about the little man pushing his glasses up his thin nose, the little man who looked like a weasel. And I thought of the large woman sweeping the blue cape off like a giant exotic bird. Molting, but still formidable.

"Me too," I agreed. "Let's stay out of it."

Famous last words.

Other famous last words: "I've got a date tonight with Buddy Johnson, that nice older man I was dancing with at the wedding."

"Father Time? Can he see to drive at night?"

"Don't be tacky, Patricia Anne. As a matter of fact, his chauffeur is taking us to the airport. We're flying on Buddy's jet to Atlanta to the opera." Mary Alice giggled. "Sounds like *Pretty Woman*, doesn't it?"

"Minus a couple of vital elements. Richard Gere, for

59

one."

Mary Alice giggled again. "I think Buddy looks a lot like Richard Gere."

Maybe he had fifty years ago. "Be sure to practice safe sex." I expected Sister to throw a sandwich at me. But I'll be damned if she didn't smile. I could hear the glub glub all the way from St. Petersburg of Bill Adams going down the toilet.

When I left Sister's house, I stopped by the Winn-Dixie for some shrimp. Fred loves shrimp Creole, and I thought it might cheer him up. On the sidewalk in front of the store were hundreds of flats of blooming annuals, marigolds, petunias, impatiens. And I couldn't resist. I did what I do every year, assumed the beautiful spring weather would hold, that there would be no more frost, and left the store with shrimp and a flat of impatiens.

Trinity Buckalew had not called or shown up back at Sister's by the time I left there to go home. "I just hope we don't hear about her on the six o'clock news," I said, getting into my car.

"I won't. I'll be on my way to Atlanta." Sister pointed in a vague easterly direction.

"What opera are you seeing?" I had made the mistake of asking.

"Lord, Mouse. Opera's opera."

I was worried about Trinity, though. It had occurred to me that she could have overheard us talking in the kitchen about Judge Haskins claiming Meg's body. We had kept our voices down, but she could have been coming to get some more Coke or something and heard us.

I called Mary Alice as soon as I got home.

"No," she said, "haven't heard a word."

"Well, if you do, call me. I'm fixing to plant some

60

impatiens, but I'll take the phone out with me."

"Okay. I guess we could call Roebuck Chapel and see if she's shown up out there."

"Good idea," I said. "Let me know."

I was hanging up the phone when I heard Sister screeching, "Mouse!"

"What?"

"Do you think I should wear a long dress tonight? Atlanta's so much more cosmopolitan than Birmingham. Maybe I should wear long."

I thought about Sister's question for a moment.

Considered how cosmopolitan Atlanta is. "Short," I decreed.

The flat of impatiens was beautiful, a mixture of red, pink, and salmon colors. I put on my jeans, got a piece of cardboard to kneel on, and sallied forth to celebrate the annual planting of the flowers. So it would be repeated again two weeks later after a freeze, and maybe two weeks after that. So what? Today the sun was warm and tomorrow was the first official day of spring.

Everybody in our neighborhood has chain-link fences. We put them in forty years ago to keep our baby boomers from toddling into the streets. Paid a lot for them. A chain-link fence was as much a status symbol as a carport. And as lasting. Now word has drifted down from those same baby boomers who were kept safe by those same fences that chain-link is tacky. We should worry. The things have been there so long you can hardly see them. They support healthy crops of honeysuckle and wisteria. They are the background for flowering shrubs such as camellias and spirea. And they still keep toddlers and animals in. Tacky? In this neighborhood, we believe good chain-links make good neighbors. Besides, in a few years, they'll be antiques. Worth a fortune.

Our particular fence is bordered by legustrum and holly. A little pruning on Washington's birthday and that's it. Every year the same daffodils, narcissus, and tulips come up. Every year the magnolia and pear tree bloom. And every year I put out a few annuals.

Woofer came and sat beside me.

"These are pretty, aren't they?" I pointed to the impatiens.

Woofer agreed that they were.

"And we're not going to have another frost, are we?"

Of course not. Woofer stretched out, his head between his paws, and watched me dig a hole with my trowel. When we adopted him from the Humane Society, the card on his cage read "Mixed." Usually they'll say "Mixed German Shepherd and Lab," or "poodle and dachshund," trying to be a little specific so you'll know what to expect. With Woofer, they hadn't even hazarded a guess, but he is a beautiful dog. Turning gray, I noticed, across his head. Old Woofer.

I needed the peaceful work. The last few days had been traumatic. The wedding, Meg's death, Fred's business problems, Trinity Buckalew, and Judge Haskins. I took a red impatien, tapped the plastic container, and turned it upside down to slide the flower out.

"There." I eased the root system into the hole and then covered it. "How about that, Woofer? Instant garden." He agreed that it looked nice.

The phone's ringing startled both of us. I pulled off my glove and answered.

"They haven't seen Trinity at Roebuck Chapel," Sister said. "And I've decided to wear long."

"Okay." I waved to Haley, who had come out of the back door. She looked bright and cheerful in jeans and a pink shirt, not tired like she does sometimes after a day in the operating room.

"Maybe she decided to go home. She might have, you know." Mary Alice's voice sounded hopeful.

"Maybe," I agreed. But I knew better. We'd be hearing from Trinity Buckalew again. "Which dress did you decide on?"

"The black velvet. It won't be spring until tomorrow and I think I can get away with it, don't you? It's the one split way up the leg."

"For heaven's sake, Mary Alice. You know you're not supposed to wear velvet after Mardi Gras. Mama and Grandmama would turn over in their graves."

"I guess you're right."

"I know I am." I thought for a moment. "How about the red crepe?"

"It makes me look fat."

I wasn't about to jump into that.

"I could wear that flowery jacket with it, though. You know the one I mean? The one with the Japanese flowers?"

"Sure. That would look great."

Haley had knelt down and was scratching Woofer behind his ears. "Where's Aunt Sister going?" she asked when I turned off the phone.

I explained about Buddy Johnson's jet and the trip to Atlanta to the opera.

"He's not that ancient guy she was moving around the dance floor with at the reception?"

"The same. Aunt Sister says he looks like Richard Gere, though, and this is just like **Pretty Woman**."

Haley laughed. "Good for Aunt Sister."

"I told her to practice safe sex."

I expected Haley to laugh again. Instead, she said, "Good idea." I looked over at her. Her cheeks were

63

turning pink.

"Are you blushing?"

Haley pressed the backs of her hands against her cheeks and grinned. "Woofer needs a bath," she said.

"You *are* blushing! Good Lord!"

"Philip's a nice man, Mama."

"I'm glad to hear he's a nice man."

"I mean a *very* nice man."

"I know what you mean."

Mother and daughter, we looked at each other over the tray of flowers. So much unsaid. So much that would never be said. Be happy. I am. Be careful. I will. I don't want you hurt. I know. Be happy. I love you. Words standing in the air between us.

"I'll go get another trowel and help you," Haley said.

"Well, Woofer," I said, watching her cross the yard. "What do you think about that?"

Woofer said it was about time.

Haley came back with a trowel, a beer, and a sheepish look on her face.

"Here," I said, handing her some flowers. "Have you heard Meg Bryan died?"

She looked shocked. "Henry's cousin who was at the wedding?"

I nodded. "Your Aunt Sister and I took her to lunch at the Tutwiler yesterday and she went over to the courthouse and either jumped or was pushed out of the ninth floor window. Maybe the tenth."

"What? She did what? That nice little lady's dead? How terrible!"

"There's more." I told Haley everything I knew from the veal medallions with orange sauce and the meeting with Judge Haskins to the peanut butter and banana sandwich and Trinity Buckalew's disappearance.

"Wait a minute," Haley said several times, making me repeat some details. Finally, "That's incredible. Where is she now?"

"Meg or Trinity?"

"Both, I 'guess."

"Meg is at Roebuck Chapel. Trinity is God knows where. Out after Judge Haskins, I assume, since she says he's Meg's murderer."

"Because Meg had the papers saying the judge's great great grandfather was a bastard." Haley shook her head in disbelief.

I took another flower from the tray and tapped it. "Meg told me that professional genealogy is a dog-eat-dog world, but she was a big dog. And Trinity said Meg's death didn't surprise her, that genealogy is a hazardous business. And at the wedding, there was a woman who jumped all over Meg for something she had found in her family tree. Called her a bitch."

"That's wild." Haley reached for another impatien. We were both quiet for several minutes. Then, "Where's Meg's computer?" she asked.

"At Sister's. So is the other briefcase. Why?"

Haley brushed her hands off and took a swallow of beer. "Well, you said Judge Haskins was working on some genealogy, too. Seems to me the first family you would look up would be your own. So I can't think this great great grandfather could have been much of a surprise."

"But he had kept it a secret. Apparently, Meg had threatened to expose it."

"Did he seem angry in the restaurant?"

I tried to remember. "No. Surprised she was there. Pleased he'd found something she'd missed. Said he would show her if she'd let him see one of her files."

"What was it he'd found? Do you remember?"

"Something about a Mobile family that Meg was researching. I can't remember their name."

"Hmmm." Haley reached for the last of the flowers. "You really don't think she committed suicide, do you, Mama?"

"My first thought was that, yes, she had. But her sister says absolutely not. And Meg certainly didn't act at lunch like she was at all depressed."

"But it's still a possibility."

I stood up and rubbed my knees. "She was so afraid of heights, she wouldn't get close to the wall up at The Club. I think someone pushed her out of the window."

Haley handed me the empty tray and trowels. "If someone did, I'll bet the reason is in that computer."

"Could be."

"Let's go get it."

"Haley!"

"Well, Mama, this is intriguing."

"What's in that computer is none of our business. Besides, neither of us knows a thing about genealogy."

"Philip does. He's done some research on his family. He knows computers, too."

I walked to the garbage can and threw the plastic trays in. Even busy doctors were finding time to look up their family histories? Was there a whole ground-swell here I had missed out on?

Haley followed me. "He showed me the Nachman pedigree chart. It's interesting."

I put the lid back on the garbage. "Pedigree chart, huh?"

"That's what it's called."

"Any horse thieves or bastards?"

"Nope. But Aunt Sister was on it. And Debbie and the twins."

"Aunt Sister on a pedigree chart? She'll be thrilled to hear it." I thought for a moment. "And who did they put down as the twins' father?"

"Left it blank." Haley grinned. "Sort of put things in perspective."

We were going up the back steps when the cordless phone that I had forgotten and left in the yard rang. Haley ran back to get it.

"For you," she said, handing it to me with her hand over the speaker. "Sounds strange."

"Hello," I said.

Julia Child's voice. "Is this the Patricia Anne Hollowell who is the sister of Mary Alice Crane?"

"Yes. Hello, Trinity."

"Mrs. Hollowell, I'm sorry to bother you, but I find myself in need of help."

"What can I do for you?"

"You can come get me out of jail. I tried to call your sister, but all I got was her answering machine."

"You're in jail?" I saw Haley stop on the top step and turn around.

"Yes. I'm in the Birmingham jail. I understand this is not the same jail where Martin Luther King wrote his famous letter, but a newer edifice. Are you familiar with its location?"

"I'll, find it. What are you doing in jail?"

"They've charged me with breaking and entering. They have been kind enough not to lock me up, though, as yet. I explained to them about my claustrophobia, and they have been most understanding."

"Breaking and entering?"

"At Bobby Haskins's house, of course. It seems he has some kind of security system that alerts the police. I told them he should be the one arrested, and I am happy to say

67

they seem to have taken me seriously and are trying to find Bobby. In the meantime, I can be released, I understand. There is a small matter of bail or something like that, but we can discuss that when you get here."

"Bail?"

By this time, Haley was standing by my side. "Who is it?"

"Trinity Buckalew," I mouthed. "I'll be right down," I said into the phone.

"Thank-you. I'll be here."

I hung up and turned to Haley. "Breaking and entering at Judge Haskins's. She wants us to come down and get her out."

"What fun!" Love was doing wonderful things for Haley, I decided. We left a note for Fred on the kitchen table explaining that we had gone to spring a friend from the Birmingham jail.

CHAPTER 6

"THE WOMAN WHO COMMITTED SUICIDE AND THE woman in jail are Henry's cousins. Right?" Haley asked on the way to town. We were in her car, since she had been parked behind me.

"His mother's first cousins, I understand. Sounds like an interesting family."

Haley stopped for a light. "You know, I've been thinking. We don't know anything about our family history, do we?"

"Would you like to? I can get you back as far as your great great grandparents on my side. Nothing spectacular. Not even landowners. Clerks and bookkeepers. Just plain nice people. Now, the Hollowells may be more interesting. Your papa said at the wedding that he would like to know more about them."

"Philip says it's good to find out about your family. In fact, he says it's something everybody needs to know. About inherited genes and stuff."

"Uh huh," I said. "Gotta watch those genes."

My knowledge of the Birmingham jail is, thank God, limited to mournful songs about letters and valleys so low which Haley sang until I told her to hush. And then, of course, there's Martin Luther King's famous letter, which Trinity Buckalew had mentioned. TV shows had prepared me for the busyness of suspects being brought in, of phones ringing, of Cagney and Lacey answering calls, rushing out. TV had prepared me for the seedy characters, the dirty floors, the screams, the bangings against the bars.

What I was totally unprepared for was the pleasant white room that could have been an insurance company or a bank. Several uniformed policemen sat at desks and either talked quietly into phones or read.

"Is this the right place?" Haley whispered.

"Must not be."

A pretty young woman in a uniform came over and asked if she could help us. We explained that we were looking for a lady named Trinity Buckalew who was being held for breaking and entering, and that we were obviously in the wrong place.

"No, you're not. She's down the hall, first door on the right. You can go on back."

"Just walk on back?"

The woman smiled. "Of course."

Haley and I looked at each other.

"Right through there," the woman repeated, pointing to the hall on her left.

"This isn't at all what I expected," Haley looked around

the room. "Where are all the criminals?"

The policewoman leaned forward and whispered, "Out on the streets." Then, grinning at our startled expressions, she said, "Y'all go on back." She turned and went to her desk.

"God!" Haley murmured. "Is she serious?"

"Probably."

"Jesus!"

"Quit taking the Lord's name in vain, Haley."

"I'm not, Mama. I'm praying."

We entered the hall, which was lined with small, neat offices. In the second one on the right, Trinity Buckalew was playing cards with a middle-aged man whose graying hair and beard looked as if they had never been touched by scissors or soap. His clothes were tatters, and the knapsack propped against the wall wasn't in much better shape.

"Gin!" he exclaimed.

"Shit!" Trinity slammed down her cards, looked up and saw us. "Well, good. Here's the rescue squad. Marty Holmes, this is Patricia Anne Hollowell and—"

"My daughter Haley."

Marty stood up politely. "Nice to meet you ladies."

"Freddie's a narc," Trinity explained. "He hangs around under interstate bridges and places like that. He's been showing me how to cheat at cards."

"A narc?"

"A narcotics agent. You know."

"I know what a narc is," I said.

Marty grinned, showing where teeth used to be. Trinity stood up and reached for her cape and hat, which were on the desk. "Well, let's go," she said.

"What about bail?" I asked. "You can't just walk out, can you?"

"They finally got Bobby and he told them I was his ex-sister-in-law and not to press charges. My car's impounded, though, and I can't get it until tomorrow. The garage is closed." Trinity swung her cape around her shoulders.

"Love that cape, babe," Marty said. "And the hat is to die for."

"Under the interstate, it probably would be."

"Too true. Not the best element."

Trinity walked over and hugged Marty. "You take care," she said. "Come see me in Fairhope."

"You take care, too, babe."

"Dear God!" I whispered to Haley.

"You praying, Mama?"

"Something like that."

"Bye, Mrs. Buckalew," the nice young policewoman called as we walked back through the office.

"Bye!"

Several of the policemen looked up and waved.

"Such nice people," Trinity assured us. Then she turned to Haley. "How tall are you, young lady?"

"Five one. Why?"

"Just wondered."

Haley looked at me questioningly; I shrugged.

We exited into a warm late afternoon. Haley had found a parking place right around the corner, and on the way to the car I asked Trinity if she had planned to stay at a hotel and if she would like us to drop her off.

"When I am in Birmingham, I always stay with my friend Georgiana Peach. She is a genealogist and a dear friend of Meg's, too. Unfortunately, she is out of town, which is why I have had to rely on your very gracious help. So any hotel you recommend will be fine."

"You have a friend named Georgiana Peach?" Haley

motioned Trinity toward the car and unlocked the door.

"A lovely Southern name, isn't it? She was named for an aunt who turned a little funny. Died a couple of years ago and left Georgiana a generous estate. Totally unexpected, I understand. Stock certificates in the attic, money in books. That kind of thing."

"I've got a family name," Haley said, "totally unencumbered with things like estates." As she opened the door, a problem presented itself. There was no way Trinity Buckalew could fold herself up enough to get in the back.

"I'll get in," I said, wondering for the thousandth time why Haley had bought this compact car.

"Stay with me tonight, Mrs. Buckalew." Haley gave me a push into the car. "I've got a sofa sleeper."

"How sweet." Trinity slid into the bucket seat. Her head touched the ceiling. "That would be very nice."

I straightened up and perched on the backseat. "Don't be silly. We've got two extra bedrooms and I've got Shrimp Creole already fixed for supper."

What else could I do? Sometimes being a Southern lady is such a pain.

"We liked your sister very much," Haley said, opening the other door and getting in. "I was so sorry to hear of her death."

"Thank-you, dear. My friend, Georgiana Peach, will be upset, too. I understand she's attending a genealogical conference in Charleston."

"Are you a genealogist, too?" Haley floored the accelerator and pulled out in front of a Mac truck. I shrieked. "Put on your seat belt, Mama," she said.

"I'm an antique dealer. Meg was the only genealogist in the family. Her business was more profitable than mine, I must admit, though I love antiques." Trinity had removed her blue felt hat and was pushing it back into shape. "Meg and I still live in the family home in Fairhope, and our sister Jo lives close by. Our sister Amy lives down the bay, and Beth—"

"Oh, no!"

"For heaven sakes, Haley. Watch where you're going," I said. "Beth lives in Hawaii with her husband and children."

"She loves it there," Trinity agreed.

Haley sighed with relief and entered the interstate heading south toward Vulcan.

"Bobby Haskins lives up there," Trinity said. "By that naked iron man."

"There are some pretty houses up there," Haley said. "Aunt Sister's is up there."

"I know. Does she have an alarm system?"

"Yes, she does," I answered.

"Well, they work. You can tell her." Trinity was silent for a few minutes, looking out over downtown. "I was going to leave Bobby a note on his refrigerator. Tell him he needn't think he was going to get away with murder. You know?"

Haley nodded that she knew. Bless her.

"In fact, I put the note under a magnet, a little red tulip it was, and was about to leave when all those policemen rushed in."

"How did you get in the house?" I asked.

Trinity snorted. "Bobby has no imagination. That's why they made him a judge, probably. There's an extreme deficit of imagination among the judiciary, you know." She snorted again. "The key was in one of those fake rocks right by the steps."

Haley turned and looked at me. That's where my key is hidden, the one she's been after me to get another hiding

73

place for. "How long have Meg and the judge been divorced?" I asked, changing the subject.

Trinity thought for a moment. "About forty years."

"Is there a Mrs. Haskins now?"

"There usually is. But if there is one currently, she wasn't at home." Trinity picked lint from her hat. "Meg was the one who got him interested in genealogy, though.

"Did Meg remarry?" Haley asked.

"She married Gregory Bryan, a prince of a man whom she treated abominably."

I hated to ask what Meg had done that was so abominable. So I asked whether they were divorced.

"Gregory is deceased. At least we think so. He went fishing one night out on Mobile Bay and never came back." Trinity sighed. "He looked like Ronald Coleman with a little mustache." She sighed again. "It was five years before I let Meg give him a fond farewell party. I kept thinking he'd come walking up the pier with that little mustache and a string of fish."

Haley wasn't as polite as I was. "What did Meg do to him?" she asked

"Always chasing around in cemeteries and libraries. She was gone so much, Gregory forgot sometimes which one of us sisters he was married to." Trinity closed her eyes and smiled. "A prince of a man. Yes, indeed."

Haley cut her eyes around at me again and grinned. She and I were thinking the same thing. If the other March sisters were anything like Trinity and Meg, Prince Gregory hadn't stood a chance.

"My husband, Ed Buckalew, was more the Jimmy Cagney type. The Yankee Doodle type, not the mean one. Loved to dance. He's gone, too. Just sat down under a pecan tree one day and died. Said he wasn't going to pick up another pecan. And he didn't."

74

Haley was suddenly seized with a suspicious coughing fit. Fortunately, our exit ramp was right ahead.

Fred's white Oldsmobile was in the driveway when we pulled up to the house. Haley hopped out of her car and helped Trinity and me unfold. "It must have been like this in the womb," I grumbled. I limped up the front steps, opened the door, and called Fred.

"Here."

I followed his voice to the den, where he sat in his recliner. An open beer was on the table beside him, and he looked at me over the pages of The Birmingham News. "How was the jail? And that was a rather cryptic note you left me. Which friend did you spring?"

"Trinity Buckalew, Meg Bryan's sister. She's coming in with Haley."

"Now?"

I didn't have to answer. Trinity swept in, all six feet two of her, her bright blue cape and hat startling in the darkening room. Fred leaped from his chair.

"He's so polite," I murmured to Haley.

"I'm Trinity Buckalew." Trinity advanced on Fred, hand held out. "Your wife has been kind enough to offer me your hospitality."

"That's great." Fred put the paper down and shook hands. "It's so nice meeting you."

"My father is a prince," Haley whispered to me.

"Don't say that," I whispered back. Then, "Let me take your cape and hat, Trinity. And make yourself at home. Would you like something to drink?"

Trinity handed me the cape and hat. "You got any Black Jack?"

"Probably. I'll see. Water? Ice?"

"Just hand me the bottle. That'll be fine. And a glass, of course."

Another fit of coughing from Haley. "I'll get it," she gasped.

"That child needs some cough syrup," Trinity said. sitting on the sofa as Haley disappeared into the kitchen.

"I'll go check on her," I said, "and get us some snacks."

In the kitchen, Haley was standing on a little foldup stepladder and looking in the top cabinet where we keep our liquor. Since I don't drink, and Fred's fond of beer, the bottles stay there a long time. "Here's some Jack Daniel's," she said. "It's dusty. Does whiskey go bad?"

"How should I know? I doubt it. Just dust it off." I reached into the pantry for some Ritz crackers, and into the refrigerator for pepper jelly and cream cheese.

"She's wonderful, isn't she?" Haley nodded her head toward the den. "I wish we had gotten a chance to know Meg better, too."

Meg's words, "I'm a big dog," came whispering into my ear. "It's hard to believe she committed suicide," I said. "In fact, I think Trinity's right. Somebody, maybe Judge Haskins, maybe somebody else like that woman at The Club, pushed her out of the window."

"That's hard to believe, too."

"I know." I handed Haley a tray for the bottle and a linen napkin. "Here. Might as well do it right."

When I got into the den with the snacks, Trinity was telling Fred what I had just told Haley, that Meg's death was not a suicide. She added that there wasn't a suicidal bone in Meg's body, and that most likely Bobby Haskins had killed her because his great great grandfather was a bastard and Meg had the proof.

"I saw it," I said, passing the crackers around. "Bastardy papers from the State of Georgia."

"What are bastardy papers?" Haley asked.

I fully expected Trinity's lengthy explanation to cross

Fred's eyes in boredom. Instead, he seemed intrigued.

"People would kill over that?" he asked.

Trinity poured a substantial shot from the bottle of Black Jack. "My friend, Georgiana Peach, who is a renowned genealogist and owns a genealogical research service, says it's more common than people realize." She held up the glass. "Cheers." Chugalug.

Fred watched with admiration. Prince of a fellow. "What do the police say about Meg's death?"

"They said they were looking into it. But they released the body to Bobby, so I'm sure that's the end of it. God only knows what he told them. But it's amazing how much influence judges have on the police."

"What kind of judge is he?"

"Probably not a very good one." Trinity poured another drink.

Fred didn't push the point. But I knew the answer. "Bankruptcy," I said. "Mary Alice found out." I eyed the glass in Trinity's hand. "Shrimp Creole in a few minutes. Soon as the rice is ready. Okay?"

"Is that an elected or appointed position?" Fred was asking as I went into the kitchen.

We ate supper in the breakfast nook. I had turned the back lights on so we could see the quince and forsythia. A few early-blooming tulips that had opened to the warm sun had closed for the night but were still bright spots of color. Woofer came out and looked at us.

"Peaceful," Trinity said.

I looked at her and saw how haggard and tired she looked. She had received the terrible news about Meg yesterday, had driven from Mobile this morning, and ended up in jail this afternoon. Haley noticed, too. She reached over and covered Trinity's large splotched hand with her small smooth one. It's times like this when I realize what a good nurse Haley must be.

"How's the ENT?" her father asked her.

And Haley blushed. "Fine."

Fred looked at me questioningly; I smiled.

Haley changed the subject. "Aunt Sister's gone to the opera in Atlanta with some old guy in his jet."

It worked. "The one she was dancing with at the wedding?" Fred asked.

"If you can call moving slightly dancing. His name is Buddy Johnson," I added. "She thinks it's like *Pretty Woman* and she's Julia Roberts and he's Richard Gere."

Fred smiled sweetly. "Good for her."

"No sarcastic remarks?"

"Of course not."

"Patricia Anne," Trinity said. "You are married to a prince. I can tell."

Haley coughed into her napkin.

We were sitting at the table enjoying an after-dinner cup of coffee when the doorbell rang. Our front doorbell rings so seldom at night that Fred, Haley, and I looked at each other, startled.

"Maybe it's a package," I said. "I ordered a bathing suit from Lands' End."

And that was how I happened to be the one to go to the door, the one to look through the peephole and see Judge Bobby Haskins standing there, the one to confront him.

"Is Trinity here?" he asked without even so much as a "Good evening."

"Yes."

"Then, here." He held out a package. "Give this to her."

"Why don't you give it to her yourself?" The judge was being too snippy to suit me.

"It's Meg."

I looked at the small cardboard box tied with ordinary twine, and tried to connect it with the woman I had had lunch with the day before. "Meg?"

"Meg. Please give it to Trinity. Tell her I had nothing to do with Meg's death."

In the dim front porch light, the judge looked as if he had been crying. "Please," he repeated. I held out my hand and took the package.

"Thank-you, Mrs. Hollowell." He turned and went down the steps. I watched him get into his car and drive off.

"Your bathing suit, Mama?" Haley stood behind me. "Let's see it."

"It's Meg." I held the box up to show her. It weighed more than I would have imagined.

"What?" Haley stepped back as if the contents of the box were suddenly going to fly out. "Are you serious?"

"Judge Haskins brought them for Trinity. He said to tell her he had nothing to do with Meg's death."

"Wow."

"Yeah. Wow."

"Why don't you wait until morning to give them to her? No use upsetting her more tonight."

"You mean after you're gone. Don't be silly, Haley. You poke around inside people's insides all day. This is just ashes."

"Tell me about it."

The package felt warm in my hands, which I knew was my imagination. I carried it into the den, and saw that Fred and Trinity had just walked in there to finish their coffee.

"What you got?" Fred smiled. "The bathing suit?"

The expression on my face alerted them, I'm sure. For a moment I just stood there, and then I put the package in

79

the middle of the coffee table and said, "Trinity, Judge Haskins left this for you. It's Meg. And he said to tell you he had nothing to do with her death."

Trinity looked at the box and then at me. Then at the box again. "Meg's ashes?"

"Yes."

What happened then was the last thing I had considered happening. Trinity Buckalew fainted. Haley, thinking

Trinity was dizzy reached to steady her and ended up on the floor underneath her.

"Lord, Mama," Haley gasped. "Look what you've done."

The next few moments were all confusion. Fred and I extricated Haley, who said she was okay and who immediately felt Trinity's pulse and looked in her eyes.

"Let's put her feet up on the sofa," she said.

"You think I should call 911?" I asked.

"No!" Julia Child's voice, weak but forceful. "Where's the Black Jack?"

I looked at Haley and she nodded yes. I ran to the kitchen and got the bourbon. This time I didn't bother with a glass, no time for niceties. Nor was one needed. Trinity, by now propped against the sofa, turned the bottle up and took a hefty swig.

"I'm sorry," I told her. "I'm sorry," I told Haley. "I'm sorry," I told Fred.

Fred reached over and put his hand over my mouth. "Hush," he said gently. "None of this is your fault."

Which was true, of course, but something in my psyche makes me feel guilty for everything that goes wrong. I am convinced that the source of this cosmic guilt is named Mary Alice. She makes me feel it's my fault if we have a picnic planned and it rains. In the current crisis, Haley's

"Look what you've done, Mama" hadn't helped.

"I'm sorry, Mama," Haley said.

"I'm sorry," Trinity said, raising the bottle again.

If the package on the table had suddenly said, "I'm sorry," I don't think I would have been surprised. Let's face it. Guilt is a universal chick thing.

Haley got a cold cloth for Trinity's head, and we helped her up onto the sofa. Fred took the whiskey bottle back to the kitchen, and I heard the cabinet door shut. Enough.

"I'm really better," Trinity said. "I just do that sometimes. Faint like that. The doctors say it's because I'm so tall. The blood doesn't make it to my head or something like that."

I looked at Haley and she nodded yes. "It's the same thing as when you stand up too quickly," she explained.

"And Bobby wouldn't come in and face me." Trinity's voice was muffled by the washrag covering her face.

"He seemed very upset. I think he'd been crying."

"It's spring. He's allergic to pollen."

"No. He was upset."

"As well he might be." Trinity folded the cloth and held it to her eyes. "I don't think I believed it until now. Meg's really gone, isn't she?" She lowered the cloth and looked at the package. "Almost." She hiccuped and sat up. "If you will excuse me, I need to use the little girls' room."

"Down the hall," I said. "Do you need some help?"

"I'm fine." She hiccuped again, stood, swayed a moment, and then headed down the hall. "I'm fine," she called back.

Fred, Haley, and I looked at each other and at the package that sat incongruously in the center of our coffee table.

"Judge Haskins really was upset," I said. "I don't think he had anything to do with Meg's death."

81

"He certainly wouldn't have killed her because she knew an ancestor of his was a bastard." Fred sat down in his recliner. "That's ridiculous."

"He might have killed her for what's on her computer, though. I still think we need to check that out," Haley said.

"But she didn't have the computer with her when she went to his office. She left it with your Aunt Sister and me."

"He tried to steal it, though. You just happened to see him and stop him."

"Wait a minute," Fred said. "Meg was doing research. She would have made backup disks of everything."

"True," Haley agreed. "But the hard drive would have everything right there."

Let them talk about their computers. I went into the kitchen and started loading the dishwasher. Ten minutes later when I came back into the den, Haley and Fred were still talking about the merits of a certain computer program.

"Where's Trinity?" I asked. "She hasn't come back?"

They looked at me blankly. I raced down the hall, expecting to see all six feet two of her dead on the bathroom floor. But the bathroom was empty. A glance in the middle bedroom told me why. Trinity Buckalew was sound asleep stretched from one corner of the bed to the other.

Haley, who had followed me, handed me an afghan, and I spread it over Trinity and slipped off her shoes.

"Size thirteen," I whispered to Haley, and turned off the light.

CHAPTER 7

TRINITY BUCKALEW WAS STILL ASLEEP WHEN I left to take Woofer for his morning walk. I had put a pair of Fred's pajamas and a new toothbrush in the guest bathroom the night before, and a peek told me she had found them. Fred had left very early, telling me to go back to sleep. We hadn't talked about his problems with Universal Satellite the previous night. In fact, Haley had stayed until after ten, and Fred had gone to sleep in his chair long before that. If he had heard anything, though, he would have found time to tell me.

The morning was sunny and still. Too still. People who live in Alabama are suspicious of warm March days when there is no breeze stirring. It means the warmth and humidity of the Gulf of Mexico are sitting right over us. A cold nudge from the north, which is inevitable in March, and tornado sirens start blasting. But that was to worry about later. The morning was absolutely beautiful with the whole neighborhood smelling of wisteria, and dogwood and cherry trees vying to see which could be brighter. Woofer, that admirable mix of every breed of dog known to man, enjoyed himself thoroughly, checking out which dog, cat, or squirrel had been by, and blazing the trail himself for the ones who would follow.

By the time we got home, Trinity was sitting at the kitchen table drinking coffee. She was dressed, but her hair was still damp from the shower. "I have a headache," she said. I reached into the cabinet and handed her the aspirin bottle.

"Your sister called. I told her I was here because of my incarceration and your kindness." She poured four aspirin into her hand; I handed her a glass of water. "She left a message. She said he's a tiger."

"A tiger, huh?"

Trinity gulped the aspirin down in the same chicken-head-thrown-back way as the day before. "A tiger," she repeated.

"She's talking about an ancient Richard Gere she had a date with last night. I'll call her and get the details," I said. "You want some cereal?"

"That would be nice. And thank-you for the pajamas and the toothbrush. I trust my overnight bag is still in my impounded car."

"You're welcome." I poured each of us a bowl of raisin bran, and brought them all to the table. "We need to call and find out where your car is and how to get it."

"I talked to my friend, Georgiana Peach, just a while ago. She got back late last night. She said she would come take me to get it." Trinity began to eat her cereal. "Fortunately, I was not the one who had to break the news to her about Meg. One of the women who works for her called her in Charleston yesterday."

I thought about the package still sitting on the coffee table. As if reading my thoughts, Trinity said, "I'm taking Meg home today."

I couldn't think of anything, to say except, "I'm so sorry."

Trinity nodded. We sat eating our cereal quietly, while outside the bay window, Spring took one giant step.

Trinity broke the silence. "Meg was a beautiful girl, Patricia Anne. You saw her as an old lady, but when she was young, she turned men's heads like you wouldn't believe."

"She was still beautiful," I said.

"And determined." Trinity smiled. "When she made up her mind to marry Bobby Haskins, he didn't stand a chance."

"I doubt he fought very hard." I got up to pour some more coffee. "How did Meg get so interested in genealogy?"

Trinity reached for the sugar bowl. "I think she always was. The Grand Hotel was a hospital during the Civil War, so there's a big Confederate cemetery right outside Fairhope, actually right behind our house. Anyway, we had a game we used to play back there in the cemetery when we were children. Yankees and Rebels. We'd take a name off a marker, you know those little white crosses they used, and make up a story for that person. Make up whole families. Meg said we were bringing them back from the dead. Beth hated it, said it gave her the creeps. She'd go along with it, though."

The front doorbell rang just as the back door opened and Mary Alice walked in.

"That would be Georgiana Peach at the front door," Tninity said.

"Y'all ordered some of those expensive peaches, too?" Sister asked. "Those third world countries are getting rich, aren't they."

"What?" Trinity asked.

"She has a friend named Georgiana Peach who is at our front door right now," I explained to Sister.

"I'll go let her in." Trinity disappeared down the hall.

"Georgiana Peach?" Sister looked at me with a raised eyebrow.

"He's a tiger?" A raised eyebrow back at her.

Sister giggled. "I'll tell you later."

Women's voices down the hall, and there was Georgiana Peach, she of the exotic name that summoned up ripeness, sexiness, boldness, a strip joint on Fourth Avenue. There she was, a little gray bird of a woman. A wren. A sparrow. Beside her, the well-named Trinity towered.

Introductions were made, coffee poured, and the four of us sat at the kitchen table.

"I can't believe it. I just can't believe it." Georgiana Peach dabbed at her eyes with a Kleenex. "I've been telling Meg she better let some of those sleeping dogs lie. You know I've been telling her that, don't you, Trinity?" Her voice matched her name, a breathy, Marilyn Monroe voice; her little-bird eyes inventoried my kitchen and yard. This woman, I thought, had known exactly where every stock certificate was in her late aunt's house. She caught my eye and looked down at her coffee.

"Yes, you did, Georgiana," Trinity agreed.

"She was on to something big. Wouldn't tell anybody."

Trinity chimed in. "Those bastardy papers of Bobby Haskins."

"Something bigger," Georgiana said.

"A woman at the wedding called her a bitch," I said. "Camille somebody."

"Atchison?" Georgiana asked.

"That sounds right."

"Meg kept her out of the DAR, I think. Made her furious. Something bigger than that, though." Georgiana Peach closed her eyes and put her fingertips to her forehead. "Let me think."

"Georgiana's something of a psychic," Trinity announced proudly.

The fingertips came down. "Sometimes I see things. But it was my brother, George Peach, who was the psychic. He hid under the house once when he was a little boy and Mama was chasing him to spank him, and he touched a drainpipe or something, and there was a loud crack, and he said a white horse came running by, plain as

86

anything. We dragged him out almost electrocuted, but he was all right. After that he could see things, though. Visions."

"You've got a brother named George Peach?" Mary Alice asked.

"I did. A twin. Killed in Vietnam. We always knew he would go early on account of that white horse. It's a sure sign." The fingertips went back to the forehead. "Let me think."

"I'll get more coffee," I said. "And who would like a sweetroll?"

Sister followed me from the table. "Flake," she murmured. But I didn't think so. There was nothing in my kitchen that those bird eyes had missed.

I got a package of sweetrolls from the freezer and stuck them into the microwave for a minute. The phone rang and Sister answered it.

"A great time," she assured the caller, giggling as if she were fifteen. "Here," she said, handing me the phone. "It's Fred,'

"Just checking to see if you're okay this morning," he said. The joys of a long marriage, the unsaid things in the most ordinary conversations.

"I'm fine. I'm fixing sweetrolls. Are you all right?"

"I'm going to run over to Atlanta. I've decided I can't let this Universal Satellite thing ride any longer. I've got to get to the bottom of the problem."

"Be careful."

"I'll be home before dark. By the way, how's our company this morning?"

"She seems okay. A friend of hers is here."

"Good. I'll call you if I'm going to be late."

"'Okay. I'll fix you a special supper."

We said good-bye and hung up. Sister was taking the

sweetrolls from the microwave, and looked at me questioningly. "He's just going to Atlanta for the day," I explained.

"He needs a jet. You can be there in a half hour."

"Shut up." I took the sweetrolls, and put them on a plate. "Bring some more coffee."

Georgiana's fingertips were still to her forehead when we got back to the table. She opened her eyes and announced that it was a man who had taken Meg's life.

Trinity nodded. "Bobby Haskins. I knew it."

I put the sweetrolls on the table. "Did you see what he was wearing?" I asked.

Georgiana's bird eyes stabbed me. "No."

" Was he young or old?" Sister was serious. She
sat down and reached for a roll.

"I couldn't tell," Georgiana said in her whispery voice. "But it was a man."

"Bobby Haskins," Trinity repeated.

I reached for a sweetroll, too. Sitting between Julia Child and Marilyn Monroe was a slightly surreal experience.

"These are good." Georgiana licked icing from her lip.

"Tell them about George Peach and the Moon Pies," Trinity said.

Georgiana smiled. "He was the Moon Pie champion of the world."

"Tell the whole story," Trinity insisted.

"Well, they have a Moon Pie Day every year in Oneonta, and George Peach just loved Moon Pies. So nothing would do but we had to go to Oneonta to see what was going on. And one of the things was a Moon-Pie-eating contest. They had this long table set up with vanilla and chocolate and banana Moon Pies, and George Peach couldn't resist." Georgiana paused to take a sip of

88

coffee. "I remember he mixed the flavors up because he figured he'd get tired of one. And, Lord! You've never seen people eat like that. Crumbs flying. Marshmallow cream all over the K-Mart parking lot. Like stepping on chewing gum, pulling up those strings with your shoes. And George Peach just stuffing Moon Pies. We knew he was going to win. One man tried to say he'd eaten fifteen like George Peach had, but he was disqualified because he hadn't swallowed the last one. Some people will do anything, won't they?"

We agreed that they would.

"But George had his fifteen minutes, didn't he?" Mary Alice said. She held her coffee cup out. "To George Peach."

"To George Peach," we responded, drinking solemnly. I glanced over at Georgiana and her eyes were brimming with tears. The unwarranted antagonism I had felt toward her disappeared like the steam from the coffee.

We sat quietly for a few minutes, each engrossed in her own thoughts and memories. Finally, Georgiana pushed her chair back. "Are you ready to go get your car, Trinity? I really must go. I've been out of the office for three days, and I know there's a stack of work waiting for me."

"Where do you work?" Sister asked.

"I've had my own genealogical research service, The Family Tree, for about a year. I have two ladies who work for me, one part-time, and we stay busy. Meg did some work for me, too. I have to get extra help sometimes, and she did some research. Of course, she had a lot of her own clients." She turned to Trinity, who had also risen. "What was she working on, Trinity?"

"I have no idea."

I spoke up. "She said it was the Fitzgerald family from Mobile, didn't she, Sister? Or maybe it was Fitzpatrick."

Mary Alice shrugged. "I don't remember."

"Well, if you really believe Meg didn't commit suicide, and I, for one, believe she didn't, you should look at what she was working on." Georgiana pulled on a green sweater that added a greenish tint to her complexion. "I know what program she usually used, if you want me to check her computer."

"The computer's gone," Mary Alice said. "Didn't I say that?"

"Gone? Gone where?" Trinity had started to rise from her chair, but sat back down.

"What are you talking about?" I asked.

"It's gone. I had it on the bed with Meg's stuff to bring over here this morning, and when I went in to get everything, it wasn't there. The rest of the stuff was, though. It's out in my car."

"Wait a minute." Georgiana sat down and stared at Mary Alice. "Let me get this straight. You are talking about Meg's little notebook computer, the one in the leather case."

"I don't think it was real leather," Mary Alice said. "And the other briefcase is gone, too. Or seems to be. I thought I put everything together so I wouldn't forget anything this morning. I was in a tizzy trying to get ready to go to Atlanta to the opera, you understand, so there's an outside chance I might have put it somewhere else. I don't think so, though."

"Shit," Georgiana Peach said. Which I took to mean that she didn't understand. "Some of the research was for my company."

"Was your burglar alarm on?" Trinity asked.

"Of course. And everything was fine when I got home." Sister held her palms up in an "I give up" gesture. "It's got to be around there somewhere. But, you know, I can close

90

my eyes and see that computer and that briefcase lying right there in the middle of that bed."

I spoke up. "Are you going to call the police?"

"Not until I've looked over every inch of that house. Some twenty-year-old cop would come in, sure as anything, and find it sitting right on the kitchen counter where I put it." Mary Alice pressed her palm against her forehead. "Dear God, I'm getting paranoid."

"Who knows your alarm combination other than you?" Georgiana asked.

"Nobody but Patricia Anne and my daughter Debbie, who's in Gatlinburg on her honeymoon." Sister turned to me. "Incidentally, she called this morning, Mouse. She said they had been out jogging. Can you imagine Debbie jogging early in the morning? And she's very happy."

I beamed. "I'm so glad. I told you Henry was wonderful, didn't I? You could tell that by the papers he wrote in my eleventh grade AP English class. I still remember one he did on *Madame Bovary*. I knew he'd make some woman a good husband right that minute, because he understood how Emma was suffering."

Georgiana got us back on track. She turned to Trinity and asked about Meg's backup disks. Where did she keep them?

"I have no idea," Trinity said. "I don't know a thing about Meg's computer stuff."

"Except Judge Haskins tried to steal it in the park the other day." I explained to Georgiana about his rushing away with the computer under his arm.

"Well, Bobby Haskins hasn't been in my house," Sister said. "Which means the computer has got to be there somewhere. It'll show up."

Trinity stood up. "You're right. And I'm not going to worry about it. You can bring it with you to Meg's fond

91

farewell party."

We all looked at her blankly.

"A party at the Grand Hotel. We don't have funerals in our family, just a fond farewell party. It's a fairly common thing in South Alabama. You can even prearrange them."

Tears sprang to my eyes. I thought of Fred's calling the wedding a "celebration of life." And it was. But how sensible to celebrate the whole of a life.

"I hope you'll come," Trinity said.

We assured her that we would, to just let us know when it would be.

"Do people get a chance to say nice things about the guest of honor? Because that's what Patricia Anne and I were doing the other night about Meg."

Meg had clean fingernails? Wasn't that what Sister had said? The ends so white they didn't look real? Lord! I could just see Sister at the Grand Hotel informing everyone of that.

"Sometimes they do," Trinity said. "Sometimes they tell the truth." She gave a wry smile. The rest of us stood up. "I'll call you," she said.

Sister said she would take Trinity down to the city garage to get her car, that she wanted to hear all about Trinity's incarceration, and was it true what they said about the Birmingham police? Surely it wasn't.

"They were ladies and gentlemen," Trinity said. "One of them who lives under the interstate taught me a great way to cheat at cards."

"We really do need to pay them more," Sister said.

Georgiana left for work in an old beige Plymouth that belied her newly acquired wealth. But the other two took off into the warm spring morning, top down on Sister's convertible, Trinity clutching her blue felt hat on her head. They left me standing on the sidewalk wondering if

Meg's ashes would make it back to Mobile Bay.

The house seemed strangely empty when I went back inside. Since before the wedding, there had been company and all the activity that goes with a large family gathering. I breathed a sigh of relief and sank down on the den sofa with the morning paper.

On the second page was the first mention I had seen of Meg's death. A small paragraph stated that a ruling of suicide had been found in the death of a woman who had leaped from the tenth floor of the Jefferson County Courthouse on Monday. The woman had been identified as Margaret March Bryan, 64, of Fairhope, AL. Mrs. Bryan, a well-known genealogist, had been in Birmingham to attend a wedding.

They obviously hadn't talked to Trinity, I thought.

I turned to the next page and read who was at the forefront of the Oscar race. Then I turned back and read the tiny paragraph about Meg again. I looked at the shoes Rich's had advertised, and then turned back to the second page again.

The paragraph was haunting. There was something about seeing Meg's death reduced to a few words that bothered me. Deeply.

"There wasn't a suicidal bone in her body." Trinity's words.

"I'm having a hard time believing Meg Bryan would commit suicide that way." Fred's words.

"It wasn't a ladylike way to do it." Mary Alice's words chimed in with the others in my head.

I read the paragraph again. A healthy sixty-four year-old woman, actively involved in work she found challenging and was successful at, a woman who had no history of depression, who had eaten a good lunch with friends and

93

seemed fine, had suddenly decided to jump from a tenth-floor window. A woman, incidentally, who was fearful of heights.

This we were supposed to believe?

Obviously, the authorities did. Judge Haskins had seen to that.

"Stay out of this, Patricia Anne." I could hear Fred saying the words. Fred, who was on his way to Atlanta. Bless his heart. With so much of himself tied up in his business.

I sighed, reached for the phone, and called the Big, Bold, and Beautiful Shoppe. I needed a sharp listener to run all this by. Someone who didn't know Trinity or Judge Haskins, or even Georgiana Peach.

"Big, Bold, and Beautiful," Bonnie Blue answered cheerily.

"Have lunch with me," I said.

"Hey, Patricia Anne. I was just thinking about you. How come you're not tutoring today?"

"Spring break." Since my retirement, I had been tutoring at a local junior high school in, of all things, math. And after all those years of grading English papers, math was a delight. "Can you have lunch?"

"Sure. The Green and White?"

"The ferns get in your food and tickle your neck."

"All right, Miss Picky. You choose. I can't be gone but an hour, though."

"How about I go by the Piggly Wiggly deli, and we take it to the park?"

"Sounds good. Don't get the potato salad with mustard."

"Okay. One o'clock?"

"Fine."

When I hung up, I felt better. Bonnie Blue Butler

always has this effect on me.

I changed the sheets on the guestroom bed, and put a tub of washing on. I ate the last of the sweetrolls and cleaned the kitchen, even mopping the floor. By the time I vacuumed the den, took a shower, fought for a parking place at the Piggly Wiggly during lunch hour, and got to the Big, Bold, and Beautiful Shoppe, I was ten minutes late. Bonnie Blue was standing in front, waiting.

"I'm sorry," I apologized.

She looked into the car. "You didn't get the mustard kind, did you?"

We found a concrete table and bench that were empty. I had brought a red-and-white plastic tablecloth, and I spread it out while Bonnie Blue checked the contents of the grocery sack.

"Umm. Polski Wyrob pickles. I love those things. Umm. Baked beans."

"I got each of us a chicken breast, too," I said.

"And diet Coke. Thanks, Patricia Anne."

We helped our plates and dived in. After all the sweetrolls, I was surprised to find how hungry I was.

"This is good," Bonnie Blue said, taking a big bite of chicken. "A good idea."

I agreed that it was. Because it was spring break and such a warm day, the park was full of children running and playing. I ate and watched them idly.

"Potato salad," Bonnie Blue said. I handed her the carton.

"I need to run something by you," I said when our plates were empty and we were putting the lids back on the cartons.

"What? You want another cookie?"

"No. You know I trust your judgment, don't you?"

"Oh, Lord, Patricia Anne. What have you done now?"

"Nothing. Not a thing. That's what I wanted to talk to you about."

"Okay. But don't do what I tell you to do and make me feel guilty."

"I promise. Now listen, because it's pretty complicated. You remember that nice cousin of Henry's that sat in as the mother of the groom? Meg Bryan?"

Bonnie Blue nodded. "Sure. The one who does family histories."

"*Did* family histories, Bonnie Blue. Past tense. The woman jumped out of the courthouse last Monday and committed suicide. Or at least that's what the authorities are saying."

"Say what?"

I had Bonnie Blue's total attention. I told her about the lunch, the veal medallion's with orange sauce, Judge Haskins, the library and the sirens, the park, the body. I told her about the computer and Trinity and Georgiana Peach and the narcotics agent who lived under the interstate.

But, most important, I told her I didn't think that Meg Bryan had killed herself.

Bonnie Blue listened carefully, nodding occasionally. When I finally wound down, she tapped her forefinger thoughtfully against her upper lip and looked over at the children playing.

"You haven't talked to the police?" she finally asked.

"No. Judge Haskins did. And Trinity Buckalew, of course. She told them she was sure the judge killed Meg."

"Well, what if you went to them and said you thought she was murdered?"

I thought about this a moment. "They wouldn't do anything. To them, the case is closed."

"Then I got myself a scrumptious lunch for telling you

what you already knew, didn't I?"

"I guess so."

Bonnie Blue narrowed her eyes. "Stay out of this, Patricia Anne."

"I will. I promise. It's really none of my business."

"You got that right. Just remember it." Bonnie Blue checked her watch. "I got to go."

We shook the crumbs from the tablecloth and threw the trash into a receptacle. A slight breeze had risen from the south. Too warm.

"Gonna storm," Bonnie Blue said.

CHAPTER 8

AND IT DID. THE WEATHER CHANNEL RADAR SHOWED a dark green front interspersed with flashing red and yellow advancing inexorably toward Birmingham from the west. Fred was coming from the east, and their arrivals were simultaneous. He opened the kitchen door just as a bolt of lightning ripped across the sky.

"Lord!" He jumped into the kitchen. "Are tornado warnings up?"

"Severe thunderstorms. And hello to you, too." I was standing at the stove stirring a vegetable taco filling that Fred is especially fond of.

He came over and kissed the back of my neck. "Hi, sweetie. That smells good."

I turned and hugged him. He was home; now it could storm. "How did your day go?" I asked.

"Well," he pulled off his coat and reached into the refrigerator for a beer, "I found out what the problem is, and it's nothing we've done here at Metal Fab. Universal Satellite is doing some restructuring, including some early retirements. The two buyers who gave us most of our orders got caught in the sweep." He sat down at the table and looked out at the storm. "Gone with the wind."

I put the taco mix on the back burner and sat down at the table across from him.

"One of them was fifty-six," he said. "I doubt the other one was much older. Both knowledgeable. Easy to deal with." He shook his head. "It's terrible what some companies will do. They'll get away with it, too."

"You think the men got a decent retirement? Or any retirement? Surely they had to give them something."

"Nothing like the salaries they were getting. They got shafted, Patricia Anne." He drank from his beer. "And you know what?"

"What?"

"They put two women in their places." He stared at the beer can as if there might be some explanation there. "Not even women. Girls. Just out of college. Calling themselves metallurgists!"

"How awful," I murmured.

Fred glanced at me with his eyes narrowed; I looked back innocently.

"One of them called me 'Pop,' " he admitted mournfully.

A crash of thunder and a sudden fit of coughing hid my laugh. Twenty years ago when I was at the height of my personal feminist revolution, I would have been incensed at the chauvinist across the table. I've mellowed, though. To start with, Fred really does respect women, and not just in traditional roles. He's very happy with our family doctor, who is a lovely woman (So he calls her a "girl." He's getting there!), as well as our "girl" dentist. He even voted for a "'skirt" for governor last time, calling her that only once, to my knowledge. So when he opens doors for

98

me or moves to the outside when we're walking down the sidewalk, I just say "Thank-you." And I'm glad he taught our sons to do the same things.

"They seemed okay," he continued, "just have a lot to learn. I asked them if they'd like to go get a drink after work and we went to a damn coffee bar. You ever hear of such a thing? A coffee bar? I swear I got a cup of coffee that could have walked in on its own legs. Juan Valdez wouldn't have claimed it. And in about ten minutes, they both had to go. One had to pick up her kid, and the other was going to the gym for a workout." Fred looked out at the driving rain. "Just as well. I beat the storm home."

"Did they sound encouraging?"

"Who knows. Guess I'll find out in a week or so."

The lights flickered and came back on. "I better get the candles," I said.

Fred drained his beer. "I just hope Malcolm and Carl are okay."

"Malcolm and Carl?"

"The guys that had to take early retirement."

I got up and headed for the den closet to find the candles. "Call them tomorrow. Find out."

"Hell, I'll call them tonight. I'm sure I've got their cards here." Fred followed me into the den and switched the TV to The Weather Channel radar. "Looks bad," he said. "Is that portable fluorescent light in the closet?"

"Here it is." I handed him the light as well as several candles. Chances were they would soon be needed. It doesn't take much of a storm to knock the power out in Birmingham.

There's a simple explanation. This is a city of trees, pine, oak, maple, cherry laurel. This is a city of people who treasure those trees, each and every one of them. Consequently, this is a city whose populace is always at outs with the Alabama Power Company. In a scene enacted dozens of times each day, a Power Company truck wheels into a driveway. Men jump out to cut tree limbs that are hanging over power lines.

We residents rush out! "For God's sake. Are you crazy? There's a bluebird nest in that tree!" Or squirrel, possum, jaybird.

"Where?" The men walk around the tree, looking up into the limbs.

"Up yonder in the next to the highest limb past the second fork. See?"

The Power Company men see. They are kind men. They agree to come back in six weeks. Probably they will be back in three because the neighborhood lights are out. "Damn Power Company!" we complain.

But so far, so good. The lights flickered several times, but stayed on while we ate supper. I told Fred about Georgiana Peach and that Trinity had left for home. I also told him about the fond farewell party, which I thought was a great idea.

"Funerals are too sad," I said.

Fred crunched into his third taco. "They're supposed to be."

"They don't have to be," I insisted.

"Of course they do. They're funerals."

I thought about how little sense this made, but chose not to point it out. Sometimes, and he would die if he knew this, Fred reminds me of Mary Alice.

By the time we went to bed, the storm had passed and a light, steady rain was falling on the skylights. Good spring rain.

The next morning, when I took Woofer for his walk, it was considerably cooler, and an occasional dark puffy cloud would skim the sun for a moment. The sidewalk was covered with cherry and pear blossoms. The dogwoods, however, had benefited from the storm. They seemed to have opened more, becoming whiter overnight.

"It's a good morning," I said to Woofer who agreed. It was such a nice morning, we took a longer walk than usual. By the time we got home, both Woofer and I knew we had been exercising. He went straight to his water bowl and I went for the coffee pot. The message light was flashing on the telephone and I checked it. It was Mary Alice saying to call her immediately. I took a long hot shower and curled up on the den sofa before I called her.

"It's me," I said when she answered.

"This is just boggling my mind, Mouse. Scary as hell. When I heard about it I said to myself 'Whoa, wait up here. What's going on?' Didn't you? Say 'Whoa, wait up here. What's going on?' "

I ran my fingers through my wet hair. "What are you talking about?"

"Judge Haskins's murder, Mouse. What else would I be talking about?"

For a moment I was speechless. I clutched the phone to my ear while Sister said, "Mouse? You okay? Mouse?"

I finally stammered, "Judge Haskins was murdered?"

"You didn't know? It was all over the TV this morning." Sister sounded delighted at my ignorance. "I'm coming right over." She hung up before I had a chance to ask her any details.

I reached for the still unopened morning paper, re moved the rubber band from it, and stared at a picture of Judge Haskins that had been made at least twenty years earlier. The headline read JUDGE ROBERT HASKINS VICTIM OF VIOLENCE. The accompanying story that had obviously been written just in time to make it into the paper gave very few details. The judge had been found shot to death in his home late last night. A friend had made the discovery and called the police. The rest of the article detailed the judge's career, using the word "prominent" at least four times.

"He was naked," Mary Alice told me a few minutes later. "He was in the living room without a stitch on. And the person who found him is named Jenny Louise."

We were sitting at the table in the bay window with the newspaper picture of Judge Haskins staring at us.

"Jenny Louise what?" I asked.

"That's her stage name. Louise. She's a stripper at Gigi's Go Go. He was shot in the forehead. Right here." Sister pointed to the middle of her forehead. "One shot."

I looked at her in amazement. "Where did you get all this? All it says in the paper is that he was a victim of violence and was found by a friend."

"Buddy told me."

"Buddy Johnson? Father Time? The jet man? How did he know?"

"This is a small town, Patricia Anne. Buddy has connections. He called me this morning and said, 'Mary Alice, you were talking about Bobby Haskins the other night and I know you'd enjoy hearing some details.' Just like that."

"He already knows what a fun person you are, doesn't he?"

"Yes, as a matter of fact, he does, Miss Smarty Pants. Now, do you want to hear the rest?"

I had to admit that I did.

"Well, it seems that Judge Haskins and his wife had been separated for about a year mainly because little Bobby was dinging Jenny Louise."

"Dinging her?"

"Buddy Johnson is a gentleman, Mouse. It's as good a word as any."

"I'll try and remember that."

Mary Alice frowned at me. I smiled.

"So," she continued, "when Jenny Louise got in last night, I guess after work, there was the judge, lying in the living room, naked as a jaybird. She said at first she thought he was waiting for her, and then she noticed the hole in his head." Sister looked thoughtfully into her coffee cup. "I guess a little rigor mortis could have set in. You know?"

I said that, indeed, I knew. "Did Buddy tell you all this?"

"Not about the rigor mortis, Mouse. He's a gentleman."

"Well, he is. But on the way over here, you know what I was thinking?"

"What?"

"That I'm glad Trinity is in Fairhope. With her barging in the house and claiming Judge Haskins killed her sister, she'd be a prime suspect."

"I thought of that, too."

"We probably ought to call her and tell her about the judge. I'm sure she'd want to know."

I got up and went into the den. "I've got the number here somewhere." I looked into the drawer of the end table. "Here it is." I handed the phone and number to Mary Alice. "You tell her. Just tell her he's dead, though. Don't get into his dinging Jenny Louise."

Sister gave me a hard look and dialed the number.

"Trinity?" she said in a moment. "Oh? Jo? You sound just like Trinity. This is Mary Alice Crane in Birmingham. May I speak to Trinity, please?"

I watched the expression on Sister's face change as she

listened intently.

"She's not?" Pause. "No. I'm sure we mis-understood." Long pause. "I'm sure she's all right." Fingernail chewed. "No. Don't worry." Pause again. "Yes, I'll call you if I see her. And you tell her to call me if she comes in today. Thanks."

Mary Alice hung up and looked at me. "She didn't go home yesterday."

I had already figured that out, and my stomach was as tightening up. "You left her at the garage, didn't you?"

"No. I waited until they brought her car. She was headed for the interstate going up Twentieth last time I saw her."

We were both quiet for a moment, thinking. Then I said, "This doesn't mean she had anything to do with the judge's death."

"Of course it doesn't." Mary Alice was studying the arm of her navy turtleneck T-shirt. "I need some Scotch tape. Bubba Cat's shedding like crazy."

I opened the kitchen junk drawer and handed her a roll of tape. "The police will be looking for her, though, for questioning."

"Maybe she got lost." Mary Alice pulled off a piece of tape and stuck it to her shirt. "She struck me as being a little dingy."

"Bad choice of adjective."

"Well, you know what I mean. Wanting me to help her find her way around and then disappearing the way she did. Wanting to know how tall everybody is."

"Maybe all her sisters are short and this is her way of adapting to the existential stress."

Mary Alice looked up from her chest. "Lord! And me without a shovel right here in the middle of the pasture."

"Trinity wanting to know how tall people are is just an

idiosyncrasy, Sister. We all have them."

"I don't." Sister pulled a piece of tape from the roll.

I let that one pass. "Well, there's no way she can be lost. You can't get lost on I-65."

"Sure you can. Remember that man last year who was going to the dentist in Pell City and got on the interstate going north instead of south and ended up in Cincinnati or somewhere? The dentist treated him for free when they found him. I thought that was nice." She held up the tape for me to see. "I think Bubba may need some hormones. What do you think?"

I shook my head. "He's just getting rid of his winter coat. And Trinity isn't wandering around up in Ohio." I sat down in the chair across from Sister. "You know, there's a possibility the police may question us, too."

"Us? Don't be ridiculous."

"Well, we were the ones who got Trinity out of jail."

"Not me." Mary Alice quit ripping tape from her shirt. "You."

"But they're not stupid. They know Meg Bryan was Judge Haskins's ex-wife. And she was your house guest."

Mary Alice looked me straight in the eyes and, so help me, had the nerve to say, "What have you gotten us into now, Patricia Anne?"

I chose to ignore her. It seems I make this choice a lot. Actually, I had just had a thought that took precedence over one of our sisterly spats. What if Trinity was the third death?

"Surely not!" Sister said when I voiced the possibility.

"Why not? They all three could have known something or had something that the murderer wanted."

"For God's sake, Mouse! You're letting your imagination go wild. Meg committed suicide, the judge's wife shot him because of Jenny Louise, and Trinity's lost."

"Too many coincidences. I'm going to get a piece of paper."

"What for?"

"To write down what we know."

"I don't know anything." Sister stuck a piece of tape to her ample bosom.

"Don't be silly." I came back with a yellow legal pad and a pencil and sat on the sofa beside her. "Here," I said. "Look." I drew three stick figures and under them printed Meg, Judge, and Trinity. Maybe it's the old schoolteacher in me, but putting things down on paper helps me think.

"Why is the judge one in the middle?" Mary Alice asked.

"Because that's where I put him. Now, pay attention." I drew a line from Trinity to Meg and wrote "sister" on it. Then I drew a line from Judge to Meg and wrote "married."

"Add 'a long time ago.' "

"I don't have room." I looked at my drawing. "Now we start thinking about any other connections. Free associating."

Sister reached over and pointed to the space between the Trinity and Judge stick figures. "Draw a line there and put 'pissed.' "

I drew the line but said, "She was pissed because she thought he killed Meg. And she thought he killed Meg because of the bastardy papers." I wrote "bastard" on the line.

"But he was into genealogy, too, so he would already have known about the papers. He wouldn't have worried about being blackmailed with them."

"Genealogy," I wrote. Which reminded me. "Did you find Meg's computer?"

"No. It's not in that house. I swear, Mouse, I've turned

106

the place upside down. I even had Tiffany help me."

Sister is the only person I know who has a maid named Tiffany. The Magic Maid. She makes a lot more money than I ever did teaching. Plus, she looks like a Tiffany, with blond-streaked hair and a fantastic shape that she keeps toned with house cleaning, so she says. I'd rather not believe it. She's also great at her job, so if she couldn't find the computer, it wasn't there.

"That's got to be important." I wrote "computer," and drew a line to it from both Meg and the judge. "Could Judge Haskins's security system have been so similar to yours that he could have worked it? By-passed it somehow?"

"I don't see how. I have my own code."

"The first six numbers of your Social Security card!"

"No one knows that but you and Debbie."

"It's the second most common code. Right after birthdays."

Mary Alice sat forward. "He could have gotten the number off any document of mine at the courthouse, couldn't he have?"

"Sure. Even jury records."

We grinned at each other.

"But he didn't have anything to do with Meg's death," I said.

"How do you know?"

"Because he said so when he brought Meg's ashes. He said to tell Trinity." I shrugged. "You could tell he wasn't lying."

"Okay," Sister accepted this. "Let's get back to the list."

But we were stuck. If Judge Haskins had managed to get into Sister's house, which was possible, and take the computer and the other files, we were still left with a big question. Why? Neither of us knew enough about genealogical research to imagine what could be in the files that would make someone want to steal them. Or commit murder.

The phone rang, and I left Mary Alice studying the stick figures and went to answer it.

"Carl and Malcolm are in Augusta playing golf," Fred said. "Carl checked his answering machine and got the message I left last night."

"So early retirement hasn't devastated them?"

"Hell no. They said for me to come join them."

"You want to?" I thought his voice sounded a little wistful.

"I told them it was too late for me to retire early."

"Sixty-three isn't too late. We could see the world."

"Dream on. We'd do good to get to a state park occasionally."

"Alabama has wonderful state parks."

"True." We were both quiet for a moment, doing a little wishful thinking, when I heard Mary Alice screech.

"What was that?" Fred asked.

"Sister's here. Did you hear Judge Haskins was murdered last night?"

"I did. That's one reason I called. Don't get messed up in this, Patricia Anne."

"Don't worry," I said.

Mary Alice screeched again. "Mouse!"

"Let me go see what she wants. I love you, sweetheart."

"I love you, too. You listen to me, now."

"Cross my heart." I hung up and went into the den. "What?"

"There's a police car out front."

"Well, my Lord! So what? They want to ask us about Trinity and Meg. Just like I said."

"Policemen make me nervous."

"Because you're always speeding."

"I am not!" Sister protested.

The doorbell rang, and I went to answer it. Opened the door to a familiar, smiling face, that of Officer Bo Mitchell Sister and I had gotten to know her just before Christmas, when we had somehow managed to become entangled in a very nasty crime at an art gallery.

"What are you up to now, Patricia Anne?" Bo grinned. "I swear, you girls are nothing but trouble."

Bo, plump at Christmas, had put on a little more weight, reminding me more than ever of Bonnie Blue. Bo's skin was darker and didn't have the coppery tones that Bonnie Blue's had. Bo was also about twenty years younger. But there was a definite resemblance, not only in their brilliant smiles, but in their attitudes. Bonnie Blue had described herself as "comfortable in her body." Bo had the same strength and assurance.

"Are you the only police officer in this neighborhood?" I asked. "How come we always end up with you?"

"Just lucky, I guess."

We hugged each other and she came into the house. "Mary Alice is back in the den," I said. "Biting her fingernails."

"Speeding again?"

"And ignoring parking tickets, probably."

"Do, Jesus. I'm gonna arrest that woman for sure."

Sister recognized Bo's voice, and came to give her a hug. I got us all Cokes and we sat at the kitchen table.

"Okay," Bo said when she had her notebook ready. "Tell me, about the jumper first." She looked at her notes. "Margaret Bryan. Says here you knew her. That she was visiting you when she decided to play birdie."

"She came up for my daughter Debbie's wedding. She's the groom's cousin," Mary Alice began.

An hour later, we had gotten to Judge Haskins delivering Meg's ashes. I fixed pimento cheese sandwiches, and we ate them while we finished the story with how we had tried to call Trinity.

"Though I'm sure she's all right," Sister said.

"She is," Bo Mitchell said. "She spent the night in a motel in Montgomery."

"How do you know?" I asked.

"Hey, give us credit." Bo flipped back several pages in her notebook. "Yesterday she bought an English coal scuttle with brass inlay on the door and some 1950 tablecloths, the white ones with a fruit border like you used to put on those formica tables with the chrome legs. You know what I'm talking about?"

Mary Alice and I looked at each other. "I still have some," I admitted.

"Well, now you know there's a market." Bo popped the last of her sandwich into her mouth and reached for a lemon cookie.

"Nothing like a humble cop," Sister muttered.

Bo grinned, took a couple of cookies, and stood up. "I gotta go. Y'all take care now."

I walked her to the door, where she suddenly turned serious. "Bullet holes in the head and bodies pushed out of buildings are not pretty, Patricia Anne. Y'all stay away from it. Okay?"

"Give me a break. We've just happened to get involved in a couple of unfortunate incidents in the past."

"Just happened, huh?"

I grinned. "The motive is something in the computer, isn't it?"

"Tell you what, Patricia Anne. I'll go surf the Internet a while and let you know."

"Smart ass."

Bo laughed her deep laugh and started down the walk. "Thanks for the sandwich," she called back.

Behind me, Sister was tearing up the paper with the stick figures drawn on it.

"Well, at least Trinity is okay," I said. "Just shopping."

Mary Alice dropped the pieces of paper into a wastebasket. "So much for your investigative theories. Let's go see how many of those tablecloths you've got."

CHAPTER 9

I WAS IN NO HUMOR TO GO DIGGING INTO THE BACK of the linen closet, and I said so. The tablecloths could just sit there, accruing in value. What was the difference between that and interest from the bank? Weren't the people who bought the tablecloths planning on their going up in value?

"Not necessarily," Mary Alice said. "They're buying them for their nostalgic value you know, there's no telling what my Shirley Temple doll would be worth if you hadn't lost it. I can just see that little white dress with red polka dots and little red leather shoes right now, plain as day."

Time to change the subject. I reminded Sister that she hadn't told me about Buddy Johnson's tigerish activities on their date.

She was happy to oblige. "To start with," she giggled, "he kept trying to run his hand up my leg at the opera."

"Maybe he thought it was his," I said. "And that it had gone to sleep."

Sister snatched up her purse, which was so heavy that it elicited a small "woof" as she straightened up.

"You know what you are, Patricia Anne? Tacky." And

with that announcement, she stomped out of the back door.

I guess I had gone too far.

I straightened up the kitchen and thought about all that had happened over the last few days. Who would ever have believed that a family history could be such a big deal? Or that a person could become obsessed with it to the point of murder? Unless there was another motive for the two deaths. Assuming they were connected. Assuming Meg was murdered.

I fished the pieces of paper from the wastebasket and put them together like a jigsaw puzzle. The fact that Trinity had shown up safe and sound, while certainly good news, changed the picture.

The phone's ring startled me.

"Patricia Anne? This is Georgiana Peach."

"How are you, Georgiana?"

"Pretty good. I'm calling to see if you've heard from Trinity. I called to tell her about poor Judge Haskins, and her sister said she hadn't returned from Birmingham."

"She stopped in Montgomery to buy some antiques, I understand."

"You've talked to her, then. She knows about Bobby."

"Well, actually, no, I haven't talked to her. A policewoman came by this morning asking about Meg and Trinity. She was the one who told us Trinity was in Montgomery."

"A policewoman?" Georgiana's breathy voice caught.

"It may be dawning on them that Meg didn't commit suicide, and that her death and the judge's are connected."

"I see." There was a long pause.

"Georgiana? You there?" I asked finally.

"Did your sister find Meg's computer?"

"She says it's absolutely not at her house. The other

stuff isn't either. The other briefcase."

"Dear God." Georgiana hung up on me. I frowned and put the phone back in its cradle. It rang again. "Sorry," she said, and hung up again.

Enough. I threw the pieces of paper back into the wastebasket, changed into a lavender-colored windsuit Fred had given me for Christmas, and headed for the mall. His birthday was next week, and he had been eying a hammock at Brookstone. Bless his heart, he deserved it. And I needed to get out of the house.

The hammock was in stock, and the Brookstone guy even carried it to my car for me. I picked Fred out a card, which took all of five minutes, and my shopping spree was over. I've never enjoyed wandering around malls for hours like Sister loves to do. She says it shows a certain lack of imagination on my part. I say it makes my feet hurt. When I walk, I want it to be outdoors, preferably with Woofer. So I was soon on my way home to a stack of ironing I had been putting off for days.

Now, it just so happens that the quickest way to my house from the mall is down Lakeshore Drive which is not located on a lake at all, but which is a very pretty name for a street, conjuring up images of mansions with green lawns sloping to water. Actually, there are some nice houses along Lakeshore. It is also where Samford University is located. Samford with the terrific genealogy program and library.

What, I asked myself, tootling down Lakeshore, would Fred appreciate for his birthday even more than the hammock?

He would appreciate some work on his family history, myself answered. Haley would be interested in it, too. Need to check those genes.

What about the ironing? I asked myself

113

It can wait, myself said.

You'll do anything to get out of ironing, I told myself. I turned on my left turn signal.

Samford University has one of the most beautiful campuses in the United States. An old, prestigious school, it outgrew its city location after World War II, and the powers that be had the foresight to move to a site in Shades Valley that allowed them to follow a master building plan. Each building, each tree, each bench and flower seems to blend into a gracious whole. The day I turned in, the Bradford pears that line the entrance driveway were in full bloom. Beds of daffodils and bright red tulips were everywhere. And, to my surprise, the campus was almost deserted. Spring break, I remembered, hoping the library would be open.

It was. The number of cars in the parking lot said so. I pulled my old Cutlass Cierra in between a Jaguar and a Volkswagen bug. Fit right in.

The genealogy department was on the third floor. I took the elevator and turned left as the sign directed me into what seemed to be a whole wing of the library. At the main desk, a pretty cheerleader-type blonde was poring over a *Bride* magazine. She was so engrossed in it, she jumped when I spoke.

"I'd like to look at some records," I said.

"Yes, ma'am. Do you need some help?" Lord, the politeness of well-brought-up Southern children does my heart good.

I looked around the room. Several people were working at tables, using microfiche tapes. Others were reading or working on computers in carrels that lined the walls.

"I'm starting to look up my family's history and I'm afraid I don't know much about, it."

"Well, I'll be glad to help you," the girl beamed.

114

"I'll do it, Emily." A tall, elegant woman in her early thirties came to the desk from the back. She was wearing a dress the color of new spring leaves, and her dark hair was pulled back simply in a barrette. Curly, escaping tendrils kept the hairstyle from being severe. She smiled at me. "You don't recognize me, do you, Mrs. Hollowell? I'm Castine Murphy. Cassie. You taught me at Alexander High."

"Castine Murphy?" I was amazed at the transformation.

"The same."

"No, definitely not the same." I looked at her admiringly.

She laughed, a nice throaty laugh. "Contacts, makeup, and a good hairstylist can do wonders."

I shook my head. "It's more than that."

Castine turned to the library assistant, who still stood between us. "I was the biggest nerd in school," she explained. "I admit it."

The girl looked shocked. "You, Miss Murphy?"

"Nerd of the world. Right, Mrs. Hollowell?"

"You were studious," I said, "not a nerd."

"Mrs. Hollowell is being kind."

And in a way, I was. Castine Murphy, poring myopically over her books, probably had topped the other students' nerd list. If the other girls' skirts were short and bought at the Gap, Castine's were mid-calf from the Goodwill thrift store. If they were reading *Love Story*, she was reading Jung's *Man And His Symbols*. Teachers see students like this every year, defiantly different, making a statement. But Castine was not one of these. She was simply herself, and I had appreciated that.

"What about her parents?" I had asked Frances Zata, the counselor, when Castine had first come into my class.

Both doctors, Frances told me. Castine was an only

child, born to them late in life, and they thought she hung the moon.

At graduation, when Will Butler, the principal, handed her her diploma, and Castine took it, saying only "thank-you," I remember wishing I had gotten to know her better.

And now Castine, who had metamorphosed beautifully into Cassie, stood before me, well-dressed, friendly, obviously successful.

"I grew up," she said.

I smiled happily. "Yes. You did."

"And you haven't changed a bit, Mrs. Hollowell. What can I help you look up?"

I explained that I would like to begin looking up Fred's family for a birthday surprise. I told her the names that he remembered, and that they were from Montgomery.

"Great," she said. "Montgomery's records are remarkably complete. A lot of times a fire has wiped out a courthouse and the old county records are lost. But Montgomery's records go back to the time when Alabama was part of the Mississippi territory. Land grants and deeds. Come on, I'll show you."

Emily went back to her *Bride* magazine, and I followed Cassie across the room.

"Are the records all on computers?" I asked anxiously.

"Some of them. But there are also copies of the originals. You don't have to know how to use a computer. It helps, though." She nodded toward a woman studying a computer screen. "Just about all the professionals use them now. There are some excellent programs available."

That reminded me of Meg. "Did you know Meg Bryan?" I asked.

"Sure. I knew Meg real well. Terrific genealogist. Was she a friend of yours?"

116

"She was up here for my niece's wedding when she died."

"That was really a shock, wasn't it? I never thought of Meg as suicidal." Cassie Murphy turned left and pointed toward some shelves. "Here are Montgomery's census records, birth and death records, and land transactions. The dates are on the side, and they're in chronological order. My recommendation would be to start with the census records. They're easy and tell you exactly when the family members first arrived there. You can narrow down the birth and death dates that way, too. Hollowell isn't a common name, so you shouldn't have too much trouble. What was your husband's mother's maiden name?"

"Haley. My daughter's named for her."

"That should be a fairly easy one, too." Cassie took down a book of census records dated 1900. "Let's see what we find here."

I followed her out to a table, where she opened the book. "You know," I said, "seeing you as a librarian is just wonderful. You always did love books."

"Oh, I don't work here. I'm a professional genealogist. I'm here doing some research, and saw you when you came in." She smiled. "I started out in computers, but got sidetracked onto genealogy. It's a wide-open field. Interesting."

"Meg Bryan said it was a dog-eat-dog business."

"It can be." She ran her finger down the index. "Here," she said. "Here's a Noah Hollowell. Your husband's grandfather?"

"Yes." I looked where Cassie was pointing.

"Okay," she said. "Get out your pencil and paper. You've started."

Three hours later when I quit for the day, my aching shoulders told me the advantage of working on the computers. Or even the microfiche disks. Lifting those heavy records was hard work. But I had the marriage date of Fred's grandparents, when they had bought the house that still stood on West Jeff Davis Avenue in Montgomery, knew that they had paid $1400 for it. I also had the birth dates of their children and the death date of a son who lived to be eighteen months old.

If my shoulders hadn't been hurting, I don't think I would have quit when I did. One piece of information made you want another. Sister and I had discovered that fact when we happened on the Tree family while we were waiting for Meg at the downtown library. And today's research was even more interesting. My children carried these genes. They would be intertwined with mine from now on.

Awesome thought. I pushed back my chair, stretched, rubbed my shoulders, and started out. At the first table, I noticed a familiar figure poring over a book: Camille Atchison, the blonde who had called Meg a bitch at the wedding reception. Maybe now that Meg was gone, she could find a way to circumvent the bad-apple ancestor who was causing her problems.

"Mrs. Hollowell? I hope you found some useful information." Cassie Murphy was standing at the front desk, elegant, cool in her green dress, talking to bride-to-be Emily.

"I did. Thank-you, Cassie. And it was wonderful seeing you."

"It was nice seeing you, too. And if you really get interested in doing research and need some help, I'd be happy to help you. Here, here's my card."

"Thanks. I could get hooked," I admitted. I was halfway to my car before I looked at the card. CASSIE MURPHY, it read, THE FAMILY TREE, with an address on

Eighteenth Street and two phone numbers. I'll be damned, I thought. Cassie worked with Georgiana Peach.

There was a message from Haley on my telephone when I got home. She and Philip were coming for supper and bringing Chinese. If it wasn't all right, call her.

I had no problem with that. I wanted to see more of this man who, obviously, was seeing a lot of our daughter.

There was also a message from Mary Alice asking me to call her.

"I thought you were mad at me," I said when she answered.

"I am. That has nothing to do with this. I think I found some of Meg's backup disks."

"You did? Where?"

"In the glove compartment of my car. Isn't that strange?"

"You're sure they're Meg's?"

"How would I know, Mouse? I just know they're computer disks and they sure aren't mine."

"But why would she put them in your glove compartment?"

"Hell, Patricia Anne. All I know is I needed a Kleenex and figured there were some in the glove compartment. When I opened it, three little blue disks fell out that say Sony Micro floppy disk Double-sided. Okay? And I don't believe the disk fairy left them there."

"You don't have to be so smart aleck." I thought for a minute. "That really is weird, isn't it? Leaving them in your glove compartment. Reckon why she did that?"

"So we would find them?"

"I guess so." Somewhere in the back of my mind, faint alarm bells were sounding. "Are you by yourself?"

"Sure. Why?"

"Because those disks could be important. They could be the reason Meg was killed. Why don't you call Bo Mitchell and tell her about them?"

"Lord, Patricia Anne, you're such an alarmist. I'm not about to call the police to come get these disks. I would like to know what's on them, though." Mary Alice paused. "Probably just a bunch of that genealogy stuff we couldn't make heads or tails of." Mary Alice paused again. "We have got to become computer literate, you know it? We could take those classes at Jeff State for old people. Don't cost a dime. We could sign up for the summer right now, and by the fall we could be on-line. You know? Getting e-mail."

While she was rattling, I was thinking. "Listen," I said, "I've got an idea. Haley is coming over tonight and bringing Philip Nachman. She said he worked on some family history and used a computer. Maybe he could help us."

"What are you having for supper?"

"They're bringing Chinese. Let me check and see if it's okay with Haley if we ask him to bring his computer. She might have other plans for after supper. I'll call you back." I started to hang up. "Sister?"

"What?"

"Don't let anybody know you have those disks."

"Good Lord, Mouse!"

"I mean it!"

"Okay! And tell Haley I want almond chicken."

I hung up and called Haley. She answered on the first ring, and I explained to her about the disks.

"Sure, Mama," she said. "I'm sure he'd like to help. Let me check, though."

In a moment she, called back. "He said fine. Are the disks IBM or Apple?"

"They're Sony." I was pleased that I had remembered this bit of information.

"I mean what kind of computer were they formatted for?"

"It makes a difference?"

"I'll tell Philip you don't know. I think he works mainly on a Macintosh. My little one here is an IBM. We'll bring both of them."

I thanked her and hung up. Sister was right. We were going to have to become computer literate.

Woofer was waiting for me. I put several dog treats in my pocket and went to take him for his walk. As we got back, Fred was pulling into the driveway. I could tell by the grin on his face that he had good news.

"The Atlanta girls came through with a great order," he announced, patting Woofer and leaning over to kiss me. "They said, 'Pop, this is because you're cute as a button. Tell your wife we think so.'"

"They did not." I kissed him back happily. "But I'm sure they thought it."

He reached back into the car and brought out a box of Godiva chocolates. "*Pour vous.*"

"Chocolates! And French with a South Alabama accent! I can't resist."

"I know. Put your canine up, woman. I'll be waiting."

And I did. And he was.

We, were the picture of decorum, though, by the time Haley and Philip arrived.

"Mama!" Haley called down the hall. "We're here."

"Come on back." I was setting the table in the breakfast nook, and Fred was outside filling up the bird feeders.

They came into the kitchen, preceded by the wonderful smell of Chinese takeout from the large sack Haley was carrying.

"Hello, Mrs. Hollowell." Philip Nachman held a notebook computer in each hand.

"Hello, Philip. Why don't you just put those on the coffee table in the den?"

"Sure."

Philip had on khaki pants and a navy and khaki striped knit shirt. The casual clothes made him look younger than he had at the wedding. But there was more salt in his hair than pepper, and the knit shirt showed the beginnings of a belly.

Haley put the sack of food on the kitchen counter, tapped on the window, and waved to her father. She was wearing a red jumpsuit that made her waist look incredibly tiny.

"There's beer and wine in the refrigerator," I said. "Philip? You want a beer?" she called.

"That would be great."

"There's wine if you'd rather."

"Beer."

Haley reached into the cabinet, got a couple of glasses, and poured two beers. I watched her in amazement. This was my daughter who, despite my protests, has drunk from a can all her life. She put pretzels onto a plate (God forbid that Philip eat out of a bag!), put the glasses and plate on a tray and carried them into the den.

Fred came in the back door, reached in the refrigerator, and got a can of beer. I handed him a glass. "Don't ask," I said.

Philip and Haley were sitting close together on the sofa. Philip jumped up and shook Fred's hand.

"Hear you're an ENT," Fred exclaimed jovially.

"That's right."

"And his office hours are over at 5:00," Haley gave her father a warning look.

"Of course they are, sweetheart." Fred beamed at Philip. "Have a seat, Dr. Nachman."

The back, door banged. "I'm here!" Mary Alice called. "Do I have to go back outside and knock?"

"Of course not, Mary Alice." The good day at the office, the greeting when he got home, and Haley's ENT were doing wonders for Fred's disposition.

"Come on in."

"Hello, Aunt Sister," both Haley and Philip said as Mary Alice came into the den. The greeting coming from both of them startled me though, of course, Philip would call her "aunt." After all, she had been married to his uncle. I tried to remember how long Sister and Uncle Philip had been married. Ten years? And wasn't he the one who had the heart attack and dropped dead in the shower? Or was it one of the others? No, it was Philip, because Sister had said he was the neatest man in the world. Right to the end.

I eyed Philip the Second, twenty years Haley's senior with the beginning of a potbelly. Heart problems are genetic.

"Hello, dear children," Mary Alice said, kissing the air toward both Haley and Philip and handing Philip three blue plastic disks.

"What are those?" Fred said.

"Computer disks that belonged to Meg Bryan, I think," Mary Alice explained. "They were in my glove compartment. Philip's going to read them."

"If I can," he said. He turned to Haley, "They're IBM. We'll have to use your computer."

"I thought you weren't going to get involved in this," Fred said to me.

"She's not." Mary Alice sat down on the sofa beside Philip. "I'm just curious about what's on these disks."

123

"Well, do you want to eat first, or look at the disks?" I asked.

"This won't take but a minute," Philip said. He handed Haley his beer and moved the plate of pretzels toward Mary Alice, who promptly took a handful. He pulled one of the small computers toward him, reached to the back, and turned it on. The machine groaned and grunted.

"What's wrong?" I asked.

"Nothing. I'm just waiting on the 'A' prompt." In a moment, he slipped a blue disk into the side of the computer and typed something.

"What are you doing?" Sister asked.

"Just typing 'Directory.' Hmmm."

"What?" Sister asked. Both she and Haley were sitting on the edge of the sofa and eying the screen. I moved around so I could see.

"There are eight files listed. But the disk is almost used up." Philip pointed to the screen, which looked impressive. "There's the auto exec file, and another file named 'Genie' that's a big one."

"She told me she was writing a genealogy program," I said.

"Then this is probably the main program, the one she was writing." Philip ran his hand through his still-abundant hair. "Let's see. There are a couple of ways to do this, but I'm going to do a soft boot and see what happens."

Soft boot. Sister and I nodded as if we knew what he was doing. Philip hit some keys, and a totally new display came up on the screen. "Wow, look at this, y'all. Nice graphics."

By this time, Fred was looking over my shoulder. "What's going on?" he asked.

"Well, we're into her program, but I don't have any

124

idea how it works."

"Damn," Mary Alice said. "Does that mean we can't use the disk?"

"It means I'll have to work on it a while," Philip said. "Hand me another disk, Haley."

This time when he slipped the disk into the computer he said, "Okay, this one is different. There are sixty-two files, probably created by a word processor."

"Try WordPerfect," Haley said. "It's on my hard drive."

Again, Philip typed some directions. "You're right. Look, ladies."

The ladies, plus Fred, looked at a letter written to someone in Richburg, South Carolina, on January 12 requesting a genealogical newsletter.

"Reckon all sixty-two are like this?" I asked.

Philip shrugged. "That's what genealogists do. Dig into every source of material they can find." He picked up the third disk. "Let's look at this one."

A new list came up on the screen. "Okay. All these files have a 'gen' extension. Must have been generated through the Genie program, the one she wrote."

"See what's on them," Mary Alice urged.

"He can't," Haley explained patiently. "He's got to figure out how Genie works."

"You mean we're stuck?"

"We can read the letters," Haley said, smiling.

Philip inserted the first disk into the computer again, and studied it. "Tell you what," he said, "my big computer is an IBM. How about I take this home and see if I can figure it out. I'd like to see what kind of program she's written. And then I can read the 'gen' files.

"And I'll print out the letters and bring each of you a copy of them," Haley said. "You could each read half of them. If Meg put the disk in your glove compartment so you would find it, there may be something important there."

"Your mama's not getting messed up in this," Fred said. "Leave her out."

Philip hit some keys that made what looked like comic book curse words come up on the screen.

"Look at that," Mary Alice said. "My feelings exactly."

CHAPTER 10

WE HAD A VERY NICE SUPPER. I PUT THE CARTONS of Chinese in the middle of the table, and we passed them around. But we ate with my good Rose Point silver. It matched the beer in the glasses better. I don't think Haley and Philip knew what they were eating. It was nice, but disconcerting.

"Just like his uncle," Mary Alice said as we watched them go down the walk to Philip's car.

"Old," Fred agreed.

"My Philip would have been one of *People's* Sexiest Men Alive if they had just known about him. Which reminds me." Mary Alice turned to Fred, who was having difficulty absorbing this disturbing information. "Buddy wants y'all to go to New Orleans with us in his jet this weekend. Actually, just Saturday night for dinner. Only takes an hour. You're not going to believe that plane. The bathroom's the best part about it, I swear. You remember the bathrooms on that plane we went to Europe on, Mouse? On Buddy's plane you have room to turn around."

I said that I did, unfortunately, remember the bathrooms on the plane we went to Europe on. My only trip to Europe. With Sister. Chernobyl blew up while we were there. Why was I not surprised?

"And you can sit in the bathroom and use the phone. Buddy says he does that a lot. Would Galatoire's suit y'all?"

"What?" The sudden jump in locations had confused me.

"Would you like to eat at Galatoire's? It's still my favorite restaurant in New Orleans. Lord, what they can do to soft-shell crabs. I don't think it matters to Buddy. He's easy to get along with."

Fred agreed that that sounded great. After Sister left, though, he said he hoped Buddy made it until Saturday. "Keep Mary Alice away from him much as you can."

"Not funny," I said. But I laughed anyway. It was wonderful to see Fred in a good humor again.

Sometime during the night, I woke up looking for the Maalox. Almond chicken and shrimp fried rice sat like a chunk of lead in my stomach. So I wouldn't wake Fred, I ended up on the sofa reading, and when I woke up again, it was eight-thirty. An empty cereal bowl in the sink assured me that Fred had had some breakfast. He had also made coffee and left the pot on "warm." I drank a quick cup and went out to get my dog, who was waiting patiently for me.

The rain from a couple of days before had washed the pollen down and made the grass grow. The sound of mowers permeating the neighborhood attested to this fact. The only clouds in the sky were a couple of jet trails, and on the mountain, Vulcan mooned us mightily. Mitzi Phizer, my neighbor, was already out in her yard working with   her flowers.

"You need one of these." She pointed to the large straw hat that shaded her face.

"I've got on sunblock. Factor one hundred, or something like that." I leaned over her fence. "What kind of flowers are those?"

"They're peonies, Patricia Anne. Just plain old peonies. I swear, you ought to join my garden club now that you're retired. I can't imagine anybody who lives in the South not knowing a peony when they see one."

"I'm so ashamed." Mitzi and I grinned at each other.

"It meets the third Tuesday. I'm serious."

I shook my head. "Not only do I not know a peony, I can hardly tell a caladium from an elephant ear. They'd kick me out. Spare yourself the humiliation."

"You're probably right. That's scandalous." Mitzi pulled off her hat and wiped her forehead with her sleeve. "It's already hot. Just think about July."

"Won't do to think about." I untangled Woofer's leash from my leg.

"Arthur and Fred both need to retire, so we can go somewhere cool in the summer."

"God's truth."

"There's not a ghost of a chance that will happen though, is there?"

"Not anytime soon." Woofer lay down across my feet patiently. "You remember Philip Nachman?" I asked Mitzi.

"Mary Alice's second husband? Sure. Nice man. Why?"

"Well, his nephew Philip the Second, acted as father of the bride at Debbie's wedding. Remember I told you about him? Anyway, I think Haley's fallen for him."

"That's wonderful, Patricia Anne! Haley's been a lost soul since Tom died."

"I think it's wonderful, too. But he's about twenty years older than she is."

"So what? You like him?"

128

"Very much. He's a widower with grown children. An ear doctor."

"An ENT? Lord! Tell her to marry that guy."

"That part pleased Fred, too." We smiled at each other.

"Is he as smitten as she is?"

"Seems to be."

"Sounds good to me. Is the age difference really bothering you?"

"Well, I keep thinking if he were her age, they would have a whole lifetime to spend together."

"Tom was her age," Mitzi reminded me. "There are no guarantees, Patricia Anne."

"True." I moved my feet so Woofer would get up. "Thank-you, Dr. Peale."

"Norman Vincent to you, honey. And any time."

I finished my walk feeling very chipper, gave Woofer his treat, poured myself a bowl of Cheerios, and settled down to read the paper. Mistake. I was in the dumps in about two seconds. Three fatal shootings, an airplane crash, and a multiple pileup on I-59 had made the front page. I put the paper down and turned on *The Price Is Right*. In a few minutes, I felt better. Bob Barker was as good for my mood as Mitzi had been. By the time a plump old lady with "One of Barker's Beauties" on her T-shirt won a Lexus, I was fine.

"The world is too much with us," I muttered, heading for the shower.

There were three phone messages waiting when I got out: a company wanting to do home repairs, Georgiana Peach saying there was something she would like to discuss with me, and Sister having lunch with Bonnie Blue and I could come if I wanted to.

I deleted the home repair message but listened to Georgiana's again. Her wispy voice had a strained, shaky quality to it, as if she weren't feeling well. I called the number she had left, but got her answering machine. Phone tag.

As for Mary Alice, she was going to the Big, Bold, and Beautiful Shoppe to buy a new outfit for Saturday night, and I needed one, too, she informed me when I called.

"I'm going to wear my red suit," I said.

"That red suit is shiny in the butt and the shoulder pads are too big. They don't wear shoulder pads that big anymore."

"Maybe 'they' don't, but I do."

"We're getting testy, aren't we? What about the outfit you wore re to the wedding?"

"Too dressy. I told you. I'm wearing my red suit."

"Well, all right. Good heavens." Mary Alice paused. "Bonnie Blue and I are having lunch at the Blue Moon. You want me to pick you up?"

"I'm busy this afternoon." Actually, I was cross. There was not a damn thing wrong with my red suit.

"What are you doing?"

"I have an appointment," I lied.

"With a doctor? Are you sick, Mouse? What hurts you?" Sister sounded so alarmed, my conscience hurt me. A little.

"Not with a doctor. I'm fine."

"A lawyer? Are you in some kind of trouble?"

"No. I am not in any kind of trouble. I'm just going to the library," I admitted.

"You have an appointment at the library? What kind of an appointment would you have at a library?"

"To discuss a program," I lied again, with the first thing that came into my head.

"What kind of program?"

Lord, when would I ever learn that lying to Sister is just

too much trouble. Sixty years certainly hadn't been long enough.

Somehow I extricated myself from my tangled web enough to satisfy her. I fixed myself a peanut butter and banana sandwich for lunch, got the notes I had made yesterday, and headed for the library.

Emily, the cheerleader, was reading a *House Beautiful* today. She recognized me and informed me that Ms. Murphy was there again today, in the reading room. Did I want to see her?

I thanked her, said it wasn't necessary, that I would be working in the Montgomery County section.

"You got it." The girl leaned forward and showed me a picture of an ornate Georgian flower arrangement on a huge mahogany dining room table. "You like this, Ms. Hollowell?"

"Too fancy for my taste."

"Hmm." She studied the picture. "I kind of like it."

Some young man, I thought, had better fasten his seat belt.

I located the section where I had worked the day before, and put my notebook on the table. One table down, I noticed, Camille Atchison was poring over a book. I moved down and sat across from her, startling myself more than I did her.

She glanced up coolly, and then looked back at her book.

"Tell me about Meg Bryan," I said in a low voice.

"Who are you?" Her green eyes appraised me.

"I'm Patricia Anne Hollowell. You were at my niece's wedding Saturday."

"Oh, yes. Debbie has done some pro bono work for the Symphony Association. I'm on the board. She's a nice woman."

"Yes, she is. What about Meg Bryan?"

"She was a bitch. I believe that's what I called her at the wedding, and I stand by it. Did she kill herself? No way. What's more, if I'd had the guts, I'd have been the one shoved her out the window. But I wasn't." Camille Atchison's cool expression hadn't changed. "Does that answer your question?"

"She did your family history for you, didn't she?"

"Wrongly and deliberately." Camille's face flushed. "Fortunately, I've been able to repair the damage." She pulled another book toward her. "If you will excuse me, Mrs. Hollowell."

I got up, started to another table, and then turned back. "I'm sorry," I said, reminding myself of Columbo, "but you really don't think there was any way Meg's death could have been suicide?"

Camille's green eyes narrowed. "I hope not. Somebody deserved the pleasure."

Well, I had asked and I had my answer. I moved to the other table and opened my notebook. Noah Hollowell, Winona Hughes Hollowell. It was fun to read about them and see what they had done with their lives, but I couldn't imagine the obsessive passion that Camille Atchison had just shown. "A dog-eat-dog world," Meg Bryan's words echoed.

I got to work. In *Death Records from Montgomery Newspapers: The Civil War Years*, I found an Oscar Hollowell as well as James and Bernard Hallowell. Oscar had died at Antietam. James and Bernard were killed in a neighborhood grudge. Actually, by the number of deaths listed for this reason, these feuds seemed to have been fairly common at the time. Their name was spelled with an "a" instead of an "o," but I decided to write it down.

"You finding what you want, Mrs. Hollowell?" Cassie

Murphy was standing beside me in a coral-colored knit dress that not only brought a glow to her skin but also outlined every curve. And Cassie had, indeed, "grown up."

"You look spectacular today," I said.

"Thank you." A flash of white, even teeth. "Can I help you with anything?"

I pointed to the Hallowell men. "The spelling is different," I said. "But not much."

"Close as that spelling is, chances are that a generation or two back, you'll find a common ancestor."

"This is fascinating. It says these men were killed in a neighborhood grudge, not the Civil War."

"There was an unusual amount of violence then because of political differences. They might have been Union sympathizers or out after some people who were."

"And we think of violence as being a modern-day thing."

"Not if you study history." Cassie waved to a man at a nearby table who was motioning for her. "That's one of our clients. Let me go see what he wants."

"I met Georgiana Peach this week. I saw by your card that you work with her."

"Georgiana's a sweetie. She's out sick today, though, and still hasn't caught up from being in Charleston. And the lady who worked part-time with us had to leave suddenly to care for a sick relative. So I'm going in all directions."

"I hope Georgiana's not very sick."

Cassie shook her head. "Just a virus, I'm sure."

So was AIDS, but I didn't point out that fact. I returned to the records, where I had just discovered Oscar Hollowell's wife was Novalene Tate. Fred and I could be cousins by marriage about twenty times removed if Novalene was the sister of my great great grandfather. In the South that counts. I made myself a note to look up Novalene. With a name like that, she shouldn't be too hard to find.

Some time later, with the beginnings of a headache, I closed the Montgomery County census records from 1850, and stretched. I looked at my watch, and was startled to see it was almost three-thirty. A glance around the room showed most of the same people who had been there when I came in hard at work. A stalwart bunch. Camille Atchison, I noticed, was either gone or had moved away from my vicinity.

Cassie was nowhere in sight, probably back at The Family Tree. Emily was leaning over an elderly gentleman's shoulder, pointing something out in a book. The elderly gentleman seemed to be enjoying himself.

The sun was warm. A good night for cantaloupe stuffed with chicken salad. Some Sister Schubert orange rolls. I headed for the Piggly Wiggly with my stomach growling. The peanut butter sandwich had left me long ago.

Consequently, I was stuffing angel food cake into my mouth when I walked into my kitchen. It was supposed to be for dessert, but what the hell, I was starving. The phone rang as I put my sack down.

"Hello," I said as best I could.

"Is this Patricia Anne?" Georgiana's fluttery voice.

"Hello, Georgiana," I said.

"You don't sound like yourself."

"I'm eating a piece of cake. Wait a minute." I chewed and swallowed. "Now," I said. "I'm sorry I missed you earlier. How are you feeling?"

There was a long pause. Then, "I think I am losing my mind."

"What? Why would you think that?" I could tell by the tone of her voice that she meant what she was saying, that she was frightened.

"Could I come talk to you for a little while? I really think I need some help."

"Should you go to a doctor? I'll be glad to take you."

"Maybe I should. But can I come talk to you first? It's about Meg," she added.

"Do you feel like driving?"

"I'll be there in a few minutes."

I put up the groceries and put the chicken breasts on to boil for the salad. Georgiana losing her mind? And something about Meg? I tore off another chunk of angel food cake and ate it.

When the doorbell rang, I was prepared for an upset Georgiana Peach. I was not prepared for the woman who seemed to have aged ten years, whose face was white and pinched, and who was obviously ill.

"Come in," I said, taking her thin arm. "You shouldn't have driven over here. I could have come to your house."

"I'll be all right," she' said weakly. "Do you have any brandy?"

"I have some bourbon. And some wine."

"The bourbon would be fine." She sank down weakly on the den sofa and pressed her fingertips against her forehead. "A straight shot."

I rushed into the kitchen and brought the bourbon back. Like her friend, Trinity, Georgiana turned the glass up and downed it in one gulp.

"Thank-you," she whispered. "I should feel better in a few moments."

"Don't you want me to take you to the doctor?"

Georgiana held up the glass, which I refilled. At the rate little old ladies were collapsing on my sofa, I was going to have to buy a new fifth of Black Jack.

This time she sipped the bourbon, looking into the

glass between sips as if it were a crystal ball. "Someone," she said, "is playing a cruel joke on me. A hideously cruel joke. Or," she gazed into the glass, "I am communicating with the dead."

I sat on the sofa beside her. "What are you talking about?"

Georgiana sighed. "Yesterday, I was feeling ill, one of those twenty-four hour things I probably picked up in South Carolina at the conference. Anyway," she gave a shiver, "I put my answering machine on and slept most of the day. Then last night, I forgot to check for messages."

She paused so long, that I finally said, "And?"

"Well, my stomach was still queasy this morning, but I knew I needed to get to the office because we are shorthanded. I was about to walk out the door when I remembered my messages." Georgiana chugalugged the bourbon that was left in the glass and gave a slight cough. Another long pause.

"Well?" I said finally. This was like pulling teeth.

"There was a message from Meg. She said, 'Help me!' "

"Meg Bryan?"

Tears welled in Georgiana's eyes. "She said, 'Help me!' "

"Wait a minute." I was trying to think of some reasonable explanation. "Did you check your answering machine when you got home from your trip? Maybe she left it while you were gone."

Georgiana nodded her head. "The message was left yesterday."

"Then you mistook the voice."

"It was Meg." Georgiana reached for the phone on the end table, "See if you can hear it." She dialed her code number and listened. "Here." She handed me the phone.

"Saturday at twelve thirty," a woman's voice said. "Call

136

me if you can't make it. Bye." Then the next message, whispered, urgent, but clear as a bell! "Help me!"

I was so startled, I almost dropped the phone.

"You heard it?" Georgiana said. "Thank God. It's a cruel hoax then, because I don't think a spirit could leave a message on a machine, do you?"

"What do I do to listen again?"

"Punch four." Georgiana reached over, got the bourbon bottle, and poured herself another shot. "I can't tell you what a relief it is that you can hear the voice. All I could think about was poor Meg caught between heaven and earth because of the violent way she died. Out there, wandering, like Cathy over the moors in *Wuthering Heights*. Calling to me for help. 'Georgiana! Georgiana!' "

I punched four and moved the bottle to where Georgiana couldn't reach it again. "Help me!" the voice whispered.

"Sounds just like her, doesn't it?" Georgiana began to cry. "Who would have done such a thing to me?"

"Done what?" Mary Alice stood in the den door loaded down with packages from the Big, Bold, and Beautiful Shoppe, as well as from Parisian. "What's the matter, Georgiana?"

"Listen," I said. I punched four and handed Sister the phone. Packages rained to the sofa as she took it.

Sister put the phone to her ear. Georgiana and I both watched her. "Help who do what?" she asked when she had heard the message.

"You didn't recognize the voice? It's Meg Bryan," Georgiana explained.

"Really? What did she want you to do for her?"

"You don't understand." I began picking up packages. "The message was left yesterday."

"So it's not Meg." Sister turned to Georgiana. "I

137

thought you said it was."

"I thought at first it was. I thought she was caught between heaven and earth like Cathy in *Wuthering Heights,* calling 'Georgiana! Georgiana!' "

Sister eyed the bourbon, bottle. "Good Lord, Georgiana, it was probably a wrong number. Besides, Cathy called 'Heathcliff!' "

"Well, I know that!"

"It does sound like Meg," I said.

"Fiddle! Y'all are sitting here letting your imaginations run away with you." Sister picked up a Parisian package. "Let me show you what I bought you, Mouse. If you insist on wearing that shiny-butted red suit, okay. But I saw this blouse and this scarf that would be perfect with it." Material poured over the chair in a rainbow. "Actually a couple of blouses. Six petite. Right?"

But Georgiana wasn't in the mood to be distracted. "Who would have played a joke like this?" She leaned forward, her arms crossed over her abdomen.

"Maybe you ought to tell the police about it," I said. I picked up the first blouse, a beautiful off-white silk with splashes of red and navy. "This is beautiful, Sister."

"I thought so. It'll dress up that red suit." Mary Alice sat down beside Georgiana on the sofa. "Dial the number and let me listen again, Georgiana."

She held the phone to her ear while I admired the second blouse, a sage-green silk, not a color I would have thought of as going with red but which I knew, instantly, would be perfect. I looked at the price tag. "Shit!"

Sister held her hand up for me to be quiet. "Nope," she said, hanging up the phone. "Probably just a kid calling around like they did in that movie. You know, the one where the guy had just killed someone and they said they saw what he had done."

"You really think so?" Georgiana rubbed her forehead. "You know, my first thought when I heard the voice was that Meg's not dead, that she needs my help. That's how upset I was. I had to tell myself that if someone is in trouble and can get to a phone, they'd call 911, not me. And then I thought, what if I'm the only one hearing it and Meg's spirit is wandering, lost, caught."

Sister caught my eye. "You got any coffee, Mouse?"

"And orange rolls."

"That sounds great. We'll bring you some, Georgiana. Okay?"

Georgiana nodded, still rubbing her forehead. Sister followed me into the kitchen.

"What do you think?" she whispered.

"About what?"

"You think it was Meg's voice?"

"How the hell should I know? You're the one who's convinced it's not."

"Well, how could it be?"

"It couldn't."

"Okay. It's settled then. Put the coffee on and come try on your blouses."

"I can't afford them."

"But I can. And I don't want you to look tacky Saturday night."

"Well, since you put it so graciously."

As we went through the den, Georgiana Peach was stretched out on the sofa snoring. I spread the afghan over her.

"You keep such strange company, Patricia Anne," Sister said. Since my arms were full of the clothes she had just bought me, I thought it would be ungracious to belt her one.

CHAPTER 11

FRED CALLED TO SAY THEY HAD A RUSH ORDER for TVA and were waiting for Athens Cartage to pick it up.

"What time will you be home?" I asked.

"I'll call you after a while. George is going to Subway to get us some sandwiches."

"Tell him to get you turkey, and very little mayonnaise. Fat-free, if they have it."

Sister, sitting on the edge of the bed, rolled her eyes. "Good Lord, Patricia Anne," she said as I hung up the phone. "Tell him to get you turkey," she mimicked my voice.

"Shut up."

"And very little mayonnaise. Fat-free."

I threw a hairbrush at her. She ducked, and it hit the wall.

"Look at that," she said. "You chipped the plaster."

"I did not." I had pulled off my glasses to try on the blouses. "Did I?"

"Just a little bit. Try on the sage blouse first."

"Too expensive," I grumbled, but I was already reaching for it.

Sister stretched out on the bed. "What are you having for supper?"

"Chicken salad. You can stay." I slipped the blouse over my head. "This has to be dry-cleaned. I hate to pay dry cleaners a fortune."

"Don't sweat."

"Girls? You there?" Georgiana's voice down the hall.

"Come on back. We're in the bedroom," Sister called.

Georgiana stood in the doorway, suddenly green as my

blouse.

"The bathroom's right there," I pointed quickly.

Georgiana disappeared, shoulders hunched.

"Gotta watch that Black Jack," Sister said.

"She's got a virus."

"I hope she doesn't spread it around." She eyed the blouse. "That looks good. I like the way it drapes across the front. Makes you look like you have some boobs. See how it does with the jacket."

I complied.

"Now try on the other one."

I complied again. By the time Georgiana had tottered from the bathroom, I had decided that I would keep both blouses. One would be a Mother's Day present, and one was for checking on Bubba Cat when Sister went to Las Vegas for some kind of stockholders' convention next month. I informed Sister of this fact.

"I don't see why you can't call it what it is—charity," she said.

I grabbed Sister's foot and mashed it forward and down. Hard. She yelped.

"Are you two having a disagreement?" Georgiana stood in the doorway again.

"No," we said together.

"Are you feeling better?" I asked.

"Some. I think I'd better run along home right away, though. I'm sorry to have bothered you. I can't tell you what hearing that voice did to me,"

"It shook me up, too," I said.

"A prank," Mary Alice said, standing up and putting her weight gingerly on the foot I had mashed. "You just go home, take some Pepto-Bismol, and get a good night's sleep."

"I suppose so."

"You want one of us to drive you?" I asked.

"I'll be all right."

I collected Georgiana's purse from the den, and Mary Alice and I followed her to the front door. "I taught one of your employees," I told her. "Cassie Murphy. I saw her yesterday at the Samford Library. Today, too."

"She's a wonderful genealogist. I'm lucky to have her." Georgiana rubbed her palm against her forehead. "She's had to do double duty the last few days with me first out of town, and then not feeling well. And my other help, Heidi Williams, had to leave suddenly. Family emergency. It's times like this I would have called on Meg." Tears welled in Georgiana's eyes.

"You'll feel better tomorrow," I said. "Get a good night's sleep."

"I know. Thank-you." Georgiana started down the walk.

"And if the Pepto-Bismol doesn't work, try Emetrol," Sister called.

Georgiana gave us a backward wave.

"You think she'll be all right?" I said, worried.

"Of course."

But Georgiana's path toward her car wasn't straight enough to suit me. "I'm driving her," I said. "You follow us." I called Georgiana's name and ran after her.

It wasn't far to her apartment, but I was glad I had decided to drive her. She sat on the front seat shivering, and I asked again if she wanted to go to a doctor.

"No," she insisted. "It's just a twenty-four-hour bug. Plus, I should have had more sense than to drink bourbon on an upset stomach."

"I shouldn't have given it to you." Guilt. Guilt.

Georgiana lived in a new development near the University of Alabama, Birmingham of charming attached town houses with businesses located on the first floor and the owner's apartment above each business. An old idea that is so practical, it had to make a comeback.

"I've been admiring these apartments," I exclaimed.

"It's wonderful. I walk downstairs and I'm at work. I'm close to the UAB library, and can hop on the Twentieth-Street trolley to get to the downtown library." She directed me to the wide alley where each town house had parking spaces. Mary Alice pulled in behind us.

"I can't thank you enough," Georgiana said.

"You're very welcome." I handed her the keys. "I'll check on you later."

"I think she ought to go to the doctor," I told Mary Alice as I climbed into her car.

"You want me to help you hog-tie her and drag her up to the UAB emergency room?"

"Shut up. I like these apartments, don't you? Above the businesses?"

Mary Alice nodded. "Real nice."

"I've been thinking I might like to start a small business."

"Doing what?"

"I don't know. Maybe a tutoring service, some editing. I don't know. I'm still sort of lost after working for thirty years."

"You need to do more volunteer work, take classes."

"I suppose."

We were both quiet going back over the mountain by Vulcan. I thought about Haley and Philip Nachman and wondered what they had found on the computer disks. I thought about Debbie and Henry and their fairy-tale wedding. I thought about Pukey Lukey, that I needed to drop him a note just to say it was good to see him. After all, family was family.

"How are the twins doing?" I asked Sister. "Missing Debbie?"

"They're fine. I've been doing the good grandmama thing, going over every day and spending time with them. Giving Richardena a break. Today Fay hit May with one of those Buzzy Bee pull-toy things and knocked a knot on her head. She had to 'time-out.' Soon as she came out, May hit her back. Anyway, they ended up identical again."

"Did you explain to them that sisters don't fight?"

"I certainly did." Mary Alice actually said this seriously.

We turned onto my street, where the yards were white with dogwood.

"You know what I've been thinking?" Sister asked.

"What?" I admired the peaceful scene, the early spring twilight.

"I think it really was Meg's voice on that phone." I didn't say anything. Sometimes, if I'm quiet, the words Sister has tossed into the air vanish into the vapors.

This, however, was not to be one of those times.

"Did you hear me, Mouse?"

"I'm afraid I did."

Mary Alice pulled into my driveway and stopped. "So, what do you think?"

"I think you've lost your mind. You've been insisting all afternoon that someone was playing a prank."

"Well, I didn't want to upset Georgiana. Besides, I've been thinking." Mary Alice opened her door. "Come on. Let's go get the chicken salad. I've got a museum board meeting at eight."

I followed her, just as I had been doing for sixty years, saying, "Wait a minute. What are you talking about?"

We walked into the kitchen. Sister slung her heavy purse on one chair, pulled another out, and sat down.

"I'll tell you what I've been thinking while you fix supper."

"Okay. I want to hear this."

"Meg Bryan is still alive."

I rinsed my hands and wiped them on a paper towel. "Then who died at the courthouse?"

"A homeless woman. Someone the murderer knew nobody would be looking for."

"Un huh." I reached into the refrigerator for the chicken and celery. "And how come the judge identified her, then?"

"She fell ten floors, didn't she?"

"With Meg's purse and clothes?"

"The homeless woman had stolen them from her."

"And the murderer just happened to come along while this was happening. This purse and clothes-snatching."

"Yes, and kidnapped Meg."

I chopped up celery. "Why?"

"To steal Meg's genealogy program, which he will sell for a mint to Bill Gacy at Microsoft."

"Gates, sister. Bill Gates. Gacy was the mass-murderer."

"Gates. The young, nice one who was so nice to his mother. For heaven sakes, Patricia Anne, you knew who I meant."

I added the mayonnaise with a sprinkle of Italian seasoning mix. "Where did the murderer take her?"

"You know those caves in the hill under Vulcan? The police have them blocked off to keep people like teenagers and drug dealers out, but from what I saw on TV, they'd still be easy to get into. That's a perfect place to hide someone, and I'll bet that's where he took her."

"There are telephones in the caves?"

Mary Alice thought for a moment. "The kidnapper had one of those tiny cellular phones in his pocket, and Meg got it. He went to sleep and she sneaked over and got it."

"You're good, you know that?"

Mary Alice beamed.

I put the chicken salad on the table. "And you've signed up for the fiction writing class at UAB, haven't you?"

"Did Debbie tell you?"

"She didn't have to." I got each of us a plate and fork and put a package of crackers between us.

"You know," I said, pulling out a chair and sitting down. "You've got one big problem with this story. If she tells where the program is, she's dead. If she doesn't, she's dead."

Mary Alice helped herself to a big spoonful of salad. "Well," she said, "you can't win them all."

The phone rang before I had taken a bite. It was Haley saying she had printed all of the Word Perfect files, that they were just letters, but Philip hadn't had a chance to work on the genealogy program.

"Did you see anything interesting?" I asked.

"Lord, no. Just letters to genealogy societies." Haley paused. "The one on top here is to the Southern Historical Press, ordering a catalog. The next one is to some organization she's joining called Heritage Quest. That kind of stuff. You want me to bring them over? Philip and I are going to a movie, and I can drop them off."

"Sure. What are you going to see?"

"Don't know." A giggle.

"My child is besotted by love," I told Mary Alice when I hung up.

"Well, if you're going to be besotted, that's the best thing to be besotted by."

"I guess so." I sat down, took my first bite of chicken salad, and chewed thoughtfully. "She'll be all right, won't

146

she? With Philip? Losing Tom nearly killed her."

"She'll be fine." Mary Alice reached over and got another helping of salad. "My Philip was the kindest, gentlest man in the world. Even when we were making love, he'd say, 'Be gentle, Mary Alice. Be gentle.' I'm sure Philip the Second is the same kind of man."

"Thank-you for sharing that," I said.

"You're welcome."

Water off a duck's back.

"They're boring," Haley said, handing me a large manila envelope, "I just glanced through them and nearly fell asleep."

"Thanks. Did you find out what movie you're going to?"

"We decided to rent one. Philip's got this thing for old movies."

Understandable. He was familiar with them. But all I said was, "Y'all have a good time."

I took the envelope into the den, and settled down on the sofa for a good read. The first letter, dated the previous October, was an order for Volume 9 of *Irish Church Records*. Okay, I thought, moving on to the second, which was dated the same day and requested information concerning a Christmas research tour in Salt Lake City at the Genealogical Society Library. The next request was for a list of unreadable tombstones in Coweta County, Georgia, which I found puzzling. If they couldn't read them, how could they list them? Some kind of scam Meg might have been investigating? I put that letter to the side and continued.

There was a letter to a woman in Ohio concerning an ancestor buried in the cemetery at Point Clear, Alabama, and a letter questioning the spelling of a German name.

My eyes got heavier and heavier.

The telephone's ring woke me up. I glanced at my watch. It was nine o'clock, so it must be Fred.

But it wasn't. "Patricia Anne?" Trinity Buckalew's unmistakable voice.

"Hello, Trinity."

"Patricia Anne, Georgiana Peach is very ill. She may be dying."

"What?" I was still half asleep. "Georgiana? She was here this afternoon. We took her home."

"She's very ill. She may be dying," Trinity repeated, giving me a chance to wake up.

"What makes you think that? And where are you?"

"I'm in Fairhope and I called Georgiana a while ago to tell her about the plans for the fond farewell party for Meg, and she said, 'Trinity, I can't talk. I'm so sick I think I'm dying.' And I said to call 911 and she said she already had."

I was totally awake by now. "She called 911? Is there somebody I should get in touch with?"

"She has a sister, but I tried her number and she doesn't answer. I hope she's with her."

"I'll find out what's going on and call you back. Okay?" I wrote Trinity's number on the corner of the letter I had been reading when I'd gone to sleep.

Damn. I tried to think what to do. Chances were that, living where she did, if she needed emergency care they would take her to University Hospital. I looked up the number, dialed it, and asked if they had a Georgiana Peach there. To my astonishment, the woman who had answered the phone hung up on me. By the time I had dialed again, I had figured out the problem.

"There is a lady," I said, "whose name is Georgiana Peach. She called 911 and may be on the way to your emergency room. Is there any way you have to check?"

"Not until they get here. Her name's Georgiana Peach?"

"That's right. Georgiana Peach."

"How about that."

"I'll call later," I said.

There was an outside chance that the paramedics were still at Georgiana's house or that she hadn't been sick enough to take to the hospital. I found her number and called it. A couple of rings, a click, and a different-sounding ring. "You have reached The Family Tree," Georgiana's voice. "We are unable to answer now, but if you will leave a message, we'll be happy to get back in touch with you as soon as possible."

"Damn machines," I muttered.

"What's the matter?" Fred was standing in the kitchen door, tired but exhilarated-looking.

"I hate answering machines."

Fred sank down into his recliner. "We made our expenses for a whole month in two hours tonight."

"That's great. Did you have time to eat?"

"Turkey, like you said."

"You want anything else?"

"'Maybe. After I wind down." He pointed to the phone. "Who are you trying to call?"

I explained about Trinity's call and Georgiana's illness. "I'm sure they'll take her to University Hospital, but she's not there yet. Trinity says there's a sister, but she doesn't answer her phone."

"Probably with Georgiana, then." Fred got up and stretched. "I'm going to get a shower." He started down the hall and then stuck his head back through the door. "Don't worry about this lady, honey. She'll be fine."

A couple of good days at work and he has the answer

for everything.

I waited a few minutes and called the emergency room at UAB again. This time the woman said that Ms. Peach had just been brought in.

"Is anybody with her? Her sister?"

"Just a minute." Turning from the phone. "Delilah! Anybody with Ms. Peach?"

I couldn't hear Delilah's answer but it must have been, "Who?"

"Ms. Peach! The lady they just brought in!" Back to the phone. "No. Not yet."

"Thanks." Georgiana's voice saying "The Family Tree" on the answering machine had given me an idea. I got my purse and found the card Castine Murphy had given me the day before. Her home phone number was on it. Working with Georgiana, she would know about the sister or anybody else who needed to be contacted.

I lucked out. No machine. Just Cassie's clear voice,saying, "Hello."

"Cassie," I said, "this is Patricia Anne Hollowell. Have you talked to Georgiana in the last hour or so?"

"I talked to her this afternoon, Mrs. Hollowell. Why? Is something wrong?"

"She's down at UAB hospital in the emergency room. Trinity Buckalew called her and she said she was so sick she had called 911."

"Georgiana's so sick she called 911?"

"And they took her to UAB. That's all I know, except nobody's with her. Do you know someone we should call?"

"Lord, I can't believe this. Wait a minute, let me think."

"Trinity said she had a sister."

"She does. Her name is Martha Matthews. But she lives

all the way up on Lake Logan Martin." Cassie was quiet for a moment. "She's got some friends from her old neighborhood that she's still close to, but I can't think of any names." Another silence. "Do they think she's having a heart attack?"

"I have no idea."

"Well, she shouldn't be down there by herself. I'll run down and see what's going on. Okay?"

"That's wonderful. Will you call me?"

"Soon as I find out anything."

Fred came into the den as I was hanging up the phone. He was wearing his navy silk pajamas that he dearly loves, and his hair was wet and slicked back. The pajamas had been a Christmas gift a couple of years ago along with some satin sheets. It seemed like a good idea at the time, very sexy, guaranteed to light the old fires. Not so. Fred slipped into bed and kept slipping right out the other side. The satin sheets ended up at the back of the linen closet.

"You still on the phone?" he asked.

I explained about Cassie Murphy, that she worked with Georgiana and was going to go see about her. "One of my old students," I added.

"Sometimes I think everybody in Birmingham is an old student of yours."

"Are you being grouchy? A hundred and forty students a year for thirty years. That's a lot of kids."

"I'm sorry. Did I sound grouchy? I'm just tired."

"Get yourself a glass of milk." Four thousand, two hundred kids. Most of whom I cared for. Most of whom had turned out fine.

Fred shuffled into the kitchen in the backless bedroom slippers he's never learned to walk in. "You want some milk?"

"No." The phone rang again. Trinity. I told her

151

Georgiana was at UAB and Castine Murphy had gone to see about her. "I'll call you, I promise, soon as I know something."

Fred settled into his recliner with the evening paper and promptly went to sleep; I tried to read some more letters from Meg's computer. Haley was right. Boring. I put them back in the envelope and picked up a novel, which I had trouble concentrating on.

At eleven-thirty, Cassie called. Georgiana had a perforated ulcer and they were going to do immediate surgery.

"There's no need for you to come down," she said when I offered. "There's not a thing you can do except sit here and worry."

"I could keep you company."

"I'm fine."

"Did you get her sister?"

"I tried, but no one answered."

I paused before I asked, "How sick is she?"

A pause before she answered. "Very sick."

"Call me if you need me."

"I will."

Fred was awake and listening. "She's in bad shape?"

"They're fixing to do surgery. A perforated ulcer." For which I had given her bourbon!

"Would you feel better if you went down there? I'll take you."

"There's nothing I can do."

But later, after I had called Trinity, after I had gotten into bed and heard Fred's breathing change into sleep, I lay awake and thought of Georgiana, the little bird with the eyes that missed nothing. I thought of her brother, George Peach, and the Moon Pie story. And I reached over and rubbed the hem of Fred's silk pajama coat like a child does a security blanket.

Down the block, a dog bayed at the moon. Another joined in, and then I heard our Woofer. He sang into the night as loudly as he had as a young dog.

"Good dog," I said, knowing that I should get up and quiet him, that tomorrow I would have to apologize to Mitzi and the other neighbors for their disturbed sleep. "Good dog."

CHAPTER 12

A CALL TO THE HOSPITAL THE NEXT MORNING gave me the news that Georgiana was in surgical intensive care in critical condition. As I hung up the phone, it rang, Cassie telling me what I had just heard from the hospital.

"No malignancy," she said, "but peritonitis. The colon was ulcerated, too. They're pumping her full of antibiotics and have her totally sedated, of course."

"What kind of chance do they give her?"

"The doctors say she has a chance. That's as committal as they'll get."

"I can't believe she got so sick so quickly. Where are you now?"

"I just got home. I'm going to get a couple of hours' sleep and then go to the office. It wasn't that sudden, though. Georgiana hasn't been feeling good for quite a while, and we've been trying to get her to go to the doctor. But she kept saying she was okay."

"Can I help you? Answer the phone for you?"

"Thanks, but I'll just put an answering message on it that says Georgiana's ill and I'll get back as soon as I can. One of the nice things about working in genealogy, you don't get emergencies."

"That's true." I asked if she had gotten in touch with Georgiana's sister.

"No. She must be out of town."

"Well, Georgiana's lucky to have you. Get some sleep now."

"Thanks, Mrs. Hollowell."

I hung up and dialed Trinity.

"Eating all those boiled peanuts," she said when I told her the details. "I swear I never saw anybody could eat boiled peanuts like Georgiana. I'd say, 'Georgiana, you are going to tear your stomach up with all those peanuts,' but you let us pass a curb market with a sign that said 'Boiled Peanuts' and Georgiana was pulling in to buy some. I declare, you could have followed her all over Alabama like Hansel and Gretel with peanut shells." Trinity paused, and with a catch in her voice, asked, "Is she going to be all right?"

"The doctors say she has a chance," I said truthfully.

"I can't lose her, too."

"You won't." My voice sounded sure and steady. Not at all the way I felt.

One more phone call, this one to Mary Alice to tell her about Georgiana. She was already gone, probably over to Debbie's to see the grandbabies. I dialed Debbie's number and Richardena, the nanny, answered.

"Hey, Mrs. Hollowell. Sure, she's here. She's been telling me about that poor lady at the wedding got kidnapped and hid in those caves under Vulcan. That poor soul."

"Nobody's been kidnapped and hidden in a cave, Richardena."

"Mrs. Crane said they had. That nice little aunt of Henry's, not big as a flea. Why would anybody treat that lady that way?"

154

"Mrs. Crane's a dingbat, Richardena. May I speak to her?"

"Okay, but you know it's God's truth there's no telling what's in those caves. Bodies. All sorts of stuff. No telling."

"Well, Meg Bryan's not one of them, Richardena. Let me talk to Sister."

"Here she is."

"For heaven's sake, Sister," I said when she answered. "Why are you telling Richardena that wild story?"

"Who says it's wild?"

"I do. Now, listen, Georgiana Peach is real sick." I told her about Trinity's call, Georgiana's surgery, and what Cassie had said about the prognosis.

"That's terrible," Mary Alice said. "Do you think it was the bourbon?"

"No more than I think it was the boiled peanuts."

"What boiled peanuts?"

"Forget it." In the background, I could hear Fay and May babbling to each other in their twin language that only they understand. "Are Debbie and Henry coming home today?"

"Yes, but what are you talking about? Boiled peanuts?"

"Georgiana Peach likes them."

"So do I. You know when I'm going to Florida, I'll go out of my way through Florala just so I can get boiled peanuts from that old guy by the railroad track with the kettle. Do they think boiled peanuts messed Georgiana's stomach up?"

"No. And it's the guy has the kettle, not the railroad track."

"Who said the guy had the railroad track?"

"Good-bye, Sister," I said, hanging up. It was too early in the morning for this.

Woofer wasn't particularly anxious for his walk. The community sing he had been involved in the night before had lasted several hours, and he thought he would sleep in.

"No, you don't," I said when he held back. "You danced and you have to pay the piper."

I let him set his own pace, though. We ambled down the block, sat on the curb once for a rest, enjoyed the smell of the wisteria. We were turning into our driveway when Bo Mitchell pulled up beside us in her black-and-white police car.

"Hey, Patricia Anne."

"Hey, Bo. You looking for me or just cruising?"

"Just cruising. Saw you and Woofer out practicing for the Olympics."

"Can you come in for a cup of coffee?"

Bo looked at her watch. "Just a minute. Let me make a call."

"I'll be in the kitchen." I put Woofer up and made a fresh pot of coffee. By the time Bo came in, I was taking some sticky buns from the microwave.

"Just what I need," she said.

I poured us both a cup of coffee and we sat at the kitchen table.

"Anything new on Judge Haskins's murder?" I asked.

"Not that I know of. His wife showed up bitching because he got blood on one of her fancy carpets. I keep hoping she's the one did it. About thirty years old. Looks like a tart."

I looked at Bo admiringly. "I haven't heard anyone described as looking like a tart in ages."

"One of my grandmama's favorite things. She'd say, 'That girl's nothing but a tart, Bo Peep. Switching her tail like a mule.'"

"And the judge's wife is a tail-switcher?"

"Switches it *all*, honey."

"I can't imagine him married to Meg Bryan," I said. "She didn't have anything to switch." Which reminded me. I told Bo about what sounded like Meg's voice saying "Help me" on Georgiana Peach's answering machine.

"Did you hear it?"

"Sure." I explained about Georgiana's visit and her illness. "It really did sound like Meg," I said. "Sister says she's not dead, that someone's kidnapped her and hidden her in those caves under Vulcan."

Bo snorted. "Might as well put her in the middle of Highway 280 there's so much traffic in those caves."

"I thought they were boarded up."

"They are." Bo held out her cup for a refill. "I'd like to hear that message."

"It's probably still on Georgiana's machine, but I don't know how to access it. Her phone's connected to her business, The Family Tree, so Cassie Murphy probably can get it. Isn't that illegal, though? Like wiretapping or something?"

"I have no idea. I just ride around in my black and white making folks feel safe." Bo Mitchell looked at her coffee thoughtfully. The dissatisfaction in her voice surprised me.

"What would you like to be doing?" I asked.

"Homicide or vice."

"Yuck."

"Something to sink my teeth into."

I wasn't going to touch that one with a ten-foot pole.

Bo got out her notebook and pen. "The Family Tree?"

I nodded. "It's Georgiana Peach's company, but Cassie Murphy is her assistant. They do genealogical research."

"They make a living doing that?"

"A good one, apparently."

"Cassie Murphy?"

"Castine, really. I taught her in high school. She's listed in the phone book, but she's asleep right now. She was up all night with Georgiana." I watched Bo jotting this down. "You think there might be something to the message?"

"I don't see how, since Meg's dead as a doornail. Deader." Bo stuck her pen back in her pocket.

"Well, do you think there's any connection between Meg's death and the judge's?"

"I doubt that, too. A judge gets shot, you got suspects coming out of the wall. Some of them switching their tails."

"But he was a bankruptcy judge!"

"Same difference. Somebody always gets mad when a case goes to court, regardless of what it is." The pager hanging on her belt beeped. Bo turned it off. "Okay if I use your phone?"

"Sure." I watched her as she went to the kitchen counter. She looked fit and attractive in spite of the extra ten pounds. And God knows, she was smart and a hard worker.

"Is it the glass ceiling?" I asked her when she finished talking.

"Nope. It's a hit-and-run on Vulcan Parkway." Then she realized what I was talking about and laughed. "Glass ceiling? More like a ton of bricks. But we gals can get there. We just have to bust our butts to do it. Don't worry about me, Patricia Anne. I'm just feeling a little sorry for myself today." She took the last sip of her coffee and started out the door. "Thanks for the pick-me-up."

"Any time." I watched her striding toward her car heading for a hit-and-run. And she wanted homicide and vice. Lord!

I straightened up the house and got out the letters that Haley had printed from Meg's disk. I realized as I started reading them that I hadn't mentioned the disks to Bo. She probably would have been interested to learn they had been stashed in Mary Alice's glove compartment. She might even have been able to read them without going to sleep, which was more than I could do.

I took the letters to the kitchen table and decided I would organize them. Letters to companies went in one stack, to individuals in another, and in a third stack I placed what seemed to be memos that Meg had written to herself. The first stack was the largest and the least interesting. A glance showed it to be principally requests for newsletters, catalogs, out-of-print books. The second stack was more interesting, but it would take more careful reading. It consisted of recommendations for membership in such organizations as the United Daughters of the Confederacy (UDC) and the DAR, as well as Sons of the American Revolution. There were also letters that must have surprised the recipients, and Meg pulled no punches. Your grandmother, she wrote one woman, was brought up before the church for adultery and found guilty. Another woman seeking admission to the DAR was informed that records showed that her great grandmother was a mulatto. I grinned, but then I sobered. There are still many Southerners who believe their family trees are strictly Caucasian and to say otherwise might be asking for trouble. Would they kill the person who said that a drop of blood, God forbid, from another race had entered the pure Caucasian stream? Crazier things had happened. I put the letter to the side to check on later.

There were many more of the personal letters, but I put them off until later and glanced at the memos. Many of them were dated, but they were in a code that only Meg would understand. For instance, under September 10, she had entered, "Bride, no. Cromwell, Cropwell. Jenkins says yes. Check." Nothing here, I thought. I glanced at the ones with the latest dates. On March 10, Meg had written, "Williams, Murphy, Bobby. Williams, Murphy, Bobby. Bobby, Murphy, Georgiana? Trinity?"

It made no sense, but something told me it was important. I knew all the names but Williams. Who was Williams? I stared at the memo, Williams, Murphy, Bobby. And then I remembered. Heidi Williams was the other woman who worked with Cassie and Georgiana. So this was a memo about The Family Tree staff, plus Judge Haskins and Trinity with a question mark.

Meg had done some work for The Family Tree, Georgiana had said. So this could well be something they were all working on. But why Bobby? Williams, Murphy, Bobby. I put this memo to the side with the questionable letters, including the one to Camille Atchison informing her of her descent from General Sherman. The rest of the letters I put back in the envelope. I would read them all later. Or make Sister help me.

The phone was ringing as I got out of the shower. It was Frances Zata, my oldest friend, who is still counselor at Robert Alexander High, where I taught for most of my career and which I still miss.

"Tell me about the wedding," she said. "I hated like everything to miss it, but we'd had this cruise planned since last September. You should have been with us, Patricia Anne. We had a ball. Tell me everything, now. What about Debbie's dress?"

"It looked like Princess Di's. Fred said that much virginal white was damaging to the retina."

"What about the bridesmaids?"

I settled down on the bed for a long chat. Finally, just

before I hung up, I thought to ask Frances if she remembered Castine Murphy.

"Sure I remember her. Bless her heart."

"Well, I ran into her a couple of days ago. She's a professional genealogist, works with a lady named Georgiana Peach who has a company called The Family Tree. She must be quite a good researcher, too."

"Castine Murphy's a genealogist?"

"She's Cassie now."

"I wondered what happened to her after her parents died."

"They're both dead?"

"When she was in college. Hit by lightning on the beach at Destin."

"How tragic! I don't remember hearing about it."

"It may have been the summer you and Mary Alice went to Europe."

"Could have been. I've blocked that summer from my memory."

"Anyway, if I remember correctly, they had just declared bankruptcy."

"You're kidding! Two doctors?"

"Hard to believe, isn't it? Some kind of land deal in Florida that went under."

"So the poor child was left without anything?" I asked.

"Maybe some insurance. I don't know whether that would have been included in the estate or not."

"Well, she seems to be doing okay. You ought to see her, Frances. Very much a lady. Thoughtful. She spent last night at University Hospital with Georgiana Peach, the lady she works for who's critically ill."

"Are you sure we're talking about the same Castine Murphy? The one who never took her nose out of a book long enough to see what was going on around her?"

"They surprise us sometimes, don't they?"

"A lot of the time. Thank God."

We said good-bye with plans to meet for lunch soon. I fixed a peanut butter and banana sandwich and sat down to watch *Jeopardy.* When it was over, I decided to go work in the library some more. Before I left, I called the hospital. Georgiana's condition had not changed.

Cheerleader Emily was actually working on what looked like a research paper. Several books were open around her, and she was jotting notes onto a yellow legal pad. "Hi, Mrs. Hollowell," she said, looking up and smiling.

"You look busy."

"It's a paper for my Twentieth-Century Writers class. You ever heard of anybody named Adrienne Rich?"

"Sure. She's wonderful."

Emily gestured toward the books. "That's what everybody says. Actually, my boyfriend and I are into diving. He's dived the Great Barrier Reef, but so far I've just been to Panama City. Anyway, when I saw this woman had written a book called *Diving into the Wreck,* I thought, well heck, that's the writer I want to do my paper on. Figured I'd learn something. You know?"

"You haven't learned anything?"

"It's all poetry!"

"See, you did learn something."

A wide smile. "I guess so."

"Hang in there." I left her to her notes, and went to the Montgomery section. On the way, I passed several people who nodded a greeting. Three days and I was becoming a fellow genealogist, one of the gang. When, I wondered, did the "dog-eat-dog" part begin? When you shook the branch of someone else's family tree?

One of Fred's great great great uncles, I discovered in West's *Montgomery County and the War Between the States,*

162

had refused to serve in the Civil War. Pursued by his own brothers who were, I suppose, going to persuade him by threats of bodily harm to support the Confederacy, he jumped into the Alabama River from a cliff. His long hair became snagged in the branches of a tree and his neck was broken. That bend in the river where he died is still called Daniel's Bend for the young man with the unfortunately strong head of hair.

The story reminded me of Absalom in the Bible. I got a Kleenex out and was sniffling a little thinking about the mother who had had to hear what had happened from her other sons, and probably a good story they made up, too, not taking any blame at all on themselves. Emily tapped me on the shoulder.

"Mrs. Hollowell, Cassie Murphy wants you on the phone."

"Thanks." I got up, still immersed in the Daniel story. He had the right, didn't he, to his own political views? But I knew the answer to that. He had siblings. Mary Alice would have chased me to the river in a minute. Dangle, baby, dangle.

"You can take it here." Emily handed me the phone across her still-open books. I answered hesitantly, afraid that Cassie was calling to tell me Georgiana had taken a turn for the worse.

"She's stable," Cassie said immediately, knowing what I must be thinking. "She keeps asking for you."

"For me? Why?"

"I have no idea. I called to see about her, and the nurse said she keeps asking for Patricia Anne. I don't know of any other Patricia Anne she knows, so it has to be you. I told the woman I would round you up."

"You mean they want me to come over there?"

"If you can. Apparently, Georgiana's pretty agitated and

they think seeing you might help."

"I can't imagine what I can do, but I'll be glad to go see her. It's five minutes every hour, isn't it?"

"Just tell them who you are. I'm sure they'll let you in."

"Okay. I'll call you when I get home. Wait a minute, how did you know I was here?"

Cassie laughed. "You're getting hooked. Bye."

I handed Emily the phone. "Thanks. Georgiana Peach is asking for me for some reason."

"I heard she was real sick. Tell her I said I hope she's better soon."

I collected my notebook and purse. The only information I had gleaned today was the story about the uncle. But that had seemed more important than all the marriage, birth, and death records I had found. Daniel's Bend. I loved it.

Coming from the bright spring sunshine into the parking deck at University Hospital is like diving into a dark cave. I turned on my headlights and crept along until my eyes became adjusted. Finally, on Level 4, I found a parking spot a block or so away from the elevator. I got out, locked the car, and very carefully made a mental note of where the car was. The trouble with my car is that it's so generic. Middle-aged, middle-sized, in a color between a gray and blue, it tends to disappear among other cars.

I hiked to the elevator, rode down to Level C, which was identified as the crosswalk to the hospital, hiked across that, and finally found Surgical Intensive Care on the seventh floor. A long hike down a long corridor led me to the nurse's station.

"My name," I said breathlessly to a pretty brunette nurse standing there, "is Patricia Anne Hollowell. I understand that you have a patient, Georgiana Peach, who wants to see me."

"Don't you just love that name?" she smiled. "Georgiana Peach." She said it again, as if she were savoring it, "Georgiana Peach."

I glanced at her name tag. Della Delong.

"You have a nice name, too," I said. "Alliterative."

"It used to be Della Jones."

"That's a fine name, too."

"Not as nice as Della Delong."

I couldn't figure anywhere else to take this conversation. "Ms. Peach? May I see her?"

"Let me check. It depends."

She didn't elaborate, and I was grateful. I sat down in a mustard-colored vinyl chair against the wall and caught my breath while she disappeared through double doors that said "No Visitors." She was back in a minute. "They say come on in."

I entered the intensive care room with trepidation. Try as I might, and in spite of Haley laughing at me, I've never been able to convince myself that hospitals are where you go to get well. For one thing, all those fluorescent lights make everyone look like they're dying. And God knows what the antiseptic smells are covering up.

"Mrs. Hollowell?" The nurse who met me was smiling as brightly as if she were inviting me into her parlor. "Ms. Peach has been asking for you. She's pretty sedated, but I think she'll know you're here."

"How is she doing?"

"Holding her own."

I supposed that was good. I didn't ask, just followed the nurse into the room filled with curtained beds on either side. I kept my eyes on her back, not glancing to the right or left. How did Haley do this every day?

"Here," she said, pushing back a curtain. "Ms. Peach?

165

You want to wake up? Mrs. Hollowell's here."

To say Georgiana looked like death warmed over is putting it mildly. Tubes and wires seemed to be attached to every inch of her and her skin was the gray of well-chewed chewing gum.

"Ms. Peach?" the nurse said, patting Georgiana on the shoulder and ignoring the fact that I had sat down quickly in the metal chair by the bed.

"What?" Georgiana's lips were so cracked that moving them had to be painful.

"Mrs. Hollowell's here. You've been asking for her."

Georgiana's eyes opened. "Patricia Anne?"

I reached over and grasped her fingers, the only part that didn't appear wired. They were freezing cold. "I'm here, Georgiana. You're going to be okay." The situation called for lying.

"I'll just leave you a minute. Don't get too tired now, Ms. Peach." The nurse slipped out through the curtains.

Her getting tired wasn't what I was worried about.

"Heidi," Georgiana said.

"It's Patricia Anne, Georgiana. You're going to be fine."

"Find Heidi."

"I don't know who Heidi is, Georgiana." But then I remembered. "The woman who worked for you? You want her to come help Cassie while you're sick?"

"Find Heidi."

"I will. Don't worry about the business. You just concentrate on getting well."

Tears coursed down her cheeks. "Bobby is gone."

"Bobby Haskins?"

"I loved him so."

"Everybody did." Wasn't that the truth! What in the world had so many women found attractive about Judge Haskins?

166

And then Georgiana answered my unspoken question. "He loved women. Truly loved them."

Okay. I could understand that. I've known a few men like that. Very few, and Fred's not one of them, thank God. Charming as those men may be, I prefer one who's selective.

"He killed Meg."

"Judge Haskins killed Meg?"

"It wasn't my fault. I loved him."

A monitor began to beep. The nurse stuck her head into the enclosure. "Visiting time's up!" she said cheerfully, as if nothing were wrong.

As I let go of Georgiana's fingers, she clutched at my hand. "Find Heidi, Patricia Anne."

"I'll find her," I promised. "I'll find her today." Given the circumstances, I would have promised almost anything. Of course, I had no idea what I was letting myself in for.

CHAPTER 13

ON THE LONG WALK BACK THROUGH THE PARKING deck, Georgiana's words, *Bobby killed Meg,* kept running across my brain like the sign across the building in Times Square. Surely not. Surely Meg hadn't paid with her life for those hundred-year-old bastardy papers.

"I told you all the time it was the judge killed her," Mary Alice said. I had stopped by there on my way home and discovered Sister and Bonnie Blue on their hands and knees on the sunporch surrounded by bright, cheerful paintings, the work of Abe Butler, Bonnie Blue's father, one of Alabama's leading folk artists.

"You did not. You said she was in the caves under

167

Vulcan."

"Well, maybe I thought for a while that she was. I can be wrong, you know." Sister picked up a small painting of an angel with a black circle for a face hovering over what seemed to be a cotton field. "I love this one, Bonnie Blue. It's different."

"Yeah, Daddy's gotten into angels. The ones of them eating watermelons are selling like hotcakes. Let me see," Bonnie Blue scooted over to a stack leaning against a chair. "There may be one in here."

"What are y'all doing?" I asked. My startling news about the judge seemed to have had little effect on these two women crawling around on the floor. These two *big* women, who were going to have to get up in the not-so-distant future.

"Picking out Henry and Debbie a wedding present. I had one all wrapped up in paper with wedding bells on it, and damned if Daddy didn't give it to his girlfriend. Here." Bonnie Blue pulled a painting from the stack. "Here's one of a bunch of angels at a watermelon-cutting at a church."

Sister and I laughed at the same time and said, "How wonderful" at the same time.

"You think that's it, then?" Bonnie Blue held the painting up and looked at it. "There's one in here somewhere of angels roller-skating, too."

"I think the watermelon-cutting is great. Henry and Debbie will be thrilled," Mary Alice assured her.

"But they don't even have faces. Look at that."

It was one of the most charming pictures I had ever seen in my life. Seven black angels in white robes were gathered around a table in the side yard of a country church. Several watermelons were on the table, and each angel either held a slice or was reaching for one. Back under a tree, one angel was pushing another in a swing. "Trust your daddy, Bonnie Blue," I said. "He knows what he's doing."

"God's truth. Making a mint on these things." Bonnie Blue rocked back on her heels. "Will you tell me how these angels are gonna eat that watermelon, though? You see a mouth?"

"Angels don't need mouths; they eat spiritually." Sister held up her hands. "Help me up, Mouse."

"Too bad you're not an angel," I grumbled. "You could get up spiritually." I took her hands and pulled. Actually, it wasn't as hard as I thought it was going to be. "The aqua aerobics is really helping, isn't it?" I said sweetly.

"Go to hell." Mary Alice turned to help Bonnie Blue, who had simply crawled over to the poppy-covered chair and hoisted herself up. "I could have done that," Sister said.

Bonnie Blue leaned the angel picture against the coffee table and started stacking the others. "That lady, Ms. Peach, she's in intensive care? Maybe she was so doped up she didn't know what she was saying."

I was impressed. Bonnie Blue had been listening to me after all.

"She recognized me."

"Tell us the whole thing again," Mary Alice said.

I started with how far you have to walk from the UAB parking deck.

Mary Alice held up her hand in the school-teacher gesture she's stolen from me. "Just what Georgiana said."

"She said, 'Find Heidi' a couple of times. And then she said she loved Judge Haskins and that he had killed Meg That's when some monitor went off and the nurse came in and ran me out."

"Who's Heidi?" Sister asked.

169

"She's the other woman who works at The Family Tree, Georgiana's research company. Remember? Cassie said she had gone to see about a sick relative."

"Who's Cassie?"

"Oh, that's right. You haven't met her. Her real name is Castine Murphy, and she used to be one of my students."

Sister groaned. *Like Fred, she thinks I've taught everyone in Birmingham.* I ignored it.

"She's a genealogist now. Works with Georgiana at The Family Tree. I've seen her over at the Samford library a couple of times. I'm looking up some of Fred's family history for his birthday." I expected a smart remark from Sister, but instead she asked about Judge Haskins.

"And Georgiana said plain as day that Judge Haskins killed Meg."

"Yes."

"Then who killed Judge Haskins?"

"How do I know? Maybe his wife. She's a tail-switcher." I explained what Bo Mitchell had said about the present Mrs. Haskins.

"If every tail-switcher were a murderer, men would be in bad trouble," Bonnie Blue said.

Sister added, "Judge Haskins's wife inherited a lot of money, wouldn't you think?"

"And hid it in the cave under Vulcan." I moved away from Sister. "How should I know if he had any money or not?"

"Wait a minute, y'all." Bonnie Blue saw where this was heading. "What was the first thing that poor sick lady asked you to do, Patricia Anne?"

"Find Heidi."

"Then that's what you ought to do."

"You're right. Cassie Murphy probably knows where she is. I'll call her."

"And I've got to go to Food World. They've got bananas three pounds for a dollar. Can you believe that?" Bonnie Blue started gathering up her pictures. Mary Alice and I helped her. Bonnie Blue looked doubtfully at the picture of the angels. "They couldn't eat bananas, either, could they?" We assured her that Henry and Debbie would treasure the painting.

We walked down the hall, and Mary Alice opened the front door. There, as if she had been waiting for us, stood Trinity Buckalew in her blue cape and blue hat.

"I came to see about Georgiana," she said, "and I realized I'm not sure where she is."

The doorway was filled with three large women, stacks of pictures, and me.

"How tall are you?" Trinity asked Bonnie Blue when Sister introduced them.

"Tall enough," Bonnie Blue answered.

I could tell they were going to hit it off.

While we helped Bonnie Blue put the pictures in her car, Trinity went in to use the "little girls' room." When we came back, she was standing at the window in the den, admiring the view. "This is so lovely," she said, turning to greet us. "Have you heard from Georgiana this afternoon?"

"I saw her," I said. "She's at University, still in intensive care. Her condition is critical but stable." I thought of the monitor going off and crossed my fingers.

"So she can have visitors?"

"Five minutes every hour. I went because she asked to see me. She wants me to find the woman who does part-time work for her." I decided not to mention what else Georgiana had said. But Sister blurted, "She said Judge Haskins killed Meg."

"Well, I'd already told you that." Trinity pulled off her

171

hat and ran her hand through her short gray hair.

"Won't you let me take your coat?" Sister asked. "Can I get you a Coke or something?"

"No, thank-you." Trinity turned toward me.

"What time are the visiting hours? On the hour?"

I nodded yes.

"Then I think I'll head for the hospital. Georgiana is my dear friend, you know."

"Well, you're welcome to come back here tonight," Sister said. "Don't even think about checking into a motel."

I followed Trinity to her car, and gave her directions to University Hospital.

"Twentieth? Right down from the statue with the naked butt?"

"You got it," I said. After she pulled out of the driveway, I stuck my head in the front door and yelled to Sister that I was leaving, too.

"Wait a minute!" she yelled back. "I'm fixing us Black Cows!"

The ultimate treat from our childhood. I hurried back to the kitchen, where Sister was pouring Coke over scoops of vanilla ice cream in huge glasses.

"I got a craving," she said. "I think it was those angels that couldn't eat." She pushed one of the glasses and an iced-tea spoon across the counter to me. Bubba Cat looked up from his heating pad inquiringly. "You'll have to eat yours on the floor," Sister told him. She scooped some ice cream into a bowl, poured Coke over it, and put Bubba down by it. He looked around, taking his time so we wouldn't think he was interested in the treat, and then dived in. So did we, sitting on stools at the counter.

"This is a wonderful idea," I said. "I haven't had a Black Cow in ages."

Sister dipped her spoon into the foam, and tasted it. "Ummm. Will you tell me why calories taste so good?"

"So we'll eat."

"You know what I think? I think some things were put on earth just for fun. Like ice cream and sex." She took another spoonful of ice cream and foam. "Georgiana Peach said she was in love with Judge Haskins?"

"That's what she said. At least she said she loved him. There's a difference."

"A big one."

"She said he was a man who loved women."

"Un huh."

Bubba Cat finished his treat and began an elaborate grooming session.

"Think she killed him?" Mary Alice asked.

"Georgiana Peach kill Judge Haskins? Of course not."

"Why not? She's loved him for years. First he spurns her for Meg, and then for various and sundry other women. She goes to tell him she knows he killed Meg but she won't tell anyone because she loves him so. And he laughs at her. It's the breaking point. She pulls out her gun, and BAM! he falls dead, his blood spattering across her shoes."

"Shut up," I said comfortably, turning my glass up and letting the foam run slowly into my mouth.

Mary Alice got up. "I really ought to write this down. I liked that blood-spattering part, didn't you?"

"Make it on white canvas shoes. The teacher will love it." I wiped my mouth on the back of my hand. "Where's the phone book?"

"Here." Sister took it from a drawer and handed it to me. "I wonder where a pencil is."

"There's one in my purse," I said. I opened the phone book to "Williams." I knew the odds were against Heidi

Williams being listed, but maybe I would luck out. I didn't. There were several "H. Williams," and a few with another initial added to the "H." Any of them could be Heidi. Or her phone could simply be listed under her husband's name. And there were five pages of Williamses in the Birmingham phone book.

"Women's names ought to be in phone books," I called to Mary Alice.

"Mine is," she called back. She came in with a notebook and pencil and sat down at the counter again. "Could the shoes maybe be tan instead of white? It's not Easter yet."

"White," I declared. I looked at all the Williamses that lived in Birmingham, and it occurred to me that if by some miracle I found Heidi, I didn't know what I would tell her. If I said, "Georgiana Peach said to find you," she would say, "Why?" And what was I supposed to say? "Damned if I know?"

"I don't know why I'm supposed to be finding this Heidi Williams," I told Mary Alice. "And there are five pages of Williamses here."

Mary Alice looked up. "You promised a dying woman."

"She's not dying. Just on the verge."

"I'm going to write it down. Dying wishes must be honored."

"Who says?"

"Mama always said so."

"Mama never said any such thing." Bubba finished his bath, and hopped back up on the counter. "I'm telling you, Sister, this cat on this heating pad is a fire hazard."

Sister paused in her writing. "The blood spatters could be shaped like huge red flowers."

"How big are the shoes?"

"Little red flowers." The pencil swept across the page.

"Heidi Williams's number will have to be at The

174

Family Tree. I'll see if Cassie's there. She probably knows it, anyway."

"Little anemones," Sister said. "Do you think enough people are familiar with anemones? You think verbena would be better?"

I shrugged and turned to the back of the phone book to the business section. "You have reached The Family Tree—" Georgiana's voice.

"Shit!" I looked up Cassie's number again and called. Another answering machine. I left word for her to call me.

"Listen to this," Mary Alice said. She held the notepad up and read, "He looked at her in surprise, the bullet hole a third eye. Then, as he fell, blood spattered like a garden of anemones across her size seven-and-a-half Keds."

"Size seven-and-a-half Keds?"

"The teacher said to sneak the description of the characters in. You don't want them looking at themselves in the mirror and describing what they see."

"Why not?"

"It's been done too much."

"God forbid. I liked that third eye, though."

"Thanks. I like it, too." Sister looked at the page admiringly.

"I've got to go fix supper," I said, sliding down from the stool. Thanks for the Black Cow."

"You want some Brunswick stew? I've still got some in the freezer we bought at the Elks' barbecue. All you'll have to do is make corn bread."

"I'd love it, and Fred will think he's died and gone to heaven." I didn't point out that she had bought the stew at the barbecue, not the freezer.

Sister walked with me to the car and waved as I started down the driveway. I saw her standing there, waving, and I slammed on my brakes and backed up. "What are you going to do tonight?" She had suddenly looked lonesome to me. That big house and her rattling around in it. No Fred. Just Bubba Cat.

Mary Alice grinned. "Buddy's coming over. The lady from By Request is bringing supper, and we're going to watch a movie in the hot tub."

"Dear God," I said, and floored the accelerator.

The phone was ringing when I came in from walking Woofer. "Philip's got the program figured out," Haley announced. "He's copied it on his little computer and we're going to bring it over after a while. Okay?"

"Sure. I'd ask you for supper, but we're just having a bowl of Brunswick stew."

"Oh, that's okay. We've got reservations at The Club. We'll bring it by before we go."

"Did he say anything about what's on it?"

"No. Just that he can get into it."

"Haley's happy," I told Fred, who walked in just as I hung up. "They're coming by in a little while to bring the computer disk. Philip figured out how the genealogy program works."

"Good." He hugged me. "I better go get a shower."

I followed him down the hall. "I went to University Hospital this afternoon. Georgiana Peach was asking to see me. She's in intensive care and looks awful, bless her heart."

"What did she want?"

"She wants me to find a woman named Heidi Williams who used to work for her. But the interesting thing she said was that Judge Haskins killed Meg Bryan."

Fred unbuttoned his shirt and threw it across the bed. "She was doped up, wasn't she?"

"Sure, but—"

"Then I wouldn't pay any attention to it." Fred reached into his back pants pocket and brought out an envelope. "Ta da!"

"What is this?"

"Open it!"

The outside of the envelope said Travel, Inc. I opened it and saw several brochures for Mexican and Caribbean cruises.

"We'll study them tonight," Fred said.

I fanned the brochures out. "I don't understand. Yesterday we were going bankrupt and today we're going on a cruise?"

"Is this not a wonderful country?" He laughed, patted me on the behind, and headed for the shower.

I looked, down at the brochures in my hand. I knew I should be thrilled, but I felt like I did when one of the children came in past curfew. I'd been so worried, that I wanted to deck him. Instead, I went into the other bathroom and flushed the toilet. The yell I heard from Fred's shower made me feel better.

We had just finished supper when Philip and Haley came by. I cleared off the kitchen table and Philip put his notebook computer down and plugged it in.

"Let me show you how it works," he said. "It's mainly pedigree charts Meg was working on. She had a neat cross-referencing system, though."

We waited a moment while the computer made its groaning noises. Then a message flashed on the screen, "Margaret Anne March Bryan. Genius I."

"That's what she called her program," Philip explained. "I copied it and all of the 'gen' files so you can look at them."

"I don't know how," I said.

"Here's how you do it. First you hold down Alt F.

Okay? Now what do you want to do? Look at your choices."

There was a list of about twenty things on the screen.

"I don't know what I want to do," I said.

"You can just wander around in it," Haley offered. "Mash the down cursor and when the one you want is highlighted, hit 'Enter.' "

"How do I know what I want?"

"Well, let's look at someone's pedigree chart. How about Efram Bates." Philip struck some keys and there was the Bates family tree. Another key listed them alphabetically. Philip selected a name, highlighted it, and said, "Let's see what Meg found out about John Harvey Bates."

John Harvey Bates was a farmer in Lowndes County, Alabama, and the father of thirteen children by three wives. He died at the age of eighty-two in 1870.

"That's great," Fred said, looking over my shoulder.

"See if there's an Atchison family in there, I said.

Philip obligingly tapped some keys. "Three. There's one listed as Atchison, Camille, one as Atchison, Camille Johnson, cross-referenced as Camille Victoria Johnson."

"Can you look at those charts?"

"Sure. I'll do Atchison, Camille first."

The same pedigree configuration came up on the screen that had been up for the Bates family. I looked over it, all the marriages, children, deaths. So much living.

"Can you do the other Camille one?"

"Sure." The Atchison one disappeared and in its place was one with the heading "Camille Johnson Atchison." At first glance, they seemed to be identical.

"I wonder why Meg had three entries for this woman?" Haley said.

"Well, this woman married an Atchison, and that's

what her children are. But she was born a Johnson. So Meg had to go back through the Johnson family."

"Oh, of course," Haley said. "So Mama is a Tate and not a Hollowell."

"I hate the way women have to change their names," I grumbled.

"You jumped at the chance," Fred said. We all ignored him.

"Talk me through this one time," I asked Philip. "Show me exactly what to do to get the charts."

"Okay. I'm going to turn it off. You just follow the instructions I've written here."

I held my breath and went right to Atchison, Camille. My audience of three applauded. "Now how do I get out of this thing?"

Philip reached over and showed me.

"Just remember," he said as they were leaving, "you can't hurt a thing. Everything's saved, and if by some remote chance you erase the whole thing, I still have the disk. So just play with it." He started down the steps and turned. "And follow my instructions."

"What a nice man," I told Fred as I closed the door.

"And an ENT, too. Now come on, let's look at those cruises."

I did, and they all sounded wonderful. We narrowed our choices down to three, watched the ten o'clock news, and went to bed. But as soon as Fred was asleep, I was back at the kitchen table with the computer on. And under Camille Victoria Johnson, I found something very interesting. In trying to leave this file, though, and go to one of the Atchison ones, I did something wrong and the words "Fatal Error" came up on the screen. That'll get your attention. I turned the computer off immediately and unplugged it.

"Fred." I whispered as I crawled into bed beside him. "I think I just killed an expensive computer."

"That's okay," he said between snores.

CHAPTER 14

THE NEXT MORNING WHEN I WENT INTO THE KITCHEN, Fred was sitting at the computer tapping keys, studying the screen like some kind of computer expert. "I thought you said you killed it," he said. "It's fine."

"What are you doing? And how come you remember my saying that? You were snoring."

"I'm just following the instructions Philip wrote down. Look, honey, here's old Darrell Dunaway married Carroll Ferguson. Named their first son Shank. I like Darrell and Carroll, but they could have done better than Shank."

I went over and looked at the screen. "How did you do that? Last night it said 'Fatal Error.'"

"The male's innate affinity with machines."

"Are you saying I messed it up because I'm a woman?"

"Something like that. The coffee's ready."

"Nice to know the affinity also goes for coffee machines. And I'll have you know I did exactly what Philip wrote down." I poured a cup of coffee and came back to the table. Fred was as having a high old time.

"Ho," he said jovially. "It gets better. Shank named his daughter Shanklette."

"He did not!"

"Yes, he did. Look at this."

"Shanklette Ferguson," I marveled, looking at the screen.

"This is great," Fred said, moving the cursor down like a pro.

"Do me a favor. Pull up the Camille Johnson Atchison file."

"Okay." He did it as if there were no problem at all. The proud male and his orderly mind! "Now what?"

"Look back in the lineage chart. What I'm looking for would be in the 1860s, maybe 70s."

He scanned down the chart.

"Slowly," I said. Then, "Wait, here it is." I read over his shoulder, "Clovis Reed Johnson married Elizabeth Ann Sherman."

"So?"

"Who was her father?"

"It doesn't say. Just says Clovis and Elizabeth had six children."

I put my coffee down and looked over Fred's shoulder. "Now look up Camille Victoria Johnson and go back to that same spot."

Fred followed Philip's instructions and zoomed right into the other file and scanned down. "Here," he said. "Clovis Reed Johnson married Elizabeth Ann Sherman. Her parents are listed on this one, though. Her father is William T. Sherman."

"Now look him up in that biographical thing."

Fred hit the keys as if he had been doing it all his life. "Okay," he read. "Sherman, William Tecumseh, born Ohio, 1820, famous as a Civil War general for his 'March to the sea' through Georgia." He looked up and grinned. "How about that!"

I nodded. "Camile Atchison is General Sherman's great great something granddaughter. Apparently, she was not pleased with the news."

"And she was trying to get in that Confederate ladies' thing?"

"The UDC. Bless her heart." But I was grinning, too.

Talk about irony!

"Looks like she'd know about an ancestor that famous.

"You mean infamous?" I sat down and picked up my coffee. "You think Clovis's mama bragged to her quilting circle about Clovis marrying General Sherman's daughter? No way. That knowledge got swept under the rug so quick the dust didn't fly."

"Elizabeth's mama probably didn't brag about her marrying Clovis, either."

"Probably not. But you want to see something strange? Pull up the plain Camille Atchison file and look for Elizabeth Sherman's parents."

Fred complied with an agility that was infuriating. "Okay, here's Clovis and Elizabeth and William T. Sherman."

"Look him up in the biographical section of that file."

"Okay. Sherman, William Thomas, born South Carolina, 1820, served in the army of the Confederacy, wounded at Shiloh. Married Rebecca O'Donnell. Six children. Lifelong resident of Greenville. Occupation, tailor. Died 1886." Fred looked up. "What is this? Two different people?"

"I have no idea. But I certainly know which version Meg Bryan gave Camille Atchison. And Camille said she had the problem worked out so she obviously got the second one too."

Fred studied the screen. "I wonder which one's right."

"I think it's interesting that there are two versions." I thought for a moment, sipping my coffee. "What does the biographical part say about Clovis and Elizabeth?"

Fred typed a message to the computer which obliged with the knowledge that Clovis Reed Johnson was a farmer and Baptist minister and had lived in Mount Olive, Jefferson County, Alabama, from 1870 until his death in 1905. There was no biographical entry for Elizabeth.

"A Baptist minister's wife in a tiny Alabama town? There's no way she would have told anyone her father was General Sherman," I said.

"If he was." Fred pushed his chair back. "This is interesting, but I've got to go to work. You want me to leave the computer on? All you have to do is punch the keys Philip wrote down."

"Sure," I said, knowing full well that "Fatal Error" was lurking in wait.

Fred leaned over and kissed me. "Bye, Sweetie."

"Bye Pop."

He grinned and bounced out of the back door. Amazing what that trip to Atlanta had done for him.

I moved to the seat Fred had vacated and read the biographical information on Clovis Johnson again. Mount Olive was a suburb Of Birmingham, so the records should be at the Birmingham Public Library.

I got a bowl of cereal and sat at the table thinking about the two versions of Camille Johnson Atchison's family tree. William T. Sherman wasn't an uncommon name. It could have been a simple mix-up. But that thought went zipping out of my head. General Sherman appearing on a pedigree chart wouldn't have been an accident. It's only been a hundred and forty years or so since the Civil War—like yesterday in Southern time. A few diehards down here still won't carry fifty dollar bills because Grant's picture is on them, and the fives don't fare much better. Mary Alice, who adores legal tender of every denomination, as do I, says thank God those folks have American Express.

So General William Tecumseh Sherman perched on a branch of Camille Atchison's family tree a mistake? No way. The name would have hit any Southern genealogist between the eyes like the rock that slew Goliath.

I finished my cereal, turned up the bowl to drink the milk, and got up to get more coffee. Cup full, I wandered back to the table and stared down at the computer. Something told me I had found something important. Something also told me I didn't know enough about computers or genealogy to figure out what it was.

The phone rang and I reached over to answer it.

"Patricia Anne?" Trinity said. "I hope I didn't awaken you."

"No."

"How's Georgiana this morning?"

"Her condition is unchanged. She recognizes me."

"Are you at Mary Alice's?"

"No. I'm at the hospital. Georgiana seemed glad to see me during the five-minute visits. And she's so sick, I hated to leave."

"You stayed all night? You must be exhausted!"

"I am. The lovely young woman who works with her, Cassie Murphy, has come in, though, and says she'll stay a while. She has suggested that I go to Georgiana's apartment. I've never stayed in her new apartment, but I understand it's close by. I'm sure it would be all right with Georgiana."

"Of course it would. Do you have a key?"

"Cassie does. I'll go sleep a few hours."

"You do that. Call me when you wake up, and I'll bring you something to eat."

"Thank-you, dear."

I started to hang up when I heard Trinity calling, "Patricia Anne?"

"Yes?"

"Georgiana keeps asking me if you found someone

184

named Heidi. Do you know who she's talking about? She seems very agitated about it."

"She's a woman who worked at The Family Tree, and I couldn't find her phone number. I imagine Cassie knows it, though. In fact, I left word for her to call me last night so I could ask her, and she didn't return the call. Why don't you ask her?"

"I will. I'll talk to you later."

I finished my coffee, put on my sweats, and went out to take Woofer for his walk. It was a perfect spring morning, bright sun, low humidity. Mitzi was already out in her yard examining her climbing Peace rose. Woofer and I stopped to speak.

"Loaded with buds," she explained." Just don't let us have another hard freeze."

"I'll do my best," I said. I started down the sidewalk and turned around. "Mitzi, what do you think about the Civil War?"

She smiled. "Doesn't keep me awake at night."

"What if you found out General Sherman was your great great great whatever grandfather?"

"Wouldn't bother me a bit. I'd just keep it a secret." She smiled wider. "Or move up north. Why? You found out he's your ancestor? Am I going to have to move?"

"Not that I know of. I don't think I want to know what's hanging on my family tree."

"Well, don't look at what's coming down the street, then."

I looked up and saw Mary Alice's car.

"She's out early," Mitzi said.

"She sure is. I hope everything's okay."

Mary Alice spotted me and pulled over to the curb, letting down the window on my side. "I am totally distraught," she said. "Get in." She didn't look distraught.

She had on a green linen jacket, and her makeup was perfect.

"I can't. I've got the dog. What's the matter?"

"Mitzi doesn't want to hear my problems."

"Sure I do." Mitzi looked very interested.

"Well, for starters, Buddy may be gay."

"Buddy's not gay. He's ninety."

Mitzi's eyebrows went up.

"Besides," I continued, "he was a tiger at the opera. You said you had to fend him off."

"True, but last night in the hot tub, nothing."

"Probably the heat and the water. Hot tubs can do interesting things to the male anatomy."

"Bill was always at his best in the hot tub."

"Maybe Buddy's taking blood pressure medicine. Heart medicine, too."

"He is. And he's on the Pritikin diet and didn't even tell me. Brought his own food, and I'm stuck with all this chicken tetrazzini. Here." Sister handed me a casserole. "Somebody might as well enjoy it."

"Gee, thanks."

"And then he asked me to marry him. And I said, 'Buddy, I know you're the second richest man in Alabama. I looked it up. But, Buddy, I marry for love.'"

"And what did he say?"

"That he appreciated my honesty, and he hoped I would allow him to woo me."

"Woo you?"

"Woo me."

"This was in the hot tub with absolutely, nothing going on?"

"Or off."

"Umm. If he's gay, why would he ask you to marry him?"

"Protective coloring?"

Mitzi leaned on her fence. "And to think I just came out to look at my Peace roses."

"Where are you going now?" I asked Sister.

"To get Tiffany at the Buick place. Her car broke down. Incidentally, Trinity Buckalew never called last night. Have you heard from her?"

"While ago. She said Georgiana Peach is just the same, and she's going over to her apartment to stay. It's close to the hospital."

"Looks like she'd have called."

"Maybe she did and you were too busy in the hot tub."

"Jackass!" Sister hit the up button on the window. I got my hand out just in time.

"Marry him!" Mitzi yelled to the departing car, her hands cupped around her mouth. "Lord, Patricia Anne," she turned to me, "the second richest man in Alabama, ninety years old with a bad heart? Lord!"

"Go figure." I took my casserole and my dog home.

After I did a minimum of housework, which consisted of making up the bed and zapping the most obvious dust bunnies with the Dustbuster, I sat down at the kitchen table and stared at the computer. I needed to know what was in it. Therefore, I would turn it on and retrieve the information I needed. I would not be intimidated by this little black box. Fred and his male's superior ability with machines. What bullshit! I turned on the power and watched the screen light up.

What I was looking for was multiple listings of any one name, such as Camille's three. Following Philip's instructions, I zoomed right to the directory and found several. One was listed as Jasper Arnold, Jasper N. Arnold, and Jasper Newton Arnold. Two generations back, I discovered that Jasper's grandfather, Clifford, was unlisted on one chart; was a farmer in Tatnall County, Georgia, where he died, on the second chart; and on the third, was a counterfeiter who died in Atmore Prison in Alabama. Three listings for Lacy Blake and Sutter Rowe provided the same disparity. An ancestor who might have been an embarrassment was washed clean.

"Okay, Meg," I said to the computer. "What's going on here?"

I got a pencil and paper and copied down the names and dates of the charts that had been changed. It didn't take a professional genealogist to recognize the snake in the woodpile here. But had this snake been the cause of Meg Bryan's death? Or Judge Haskins's murder?

While I was in the shower, I thought about the obvious advantages of changing a name on a family tree. General Sherman's name on the Johnson lineage chart had kept Camille Atchison out of an organization she felt passionately about belonging to. But if General William Tecumseh Sherman became William Thomas Sherman, a Georgia farmer wounded in service to the Confederacy, could Camille take the revised pedigree chart and say, "Big mistake. Clean slate," and be admitted? How much proof would she have to come up with?

And then there was the flip side of the coin. If a family tree could have rotten apples plucked off, it could also have some grafted on. And how much would a person to whom ancestry was a matter of pride pay to have a Benedict Arnold expurgated from his pedigree chart? And would he keep paying? This could be a field ripe for blackmail.

I poured shampoo into my hand. Surely this wasn't what Meg Bryan was doing. Or was it? She had given the chart with General Sherman's name on it to Camille Atchison. Camille said she had had it "straightened out," obviously with the "'farmer in Georgia" version. I lathered my hair with the special shampoo I use for curly hair. Some ancestor had forwarded his genes for curly strawberry-blond hair (now mostly gray), along with a million freckles, to me. Another had bequeathed straight brown hair (now curly strawberry-blond) and olive skin to Mary Alice. So what? I stood under the cascading warm water and realized that knowing who these progenitors were would never be the passion for me that it was to the people in Meg's computer.

And then I thought of the boy who fell from the cliff and was hanged by his hair. The stories. Now those I could get hooked on. All the stories of the world are found in each family. A walk through any cemetery is a walk through the world.

"Records for Mount Olive?" the librarian in the Southern History Department at the Birmingham Public Library said. "We've got some. But your best bet would be over at the courthouse."

"This man was a Baptist minister," I said, "in the late 1800s."

"The Alabama Baptist Convention has very complete records, too," she said. "I think they're at Samford University." She got up from the same desk, I swear, where I had sat forty years earlier clipping newspaper stories for Miss Boxx, who still appeared occasionally in my anxiety dreams. "Our records are back here."

I followed her to the back of the room. Her skirt, I figured, was one-fifth as long as mine had been forty years ago.

"What is it you want, exactly?"

"I'm trying to find out all I can about a man named Clovis Reed Johnson and his wife, Elizabeth."

"Were they born in Jefferson County?"

"I don't know," I admitted. "He might have been. I doubt she was."

"Well, like I say, most of the Jefferson County records are over at the courthouse. If you don't find anything here, that's where you need to look."

"Thanks." I put my purse and notebook on a table as the woman walked off. In her green miniskirt and matching tights, she would have been at home in Sherwood Forest, Miss Boxx, the ultimate librarian and founder of the Southern History Department, scowled down at her from her portrait on the wall.

It didn't take me long to realize that the woman was right about the records. I found a 1900 census list that had Clovis R. Johnson and Mary C. Johnson listed with four children ranging in age from six to eighteen. Had Elizabeth died? Probably. There certainly wouldn't have been a divorce.

"Death records?" the wood nymph said when I asked her. "They're over at the courthouse. We're going to get all that kind of stuff put on the computer some day, so all you'll have to do is call it up right here." She pointed vaguely toward a couple of computers that sat, unused, on a table. "But right now you're going to have to go over to the courthouse. Up on the tenth floor. Archives Department."

I cut across the park to the courthouse, remembering that the last time I had been in this park, there had been emergency vehicles flashing their lights and Judge Haskins running to tell us Meg was dead. Today a few people were sitting on benches or by the reflecting pool, eating lunch or just enjoying the spring sun. A tranquil scene.

The lobby of the courthouse was dim and cool after the brilliant sunshine outside. I found the elevators and

190

pushed the button for the tenth floor, realizing that the reason Meg had been on the tenth floor was probably because she was looking for something in the Archives Department. I shivered.

The tenth floor seemed deserted. A double glass door at the end of the hall looked promising, though. I walked toward it and saw that it was, indeed, the Jefferson County Archives and History Department. I pushed the door open, and a woman looked up in surprise from behind a tall counter.

"I'm looking up a family," I said, "They lived in Jefferson County in the late 1800s."

The counter, I realized, was average height; the woman was very short. "Sure," she said. "What do you want? Births, deaths?"

"Deaths. I need to find out when a man's first wife died. But I need the marriages, too."

"What's the name? Some of those records are alphabetized. Just some of them, though."

"Johnson. I need all I can find on a woman named, Elizabeth Sherman Johnson. Her husband's name was Clovis Reed Johnson."

"What is this? You're the second person this week wanting to know about Elizabeth Sherman Johnson. What is it with her?"

"Really?"

"God's truth." The short woman opened a door in the counter. "Come on back. I don't think I've even put those records up yet."

The woman was as wide as she was tall. I followed her down aisles lined with record books, where small stepladders attested to the way she reached the ones that were over five feet high.

"What did this person look like?" I, asked. "The other

one who wanted Elizabeth Johnson's records."

"Little bitty. Gray."

"Did she look like Jessica Tandy?"

"You know, she did. Thanks. I kept asking myself, 'Aileen, who is it this lady reminds you of?' And for the life of me, I couldn't think of it. And that was it exactly."

It was Meg. It had to be. "Did she sign anything in order to look at the records?"

"No, honey. They're here for the looking. She didn't stay but a minute, anyway."

Coming from between the aisles, we came into an area with several tables and windows that overlooked the park.

"There they are," Aileen said, pointing to a couple of large record books on the table. "I know those are the same ones." She opened the nearest one. "Let's see. Johnson, Clovis. That's an unusual name, isn't it?"

"It's his wife, Elizabeth Sherman Johnson, when I'm really interested in."

"They list them by the man, honey. Makes me furious." She ran her finger down an index. "Here's Clovis, page 219. Elizabeth should be attached. What's she done, anyway, to warrant all this attention?"

"Nothing that I know of. It's a family-tree thing."

"Family trees are for the birds." Aileen laughed at her own wit while she opened the heavy record book. I reached over to help her.

"Page 219, 219," she murmured, turning the pages. "Pages 218, page 221. Page 219?"

"What?" I asked.

"There's not a page 219." She turned back several pages and looked through again.

"Let me see," I said. She moved over and I turned the pages. 218, 221. No 219 or 220. "Is there any way it could be misnumbered? Out of place?"

"With these records, sure. But look here." Aileen, whose eyes were much closer to the book than mine, pointed. Close to the binding were a few jagged edges of paper.

"Somebody tore it out?" I asked.

"Somebody tore the son of a bitch out! Brenda!"

A voice from the stacks answered, "What? I'm dusting."

"Come here."

A tall thin woman with a red feather duster in her hand appeared from between two of the aisles.

"Look at this," Aileen pointed. "They've done it again."

Brenda came up, looked at the ragged edge, and shook her head. "Computers," she said.

"Well, I know what the answer is, Brenda," Aileen said. "How many you going to donate?"

"What laws are they breaking?" I asked. "Tearing these pages out."

"Every law in the book. Ticks me off to hell and back."

"Me, too," Brenda said.

"Well," I put my notebook back in my purse, "I guess I'll try Samford. Clovis was a Baptist preacher."

"Gonna have to put these things under lock and key," I heard Aileen telling Brenda as I left. For starters, she could try not leaving them lying out on the desk for days, I thought.

On the way to the elevator, I passed a ladies' room and decided I would be more comfortable if I took advantage of the facilities. When I entered, I found myself in what was the courthouse tenth-floor equivalent of the teachers' lounge at Alexander High. And like all teachers' lounges, it was furnished with a couple of chairs and an old sofa salvaged from someone's basement. In this case, they matched, though, rattan with faded flowered cushions. A coffee table with a cracked glass top and a nice, built-in makeup counter completed the furnishings. In the next room were four toilet cubicles and sinks. The courthouse is a nonsmoking building, but word hadn't gotten up to the ladies' room on the tenth floor. Smoke hung heavy in the air in spite of the window opened wide to the spectacular spring day.

As I was drying my hands, I walked to the window and did a double take. This was where Meg jumped. Or was pushed. I glanced down again. The view made me dizzy and I backed away, but below me was the exact spot where her body had landed. I looked around the room as if expecting some answers.

The door burst open and two young women came in laughing.

"Hi," they both said to me as they took out their cigarettes and plunked down in the chairs.

CHAPTER 15

I WAS AS STARVING. I WAS STARVING FOR FAST, FATTY food. I went through the drive-in at the Green Springs McDonald's and ordered a Big Mac and a chocolate milkshake. Then I took them home, pulled off my shoes, and settled down to eat and watch *Jeopardy*. I knew the answer to the Final Jeopardy question and that, plus more fat than my digestive system usually had to cope with in a week, cheered me up. So did a message on my answering machine from Debbie that they were home, very happy, and I should give them a call.

"The most wonderful honeymoon in the world," Debbie bubbled. The quaintest inn, a wonderful fireplace in their room with a fire every night, a wonderful view of the mountains from rocking chairs across the porch. And a wonderful husband to share it with.

"I'm glad you had a wonderful time," I said.

"Thank-you, Aunt Pat," Debbie said, seriously, a sure sign of how rattled she was. "I talked to Haley, so I know about her and Philip. I think that's wonderful."

"Wonderful," I agreed. "And your mother got a marriage proposal."

"So I hear. I think it's—" Debbie paused.

"Wonderful?"

"Well, sure. He's getting on up there in years, though, isn't he?"

"Honey, you know that game on *The Price Is Right* where they play yodeling music while the little mountain climber chugs up to the top? And he falls over, clunk, when you overbid?"

"You're saying Mama better bid carefully?"

"Something like that. On the other hand, who knows? Buddy Johnson may outlast us all. You need to come over when you can. We've got a lot of catching up to do. This has been a busy week."

"So I hear. I couldn't believe Meg Bryan's death. She seemed fine at the wedding."

"That was just the beginning," I said.

"Well, could you and Uncle Fred come to supper tomorrow night? Henry wants to try out a new lamb recipe. I think Haley and Philip will be here, and Mama. We can hear about everything."

"That sounds wonderful," I said. We made a date for six o'clock so we would have a chance to see the twins before their bedtime.

I had been talking to Debbie at the table where I had stacked the letters from Meg Bryan's computer disk. I picked up the one on top of stack three, with the names, Williams, Murphy, Bobby, Trinity, scribbled on it. It reminded me that I hadn't found Heidi Williams like I had promised Georgiana Peach. I called Debbie back and asked her if she had a city directory.

"Sure. Right here."

"See if there's a Williams, Heidi listed. She's not in the phone book under the name Heidi, but the city directory lists wives' names separately."

"Just a minute, Aunt Pat. Talk to Fay while I'm looking."

A conversation with a child who has just turned two is exhausting. Not that Fay didn't talk; she talked a blue streak. But I didn't have the foggiest idea what she was telling me. Consequently, my side of the conversation consisted of "That's right, darling." I was glad when Debbie rescued me with the news that Heidi was, indeed, listed, and did I have a pencil?

I did and was rewarded with both Ms. Williams's phone number and address. Bless the city directory people. I called the number and got the usual answering machine. Heidi had such a strong Southern accent, her voice could have been a study for a linguistics class. Most people think Southern accents are all alike. Not so, as any Southerner can tell you. Heidi's voice was straight from the Tennessee mountains. I left a message for her to call me, and told her that Georgiana Peach was sick at University Hospital and was trying to get in touch with her. I stuck the card with the phone number and address in my purse, then turned back to the letters. The last one I read before my eyes closed in a delicious nap was one in which Meg was questioning the contraction of Pollack into Polk. Was James K. Polk's original family name Pollack? The sandman cometh; I embraced him.

An hour later, I awoke feeling like hell. I had been too sound asleep for too short a time. My head ached slightly,

I had a crick in my neck, and the Big Mac seemed to have wedged sideways in my esophagus. I got up stiffly and went looking for the aspirin and Maalox, which I promptly spilled on the kitchen counter. Damn. Why is it that sleeping in the daytime seems such a great idea but leaves you feeling like a zombie?

I was holding a wet paper towel against my face when the phone rang.

"Patricia Anne?" It was Frances Zata, my friend, the counselor at Robert Alexander High. "You know we were talking about Castine Murphy?"

"I knew you would be happy to know she's turned out okay."

"Well, I went back and pulled her record here at the school. She went to Vanderbilt. Did you know that? And here's a letter from Vanderbilt in her file that she graduated magna cum laude."

"Nobody said she didn't have a brilliant mind," I grumbled. "She just did what she wanted with it."

"Were you asleep?"

"Just waking up," I admitted. "My head's loggy."

"Oh, but the idea of being able to take a nap," Frances enthused. "I've decided I'm definitely retiring this year. Why shouldn't I? I've put in my thirty years."

"You'll miss the kids," I warned. "And the school."

"About as much as you do."

Which was quite a lot. There was a large hole in my life that I still hadn't filled.

"Anyway, you know I told you her parents were killed by lightning while Castine was in college?"

"Yes, and that she didn't inherit the money everyone thought she would. She still got to finish school, though?"

"Apparently, thanks to that judge that was murdered the other day. Judge Haskins. He became her guardian.

197

This letter is a copy of one Vanderbilt sent to him saying congratulations, that Castine was in the top five percentile of her class and would be graduating with honors."

My head wasn't loggy anymore. In fact, I felt very alert. "Judge Haskins was Cassie's guardian?"

"Fortunately, since her father had just declared bankruptcy before he died. I guess she could have done it, but that child would have had a tough time getting through school without some help."

"Judge Haskins was a bankruptcy judge," I said, putting two and two together. "I'll bet that's how he met her."

"Lucky girl," Frances said, "to have the judge step in like that."

"Hmmm."

"Anyway, I thought you might like to know, so if you see her again you can express your sympathy about the judge's death."

"Thanks." I heard bells ringing in the background.

"Gotta go, Patricia Anne. See you soon."

I hung up the phone and said, "I'll be damned." I picked up the note Meg had written with Murphy, Williams, Trinity, Bobby, Georgiana on it. Can of worms, I thought. And getting curiouser and curiouser. So Judge Haskins had been the teenager Cassie's guardian. That relationship should have been an interesting one. Or maybe it wasn't. Maybe it was strictly business and paternal goodwill.

Yeah, right.

Maybe I should warn Frances that when you retire you become cynical, start talking to yourself, and minding other folks' business.

I had promised Trinity I would bring food over later. She could probably fill me in on the Cassie-Judge Haskins relationship. Her version of it, anyway. I divided the chicken tetrazzini Sister had given me, putting part of it in a small casserole for Trinity. Not enough. I needed a green salad, but my only lettuce was yellow around the edges and limp as a bad perm. I stuck the casserole back in the refrigerator, combed my hair, slapped on lipstick, and headed for the Piggly Wiggly.

The paper with Heidi Williams's address and phone number on it fell out when I reached in my purse for my money. Hollywood Boulevard. Just a couple of blocks away. She hadn't answered the phone, but what the heck. If she was out of town, maybe some neighbor knew where she could be reached.

I swung onto Hollywood, watching the street numbers. Heidi's address was Apartment B in a complex of six apartments that formed a "U." The stucco exterior said 1920s, but, like most of the homes in this area, the complex was well-maintained. From the sidewalk that ran along the street, another large sidewalk led into the middle of the "U" and neatly bordered sidewalks branched to the front doors of the individual apartments. These apartments, I knew, would have high ceilings and arched openings between the living room and dining room. There would be dentil molding throughout, and glass in the front of the kitchen cabinets. These apartments, in this neighborhood, did not come cheap.

I slowed, trying to decide whether to go knock on the door. An elderly man sitting in a wheelchair in front of one of the apartments waved at me. I waved back. It was a nice day to be out enjoying the sun.

He waved both arms, trying to get my attention. I stopped and let the window down.

"Hey!" he yelled, propelling himself toward me. "Hey!"

I got out to meet him, though he seemed to be having no problem getting around.

"You the woman from the Humane Society?" he asked.

"No. I'm just looking for a woman named Heidi Williams. Why? Is something wrong?"

"It's her dog. Mrs. Williams's. It's been howling for two days. I swear I think that woman went off and left that poor animal without any food or water."

"Nobody has a key to her apartment?"

"None of the neighbors has a key. I'm the only one around during the day, so I promised I'd call the Humane Society." He swung his chair around and headed back toward the apartment. He was not as old as I had first thought, but rather in his early fifties; his withered legs were the recognizable legacy of childhood polio. He seemed to assume I would follow him, which I did.

"Right here," he said, pointing to Apartment B. "Listen."

He didn't have to tell me to listen. Plaintive wails, interspersed with yelps, were emanating from the apartment.

"My God!" I said. "When did you call the Humane Society?"

"This morning. They said they couldn't go in the apartment, though, and I should call the police. So I called the police and they said they'd get hold of the Humane Society. Back and forth. Back and forth."

"Maybe Mrs. Williams is sick in there." I hated to say what I was really thinking. "When did you see her last?"

"Don't know." He suddenly held out his hand. "Bill Mahoney."

I shook his hand. "Patricia Anne Hollowell."

"And she's not dead, if that's what you're thinking. Hot as it is, we'd have known."

I let that pass. "Did you ask the police to come check?"

"I told them about the dog. They said they'd call the

Humane folks. I kept thinking they'd show up together, but they haven't."

I walked up the sidewalk to Apartment B. Draperies were drawn across what must be the living room windows. I tried to peep through them, but I couldn't. The windows on the side were too high to look in, and the poor animal inside, sensing my presence, howled even louder.

"It's enough to make you cry," Bill Mahoney said when I came back from my excursion around the apartment. "She's the cutest dog you ever saw."

"Mrs. Williams has never done anything like this before, has she?" I asked.

I have no excuse for what happened then. Here he was, worried about the dog and not the woman, and it suddenly infuriated me. "Did you explain this to the police? Did it occur to you she might be lying in there sick? Needing help from her neighbors? No. You were going to let her die and wait until her body smelled? What's wrong with you, man? And where's your phone?" My voice was shaking with anger.

"Apartment A. And you listen, lady, I'm a good neighbor."

He probably thought he was. At least he was trying to get the dog out. Damn. What the hell was I doing beating up on a man in a wheelchair? He had enough troubles without me adding to them. I willed myself to calm down as I followed him down the sidewalk to his apartment.

"Here," he said, opening the front door for me. I found Bo Peep Mitchell's number and called it. "A semi-emergency," I told the operator, and gave my name and the number of Bill Mahoney's phone.

He had followed me into his living room, which was filled with all kinds, of exercise machines.

"You want a Coke?" he asked as I hung up the phone. I shook my head no. He wheeled into the kitchen and came back with one. "I guess I just never thought about Mrs. Williams being sick."

"Sorry I jumped down your throat," I apologized.

"It's okay. I guess I should have. I just assumed she was gone and I'm sure the other neighbors did, too. I've been getting her newspapers and mail." He put his Coke on a table and picked up a couple of barbells. Up. Down. Up. Down.

The phone rang. Bo. She was only about six blocks away, she said, when I explained the situation. She'd be right along.

"The police will be here in a minute," I said.

"You really think Mrs. Williams is in there sick?" Bill Mahoney asked.

"I hope not." My anger was gone. Bill Mahoney had enough problems. Let him go on thinking he was a good neighbor. He had done more than anyone else in the apartment complex. "I'm going to wait outside," I said.

"I think I'll stay here."

Ah hah. Afraid of what they were going to find.

In a few minutes, Bo's black and white pulled in behind my car.

"What's up?" she called, coming up the sidewalk.

"Listen."

"You called me to hear the Hound of the Baskervilles?"

I explained to Bo what had happened, and she made the same tour around the apartment that I had made.

"Can't you just go on in?" I asked.

"No, Patricia Anne. I can't just barge into someone's house. I'd be out of the police department and on my butt. There's more to it than that, girl."

"Well, do something. What if the poor woman had a

202

stroke or something?"

"I'll do something. Give me time." She looked around. "Where does the Good Samaritan live?"

"Apartment A."

"I'll go talk to him for a minute."

Bill Mahoney was waiting for her. I saw him open the door. I sat on the front steps of Apartment B. The poor animal inside had calmed down. There was an occasional whimper, but not the earlier wails. "We'll get you out soon," I whispered.

When Bo came back, she explained that another officer was on his way with a warrant to open the apartment, that there did, indeed, look as if something were amiss inside. She also wanted to know what I was doing there.

I started with Georgiana Peach's intestinal problems and ended up with how expensive lettuce was in March at the Piggly Wiggly.

"Okay," Bo said. She sat down on the steps beside me.

"Can you imagine," I said, "that no one in these six apartments has seen this woman in several days, her papers are piling up and so is her mail, and they wait until her dog starts howling to check on her? And even then, it's the dog, not the woman, they're worried about."

"People like dogs," Bo said.

"You don't think, they liked Heidi Williams?"

"How do I know? People don't want to get messed up in other folks' lives. Scared they'll step on other folks' toes or get their own stepped on. Dogs are different. They're just dogs." Bo sighed. "Don't be rough on these people, Patricia Anne."

"It makes me sad," I said.

"Me too," Bo agreed.

A second police car pulled up, and a handsome middle-aged man with a handlebar mustache got out.

"Rambo, my man," Bo called to him.

"Bo Peep, my woman." The policeman came up the sidewalk and was introduced to me as Gaston Rambo.

"God's truth," Bo said. "Imagine having to live with that."

"Beats Bo Peep," Rambo smiled. The dog inside the apartment began to moan again. "You ready to see what's going on?"

"Expect we better." Bo got up. "You better wait out here, Patricia Anne."

"I'm not horsing to go in," I said. I sat on the steps. Bill Mahoney had wheeled himself out to the sidewalk again. Together we waited.

"Here," Bo said in a minute, handing me a small brown and white mixed breed dog. "So far so good."

I held the trembling little dog. It was amazing that something this tiny could have made such a noise.

"Her name is Doodle," Bill Mahoney called.

"It's okay, Doodle," I whispered. "You're going to be okay now."

"I'll get her a bowl of water." Bill wheeled back into his apartment. I got up, carrying the dog, and went over to his porch. "Here you go, Doodle," he said, taking the dog from me and setting her before an orange Tupperware bowl. She drank the whole bowl of water and half of the refill Bill brought. "You think she'll eat some Dinty Moore stew?" he asked.

"I think she'd love it."

We were on Bill's porch watching Doodle finish the last of a large can of Dinty Moore when Bo and Gaston Rambo came out.

"Everything looks okay," Bo said. "The dog was just hungry and thirsty. She left quite a few opinions of the way she was being treated for her mistress."

Bill Mahoney looked relieved, and I'm sure I did, too.

"Either one of you know anything about her family?" Gaston Rambo asked.

"Castine Murphy down at The Family Tree might. That's where she worked. And Georgiana Peach, but she's in intensive care at University Hospital."

"Well, we need to follow this up," Bo said. "Bill here says she's never done anything like this before."

"Never," he repeated. "Can Doodle stay with me until Mrs. Williams gets back?"

"I thought you wanted her to go to the Humane Society."

"I just wanted them to rescue her. Come here, Doodle." One jump and the little dog was in Bill's lap.

"Sounds good to me," Bo said.

"You want me to go get her some dog food?" I asked.

"There's probably some over in Apartment B," Bo said. "Come on, Patricia Anne, let's look."

"I'll see you later, Bo," Gaston Rambo said. "I'll write the report on this."

"Thanks."

I followed Bo over to Heidi Williams's apartment. "What is it?" I asked. "You don't need me to help you pick up a can of dog food."

"You can help me clean up dog doo."

"Yuck."

"We don't want Mrs. Williams coming home to a messy house," Bo said.

We entered a living room that was totally in order. "Reckon there's a Mr. Williams?" I asked Bo. "I forgot to ask Bill Mahoney."

"Look around you, child."

Bo was right. This was a woman's house with frills and pillows and lacy curtains. It was the house of a woman who should own a cat, not a Doodle. But a Doodle was what she owned, and a Doodle had made a mess on the backporch, close to her empty water and food bowls.

"I'm not liking what I'm seeing," Bo said.

"I'm not either," I said, eying the mounds of Doodle doo and the yellowed, drenched newspapers.

"I mean the way this woman has disappeared. A woman with heart-shaped pillows on her bed and a Laura Ashley comforter and draperies does not go off and leave her dog."

"Is this a Bo Mitchell theory?"

"Nope. It just doesn't fit. One thing you learn in police work is that things fit. If they don't, you can bet something's wrong."

"Pure brilliance," I said. But my grin was half-hearted. "How old is Heidi Williams?"

"How should I know? She was your friend."

"I didn't know the woman from Adam's house cat. I was getting her for Georgiana Peach."

"You got, strange friends, Patricia Anne."

"God's truth. Just keep shoveling, Bo Peep."

We worked for a few minutes. "Least Doodle stayed in the same area," Bo said, rinsing out the mop.

"She looked like a nice little dog."

"Yes." Bo swished the mop across the floor. "What do you know about Georgiana Peach, Patricia Anne?"

"I never met her until this week. She's a genealogist, an old friend of Meg Bryan and her sister. She seems very nice. Why?"

"You know anything about her and Judge Haskins?"

"I know she was fond of him."

"Reckon there was any reason she might want to kill him?"

"Not that I know of. Why?"

"They found the murder weapon. It was a pistol registered to her."

"To Georgiana? Georgiana had a gun?" I was so startled, I almost dropped the bottle of Pine Sol I was holding. "Where did they find it?"

"At the house next door to the judge. In the swimming pool."

"My Lord!"

Bo folded her hands over the end of the mop and propped her chin on it. "You like her? Georgiana?" she asked, looking at me.

"Very much."

"Well, don't stay awake tonight worrying The gun in the swimming pool? Doesn't fit."

CHAPTER 16

WHETHER GEORGIANA'S GUN BEING THE WEAPON that had killed Judge Haskins and being found in the swimming pool next door fit or not, it was something to worry about. At home, fixing the salad, moving around the familiar kitchen, I worried about it. Georgiana's words, *I loved him so* and *He loved women, truly loved them,* echoed in my thoughts. Surely she hadn't loved him so much that the thought of him dinging a twenty-four-year-old Jenny Louise had driven her over the edge. From what I had learned, dinging twenty-four-year-olds had been a hobby of Judge Haskins. Because "he loved women, truly loved them." Bullshit. He was a horny old bastard who was lucky to have lived as long as he did without a bullet between his eyes.

I slapped the food on a tray and headed for Georgiana's apartment. Trinity opened the door before I knocked.

"Good," she said, "I'm starving."

I handed her the tray with the chicken tetrazzini tossed salad, and a piece of Sara Lee cheesecake I had found in my freezer. "Hello, Trinity."

"You're out of shape," she said. "Just huffing."

"Steep steps." The back steps that led to the outside doors of the apartments were, indeed, steep.

"Come in a minute and get your breath."

"Thanks," I said. I pulled out a kitchen chair and sank down. Georgiana's kitchen was small, but bright and airy. The cabinets and appliances were white, and the floor tile was white with a peach-colored geometric design. The table where I was sitting was made of heavy glass atop two pieces of humorous garden statuary, two rabbits with their arms uplifted. The four cane bottom chairs, which had probably been purchased at a thrift store, had been painted in a dozen bright triangles, circles, and stripes. It was the kitchen of an artist.

"I love this room," I said. I wondered if Trinity knew Georgiana had a gun.

"The whole place is spectacular," Trinity was already sticking the chicken in the microwave. "The office downstairs is, too. I keep telling Georgiana she missed her calling."

"She decorated this?"

"She did it all." Trinity reached in a cabinet for a plate. "You want some iced tea?"

"That would be great. Have you heard from Georgiana this afternoon?"

"Cassie Murphy called and said she was about the same. Maybe a little better. She had to leave, so I'm going over there after a while." Trinity brought me a glass of iced tea and some lemon.

"Did Cassie say she was coming here to the office, by

any chance?" I explained to Trinity about Heidi Williams, leaving out the Bo Mitchell part, and saying that perhaps Cassie or Georgiana knew a relative.

The microwave dinged and Trinity got up to retrieve her chicken tetrazzini. "She said she was going to the library first. Georgiana's address book is in the living room by the phone, though. Maybe there's something in there."

"I'll go look," I said.

Granted, the apartment was new and the paint was fresh and the carpet clean, so even I could have made it look okay. But what Georgiana had done to that room was, indeed, spectacular. I wandered around, admiring the subtle blend of antique and new. The old wicker library table with the Lucite lamp, pictures by Birmingham artists whose names I recognized, and a poster of a music festival. Above the fireplace was a small Wild Goose Chase quilt done in bright shades of peach and green. Trinity was right, I thought. Georgiana was a decorator.

Even the address book was not the same one everybody has from the Metropolitan, the Mary Cassatt painting of a woman licking an envelope. Georgiana's was a photograph, a close-up of the back of a pink shell that took a moment for me to figure out what it was. I was admiring it and the pillows on the sofa so much that I almost forgot who I was supposed to be looking up.

"Find it?" Trinity called.

"I'm just admiring everything."

"Told you she missed her calling."

"You're right." I opened the shell book to Williams and found the same number and address that Debbie had given me from the city directory. "It's not here," I said, carrying the book back to the kitchen, where Trinity was sitting at the table eating.

"This is wonderful," she said, holding some chicken

tetrazzini up on her fork.

"Thanks." No use explaining Mary Alice's caterer had done it.

"Maybe there's something down in the office. A work file," she suggested.

"Can we go down there?"

"Right out the living-room door and down the steps."

"There's no burglar alarm or anything?"

"There is, but it's not on. Cassie said she would come by later and set it. Just the office part. It's locked from the outside, but from here, you can walk right down."

"The records are probably all on computer," I said.

Trinity poured some more ranch dressing onto her salad. "There's some file cabinets and a rolodex."

"I'll go look," I said. "Right out the living room?"

Trinity nodded, her mouth full of lettuce.

The office was neat and attractive, decorated in the same shades of peach and green as the apartment above it. The three desks were white, as were the bookcases and filing cabinets. A small sitting area held a wicker love seat and a couple of wicker rockers with coordinating cushions. Comfortable. Pleasant. On the wall above the love seat was a collage of antique valentines.

"Oh, my," I said admiringly.

"It's lovely, isn't it?"

I jumped guiltily. I hadn't heard Cassie come in behind me. "Trinity said it was okay to come down here," I explained, feeling like a kid without a hall pass.

"Sure it is. What are you looking for, Mrs. Hollowell?"

"I promised Georgiana I'd find Heidi Williams, and I located where she lived, but she's not there and, according to a neighbor, hasn't been for several days."

"Let's see." Cassie had her hands full, a large purse, a small computer, and a briefcase. She put them on a desk and flipped through the rolodex. "This just has her address."

"What about her application for a job? Don't you have to put next of kin on Social Security?"

"I don't remember. Let me see if I can find it." She went over to a file cabinet and pulled out a drawer. "Williams. Williams. Nope." She came back to the desk. "Maybe it's on the computer." She turned a computer on that was on a side counter. The usual groaning and humming ensued. "Williams. Williams. Here's a Brenda Williams. Most of this is stuff we're working on, though. Georgiana has a CPA who does the books."

"He'd send the records back to her, though."

Cassie turned the computer off. "I'm sorry, Mrs. Hollowell. I have no idea where Georgiana keeps stuff like that." She rolled her shoulders backwards and rubbed her neck. "I'll look harder tomorrow. I just came by to set the alarm system."

"You look exhausted," I said.

"I am. I need to go to the library, but I think I'll stop by Subway and get a sandwich and head home."

She gathered up her purse and small computer.

"Here," I said, "let me help you." I picked up the briefcase, followed her into the hall, and tucked it under her arm. "How was Georgiana when you left?"

"Her temperature has shot up." Cassie shrugged. "They're switching to another antibiotic. I guess we'll just have to keep our fingers crossed." She turned toward the alarm panel beside the door. "You need to go back upstairs before I set this," she explained. "The sensors include the foyer. Tell Trinity I'll talk to her later."

"I will. You go home and get some rest."

Trinity was eating her cheesecake and drinking a cup of coffee when I came back into the upstairs apartment.

211

"Want some?" she offered.

I shook my head and said I needed to get home, that Fred would be home soon for supper.

"Men!" she said.

"I like them."

"Oh, I do, too. I just hate to feed them."

I sat back down at the kitchen table. "Tell me about Judge Haskins," I said. "And Meg."

"Nothing to tell. They met in college. His family was trash, honey. I mean trash. But he'd pulled himself up by his jockstrap and was in law school."

"You mean his bootstrap?"

"I meant what I said. I think he was the first guy Meg ever slept with, and she thought she had to marry him. She adored him. Bobby used Meg as a steppingstone, but, in a way, I think he loved her, too. Always did. He was just screwed up. Smart, but screwed up."

"How long were they married?"

"Seven years? Eight?" Trinity shook her head. "She finished putting him through law school and taught him manners. But, I swear, Patricia Anne, trash will rise to the surface. You know it."

"But he got to be a judge."

"Tell me about it." Trinity got up and rinsed her coffee cup.

"Do you really think he killed Meg because of the bastardy papers?"

"At first I did. Bobby set a store by that trashy family of his, Lord knows why. But Georgiana says Meg knew something Bobby was mixed up in. I don't have any idea what. But whatever it was got both of them killed."

"But she ran into him accidentally at lunch."

"Hah. Whose idea was it to have lunch there? You didn't know my sister very well."

212

"I think it was Mary Alice's idea."

"You want to bet? I'd stake my life on the fact that Meg knew where he was having lunch. She just 'accidentally' ran into Bobby every time she came to Birmingham."

"And Georgiana loved him, too." This was a statement, not a question.

Trinity shook her head yes. "There's just no accounting, is there? Even I had a hankering for the old fellow at one time."

The phone rang while I was thinking about this. Trinity didn't answer it. Instead, Georgiana's voice came on with The Family Tree message. We heard a woman asking Georgiana to call her when she got a chance. But while the woman was leaving her message, I remembered the voice that had sounded like Meg's saying, "Help me!"

"Have you listened to the messages?" I asked Trinity.

"No. I figured they were all that genealogy stuff."

"Well, there's one here I want you to listen to." I ran the tape back, but I couldn't find the "Help me!" message.

"What is it?" Trinity asked as I wandered through "that genealogy stuff."

"Just a message I thought you might be interested in. Nothing, really."

She was getting her things ready to leave and didn't question me any closer, for which I was grateful. How do you explain a dead sister's voice saying, "Help me?" And how do you explain the initials MMB on a briefcase that obviously had a small computer in it and which was being carried by Castine Murphy?

After supper I startled Fred by telling him I was going over to Sister's for a while.

"Why?" he said. "Just wait a while and she'll show up. What do you need to see her for, anyway?"

213

"About the trip to New Orleans."

"Why don't you just call her?" He looked at me over the paper. He would be dozing in ten minutes; he and I both knew it. But while he was dozing, he wanted the television on and me reading or sewing across from him.

"I did. I want her to check out the dress I'm going to wear. Besides, her masseuse is there."

"Her what?"

"The woman who gives Sister massages. She says she can work me in one."

"I'll give you a massage," Fred said. "I don't want you out running the streets at night, Patricia Anne. It's too dangerous."

"Old coot," I said, "I'll be home by the time you finish your paper." I kissed him and went out into our crime-ridden neighborhood, which was filled with joggers and neighbors talking over fences in the late twilight. I forgot to bring a dress to show to Sister, but fortunately, Fred didn't notice.

Mary Alice met me dressed in a terry-cloth robe. "You're late," she said. "Francine had to go."

"That's okay. I can't stay long, anyway. I just needed to run something by you."

"What? Come on back to the kitchen. I haven't had supper yet."

I followed her and sat on the stool by Bubba Cat's heating pad. I laid the manila folder I had brought from home beside him, and he looked up and yawned a greeting. "I think," I said, "that I know who has Meg's computer and briefcase."

"Who?" Sister opened the refrigerator door and looked in. "I guess I need to eat this chicken tetrazzini. They made enough for an army. Does that Pritikin food come already fixed, or is it recipes you fix yourself?"

"Damn it, Mary Alice. Did you hear what I said?"

She looked up, startled. "I asked 'who.' "

"But you aren't paying any attention, and this is important."

"Can I put this casserole in the microwave, or should I stand at attention?"

"Stand at attention, damn it. Cassie Murphy has the briefcase, and I'm sure the computer was in it."

"How do you know?" She slid the casserole into the microwave.

I explained about being in The Family Tree office looking for some information on Heidi Williams, and Cassie walking in. "I handed her the briefcase," I said, "and you could feel the little computer in it. And right on the flap were the initials MMB."

Sister took the casserole from the microwave, came to the counter, and sat on a stool, which groaned in protest. "I have got to lose some weight," she said.

No way would I touch that.

"You're sure it was Meg's?" she asked.

"I'm positive. Now how did Castine Murphy get it and why?"

"Hmm." Sister took a bite of casserole, rolled it around her tongue, and grabbed a glass of water. "Too hot."

"Anyway, I think she's messed up in whatever's going on, and I think"—I pushed the manila envelope of letters toward Sister—"that the answer is in here."

"I thought you said you'd read them."

"I started to, and they kept putting me to sleep. I need you to help me."

"But what are we looking for?"

"I don't know. I stuck a couple of them aside that looked like they might be questionable. They're on top." I got up and got a Coke out of the refrigerator. "But you know what I found on Meg's computer disk?"

Sister shook her head.

"Family trees that have been doctored." I came back to the counter. "You remember Camille Atchison, who called Meg a bitch at the wedding?"

"I found out she's Buddy's daughter," Mary Alice said.

"Your Buddy Johnson's daughter?"

"I'm afraid so."

"You've got to be kidding." But then I remembered that the files were listed as Camille Johnson Atchison.

"No, I wish I were. What about her?"

"Well, apparently she wanted to get into the UDC, so she went to Meg to have her lineage authenticated, or whatever they call it. Anyway, Meg found out that the principal ancestor Camille had in the Civil War was General Sherman."

Sister put her fork down and stared at me. "General Sherman? Buddy's kin to General Sherman?"

"I don't know. There was another lineage chart that had another Sherman on it in place of the general. A farmer in Georgia who fought for the Confederacy."

"I'll bet that's the right one." Sister looked happier.

"That's not the point," I said. "It's the fact that someone has changed the records."

"Can they get away with that?"

"As long as they do away with supporting evidence." I told Sister about my trip to the courthouse and the missing papers for Clovis and Elizabeth Johnson.

"But wait a minute," Mary Alice waved a fork at me. "This could work both ways, couldn't it? Say you were an unethical genealogist and you truly found General Sherman or Adolph Hitler on somebody's family tree. You could have the client pay you to clean it up. But you could also stick General Sherman's name in where it really

216

didn't belong. Blackmail them that way. Wow."

"Sure they could. I think that's what Meg was talking about when she said it was a 'dog-eat-dog' business."

"You think she was involved in changing the charts?"

"I don't know." I sipped my Coke. "I think she thought Bobby Haskins was and was trying to protect him."

"Why?"

"Why was she trying to protect him? He was her first love. You remember Odell Martin in a special way, don't you?"

"Who?"

"Let's read the letters," I said.

An hour later, we had come up with nothing. Mary Alice put her last letter on the stack and said, "I'm about to fall out, I'm so sleepy."

I yawned, too, and stretched. "I didn't tell you about going by Heidi Williams's apartment this afternoon," I said. "You know the one Georgiana Peach keeps asking about? She wasn't there, and she'd left her dog locked up for several days. Bo Mitchell came and let the dog out."

"Hmm," Sister said, "was she all right?"

"The dog? Thirsty and hungry. A neighbor's got her. But I forgot to tell you the most important thing. Bo also told me Georgiana Peach's gun was the one that killed Judge Haskins, that they found it in the swimming pool next door."

"Really? Why would you shoot somebody and throw the gun in the next door pool, where it would be found in a minute?"

"I have no idea," I admitted.

"Unless you wanted it to look like somebody was setting you up. Is Georgiana that devious?"

"I don't know Georgiana well enough to say."

"I'll bet she is. And she's making it so obvious that

nobody will believe she's guilty."

"I don't know," I said. "I just don't know."

"But it's possible."

I shrugged. I didn't want it to be. I liked Georgiana Peach.

"Okay," Sister said, "back to business. Mouse, did you find any letters to the American Genealogical Society?"

I looked up. "No. Why?"

"This last one is to a Mrs. Winona Grafton at the American Genealogical Society, thanking her for being so prompt in her reply and saying she is looking forward to their meeting in Atlanta March twenty-sixth. That's next week."

"Let me see," I said. "When was it dated?"

"The thirteenth. That would have been the day before Meg came up here for the wedding."

I took the letter and read it. "This could be about anything," I said.

"Maybe it wasn't the judge, but the women from The Family Tree who were changing records and stealing stuff from the library."

"It's a possibility," I admitted. "I'm sure that national genealogical organization polices itself. Meg could have been reporting them."

"Another possibility is that Heidi Williams and Meg are both dead."

"I thought of that, too." I shivered.

Mary Alice got up and walked to the window that looked over the city. "They're in the caves under Vulcan, Mouse."

I knew that was ridiculous, but I shivered. I walked to the window, stood beside Sister, and looked at the iron statue on the mountain. He looked larger at night, lighted against the dark. Beyond him, in the east, Venus dipped to the horizon, bright and beautiful.

"Did you know Venus was Vulcan's wife?" I asked.

"I think I missed out on that crucial bit of knowledge."

"Well, she was. And he adored her. All her love affairs maddened him."

"Maddened him, huh?"

"He forged magic weapons against her lovers."

Sister turned and looked at me. "We have got to get you on *Jeopardy*."

"No. But listen, it's an interesting story. He's crippled because his jealous stepmother, Hera, threw him off Mount Olympus because he was Zeus's illegitimate son."

"Are you trying to tell me that dysfunctional families are nothing new?"

I thought about that for a moment. "You know what's wrong with us, Sister?"

"You're going to tell me, aren't you?"

"I don't think our family was dysfunctional enough. Just think about it. Mama and Daddy loved us both and never mistreated us. And we didn't have much money, but we didn't know the difference because nobody else had any, either. We weren't prepared for the harsh, real world."

"You've really had a harsh real world with Fred. 'Yes, Patricia Anne. Whatever you say, darling.' Besides," Sister dodged my elbow, "we were dysfunctional enough for you to steal my Shirley Temple doll."

"I never stole anything but a fork from Loveman's Tea Room, which Mama made me take back and apologize for." I was looking at Sister, but a flash of light at the corner of my eye made me look back at the window. To our right, well down the mountain, a light flashed intermittently.

"What's that light?" I asked. "I didn't think there was

219

anything down there."

"There are some paths. Probably someone with a flashlight looking for a lost dog or something."

"They can't climb up here, can they?"

"Not unless they want to break their necks."

"But it could be done."

"No, Patricia Anne. It could not be done. And even if it could, that's why I have the burglar alarm."

"The alarm somebody knows the combination for, or Cassie Murphy wouldn't have Meg's briefcase."

"Quit worrying. Sit down and I'll get us some ice cream."

An hour later, as I was going to my car, I heard Sister say, "Mouse?" I looked back to see her silhouetted in the door. "You really are adopted, you know."

I hoped she could see my middle finger pointed heavenward.

CHAPTER 17

FRED WAS ASLEEP ON THE SOFA WHEN I GOT home. I covered him with an afghan and went to take a shower, hoping the warm water would relax me. It didn't. I put on my robe and went to the kitchen for some milk. Fred didn't move. I took the milk back into the bedroom and called Georgiana's number.

For once, I didn't get the recording. "Hello," Trinity said.

"It's Patricia Anne. How's Georgiana?"

"They're terribly worried about her. The infection isn't responding to the antibiotics like they had hoped. I saw her at nine o'clock, but I'm not sure she knew who I was. The doctor told me to come on home, they would call me if there were any changes." Trinity's voice broke. "I don't think she's going to make it, Patricia Anne."

"Oh, Trinity, I'm so sorry."

A deep sigh. "So am I."

"Trinity? I need to ask you a question. How much work did Meg do for Georgiana? Do you know?"

"Not exactly. Meg didn't come to Birmingham often, but with all the computers and faxes they've got now, she didn't need to. I think she did a pretty good bit of research for her in South Alabama and Mississippi.

"Before she came to the wedding, did she say anything about doing some work for Georgiana while she was here?"

"She said Georgiana was going to be out of town. I remember that because I thought she might stay with her. Why?"

"Just wondering."

"You can't think Georgiana had anything to do with Meg's death? If you are, you can erase that thought right now. Not Georgiana. I'd trust my life with her."

Perhaps that's what Meg did, I thought. But I had already upset Trinity too much. "Of course I wasn't thinking that," I lied. I told her to call me if Georgiana's condition changed (a nice euphemism for if she died), and had hung up when I remembered I hadn't asked her about Castine Murphy.

Mary Alice and I had come to several conclusions. First and foremost was that Meg had discovered that Georgiana Peach and probably Castine Murphy, too, were doctoring family pedigree charts and either blackmailing clients or charging large amounts to change them. They were also changing, stealing, or tearing out pages from the records at the courthouse that would disprove their claims. Was this some kind of federal offense? Stealing public records?

Probably. And blackmail certainly was. Meg had left the computer disk to show the changes in the charts, as well as the letter about the meeting with the woman from the American Genealogical Society.

"Stool pigeon," Sister said with satisfaction. "She was about to squeal and they doffed her."

"You mean offed her. You've been watching way too much of the old movie channel," I said. But it made sense. "What about Judge Haskins, though?"

"He knew Georgiana and Cassie had killed Meg and was about to squeal and they doffed him. Besides, Georgiana was still enamored of the judge and jealous of Jenny Louise."

I looked at Sister. "They doffed him while he was dinging Jenny Louise? Come on, Sister. Where do you get these words?"

"You doff your hat. Same thing."

"Then Heidi Williams? Where is she, and why does Georgiana want her?"

"Heidi knows the truth about Meg's murder, and she ran because she knew her life was in danger."

"They might doff her."

"Of course."

I had to agree that that made sense. "But what about Meg's voice on the answering machine? The 'Help me'?"

"Wrong number," Sister announced in her don't-bother-me-with-such-trifles voice.

"I'll call Bo Mitchell in the morning and run this by her."

"Don't run it by anyone else," Sister warned.

"I'm not anxious to get doffed," I said. And that was the way we left it. A lot of strings were hanging loose in this version, strings that would trip us up in a minute.

"And how in the hell did we get mixed up in it?" Sister

222

asked.

"Just being polite."

I roused Fred from the sofa and he shuffled down the hall, grumbling that I had awakened him. In two seconds flat, he was snoring again. As for me, I lay beside him all night, drifting in and out of a light sleep. At six o'clock, I was up making coffee, and by seven I was out walking Woofer.

Sometime during the night, a heavy fog had settled over Birmingham. This is a fairly common occurrence here, as the humidity from the Gulf of Mexico rushes up and bumps into the mountains. Woofer especially enjoys our walks on these days, and this morning we took our time. Fog always activates messages left by other animals through the years, and Woofer wants to stop and read them all, as well as answer them.

Fred's car, with its lights on, pulled up beside us. "'Hi, sweetie, you okay today?"

"I'm fine. You?"

"Fine. I'll call you later."

Mitzi Phizer had just come out to get her paper, and waved at Fred. "Such a nice man," she said. I agreed.

I still say that everything that happened that day wouldn't have happened if it hadn't been Bo Mitchell's day off. I called the station as soon as I got home, and was informed that Bo was off, but would I like to talk to someone else? The only person I could think of was the Rambo guy. So I made the decision to wait until the next day, when I could talk to Bo. Then I sat down at the kitchen table with the morning paper. One of the stories on the front page was the questioning of Judge Haskins's wife, Moira, 37, concerning his murder. Moira (what kind of a Southern name was that?) had not been visiting her relatives as was first reported. Also being questioned was

Jennifer Louise Hall, 24, who discovered the body.

I shook my head. How had a lady like Meg Bryan ever gotten mixed up with a womanizer like Bobby Haskins? Surely he had been the same when he was a young man.

The phone rang. Julia Child's voice. "Georgiana is rallying. She told me where to find the information on Heidi Williams. Her mind is very clear this morning."

"That's wonderful news," I said. "Is it down in the office? You'll need to know the alarm combination."

"I have it. I was hoping you might have the time to go get the information, though. I want to stay here at the hospital. They're letting me sit by Georgiana's bed most of the time, and she finds it comforting."

"Sure." Being polite. "Does she have a key hidden somewhere, or do I need to come by and get one?"

"In a fake rock in a flowerpot by the door."

Dear Lord. I wrote down the alarm combination and went to get cleaned up. I wanted to talk to Heidi Williams before I reported her whereabouts to Cassie or Georgiana. I was getting dressed when the phone rang again. This time it was Haley.

"Why aren't you at work?" I asked.

"I am. We're taking a break between cases. We just did a five bypass one. The Roto-Rooter man couldn't have gotten through those arteries."

That put a lovely picture in my mind.

"I just wanted to tell you I want to make Papa's birthday cake. I saw Martha Stewart do one on television last night that was a vegetable garden. All the little vegetables were made out of marzipan. The little cabbages were wonderful."

"You want to decorate a cake with marzipan vegetables?"

"It looked like fun. I'd love to. There were little carrots

224

and eggplants and a picket fence. The dirt was chocolate. Isn't that cute? You haven't ordered one yet, have you?"

"No. I was going by Savage's this morning."

"Well, let me do it. Where can you buy marzipan?"

"Vincent's Market."

"Thanks, Mama. We'll see you tonight."

Marzipan cabbages! She was going to make marzipan cabbages and didn't know where to buy marzipan! Love had done a number on Haley.

I called Sister to see if she wanted to go with me to locate Heidi, but she wasn't home. I left word that I was going to The Family Tree and would call later. I also said I had tried to reach Bo Mitchell and it was her day off. She might want to run our theories by a guy named Rambo.

The little shops with the apartments over them were so attractive that I admired them again as I went by, thinking it would be nice to have a business of some kind. One that was open two days a week. Maybe a consignment shop. Or a very special antique shop where you could hit all the garage and estate sales, grab the best stuff, and resell it. All kinds of collectibles. Mary Alice served on the board of every charitable and art group in Birmingham, but that wasn't my cup of tea. Maybe when Frances Zata retired, she and I could get together on some project.

I pulled around to the back and parked by Georgiana's car. The key was in the fake rock just as Trinity had said. I let myself into the apartment, which was beautiful and light even on a foggy day. It was a happy apartment, I realized, as I admired the colorful ladder-back chairs that Georgiana had painted. I found myself hoping that whatever was going on with The Family Tree, the record changing, the murders, that Georgiana Peach wasn't involved.

The panel for the downstairs alarm was just inside the door of the upstairs apartment. I took the combination from my purse and opened the panel. I certainly didn't want to make a mistake here and set off a burglar alarm.

But the alarm wasn't on. A green light shone brightly at the top of the numbers. Across the light was the word "Clear." No mistaking the message. I opened the door and walked down the steps to The Family Tree office.

If I'd had any sense at all, I'd have turned around and hauled ass when I heard the music, Vivaldi's *Spring*, coming from the office. In fact, I should have hauled ass when I saw the green light on the alarm. Truthfully, I don't know what I was thinking of, maybe that Heidi had shown back up or that Cassie was a nice person after all and I was mistaken. All I know is I heard the light, airy music flowing out into the two-story foyer with its palladian window, and I traipsed right into the office with a smile on my face to see who was there.

"Oh, my God!" Meg Bryan exclaimed from the love seat.

"Shit! I forgot to set the alarm." Cassie was sitting in front of the computer we had looked at the day before.

I looked around calmly. The office was, indeed, lovely. The rug—why hadn't I noticed the rug the day before? It was an emerald green with a border of peach flowers. Were they peonies? Mitzi would know. And Cassie with her hair in a French braid today. It looked terrific, elegant, as did her yellow linen jacket with the sleeves pushed up. And Meg, frail little Jessica Tandy Meg, the Southern lady, seated at the coffee table, her hands, veined and mottled, fluttering toward her throat.

And then I turned to Meg and said one of the stupidest things I've ever said. "You're not dead, are you?"

Her fingers caressed the sides of her throat. "Of course I

am. My ashes are in Fairhope right now, thanks to my dear sister."

I sank down in a wicker rocker, my palms pressed to my chest, where my heart was pounding. Calm, Patricia Anne. Stay calm. "Trinity is very upset because she thinks you're dead," I managed to say in a voice that didn't sound like mine.

"You hear that, Cassie?" Meg asked.

Cassie came over and sat in the other wicker chair. "I hear it. Sad, isn't it?"

Meg turned to me. "Did Trinity tell you she slept with both my husbands?"

"Of course not," I lied. "All I know is she fainted when Judge Haskins brought us your ashes."

"Dear Trinity. I'll bet she shopped for antiques on the way home so she could write the trip off."

I didn't say anything and Meg laughed. "She did, didn't she? What did I tell you, Cassie? I knew she would."

Cassie smiled, a faint smile. "Meg," she gestured toward me, "we have a problem here."

Meg smiled back. "We certainly do."

"I'm not a problem for you," I said, standing up on shaky legs. "Y'all just go on with what you're doing. I need to go run some errands."

"Sit down," Meg ordered. Her face no longer reminded me of Jessica Tandy. Maybe a warden from a women's prison movie. I sat.

"What's going on?" I asked. "I don't know what's going on here."

Meg and Cassie both laughed, as if I had told a wonderful joke.

"Spring cleaning," Cassie said. For the first time, I noticed three cardboard boxes with "Twelve Litres, Canadian Mist" printed on them.

Meg held up a delicate cup. "I'm taking a coffee break, though. Would you like some, Patricia Anne?"

I shook my head no. It had occurred to me that I needed to get out of here, and fast. I looked toward the front door. Maybe it was unlocked? I could kick the coffee table over and run like hell, hoping the overturned table would get in their way.

"Cassie," Meg asked, "do you know what Patricia Anne is thinking?"

"Of course." Cassie turned toward me. "The front door's locked, Mrs. Hollowell. Forget it."

The Vivaldi came to an end, and there was a moment's silence before Beethoven's Sixth began.

"Nice tape," Meg said, tilting her head slightly toward the music.

"Victoria's Secret," Cassie explained. "Buy twenty dollars' worth and you can get the tape for, I think, three dollars. Something like that. It's a good deal."

"Hmm." Meg sipped her coffee while I marveled that such glorious music could be so threatening.

"Georgiana said Judge Haskins killed you," I said.

"She meant it metaphorically. And truthfully."

"Would y'all like to tell me what's going on?" I asked.

"Not especially, but I guess we'll have to, don't you think, Cassie?"

"Why?" Cassie asked.

"It would be polite, Cassie. Remember the definition of good manners is not making someone uncomfortable, and I get the impression that Patricia Anne is very uncomfortable right now."

"I have to go to the bathroom," I said.

"Right through that door," Meg smiled. "Leave your purse here."

There were no windows in the bathroom, as Meg well

228

knew. There was a framed poster of Monet's Garden above the toilet, and a mirror above the sink. Could I break one and come charging out with a piece of glass? Take off my blouse, wrap it around my hand and hit the mirror hard enough to break it? Break every bone in my hand?

"Don't try anything, Patricia Anne," Meg called through the door. "I have a tiny pistol in my pocket. Loaded, I assure you, and very lethal. I can assure you of that, too."

My fear was becoming tempered with anger. I opened the door and said, "I want to know what the hell's going on. You have no right to treat me this way."

"You are so right, dear. It's abominable. And you and your sister were so nice to me at the wedding." Meg sat back down on the love seat and motioned for me to sit in the wicker rocker again. Cassie was kneeling at a bottom file, riffling through manila folders. Occasionally she would take one out and put it into a Canadian Mist box. Anyone looking in, hearing the music, would have thought it a peaceful scene, two old ladies talking while a younger one leisurely went about her work.

"It's Heidi Williams who's dead, isn't it?"

Cassie looked up from the floor. "Splat."

"Don't be crude, Cassie." Meg pleated the full skirt of her blue shirtwaist dress as if she were folding a paper fan. "Yes, I understand Heidi is going to be given a fond farewell party at the Grand Hotel next week. I'm sure it will be nice."

"But why?"

Meg leaned forward. "Because I needed to be dead. Heidi was my age, my size—"

"Wearing your clothes," Cassie added.

"Carrying my purse." Meg turned toward Cassie. "You

know, I still wonder if a woman would jump carrying her purse. I think we should have left it in the restroom."

"Doesn't matter," Cassie said.

"I guess not. It was a good Aigner purse, though. I just wasn't thinking."

"Wait a minute," I said, "let me get this straight. You made Heidi Williams put on your clothes and then you pushed her out the window?"

"Well, just my jacket. Heidi always wore flowered dresses like the one I had on that day. They were enough alike."

I thought of the Laura Ashley apartment, the little dog.

"Heidi wasn't blessed in the brain department," Meg said, "and I gave her a song and dance about trying on my jacket because I was going to order her one since she had admired it so. I needed to see if the size was okay."

"She believed that?" I closed my eyes, willing the tears not to come.

"Of course. It was to be a gift for all her help."

"Heidi had turkey brains," Cassie said.

Meg giggled. "Yes, she did, didn't she?"

I remembered that day vividly, the anguish on the judge's face as he ran toward Sister and me. I turned to Meg. "The judge really thought it was you, didn't he?"

"We figured he wouldn't look too closely. Bobby was as easy to read as a book."

"That's the truth," Cassie agreed.

"The extent of his grief was a pleasant surprise, though. I thought that was sort of sweet, didn't you, Cassie?"

"I guess so."

My mind was not working right. The shock of walking right into Meg and having her calmly admit to killing Heidi Williams had knocked me for a loop. "Calm down, Patricia Anne," I kept saying to myself over the other

230

message my brain was sending out, "You're in a hell of a situation, Patricia Anne."

"How's it going, Cassie?" Meg asked.

"I'm about through."

"Why did you need to be dead?" I asked Meg.

"So I could kill Bobby, and Georgiana would spend the rest of her life in prison for it."

"Georgiana?"

"Let me tell you a story, Patricia Anne, quite an old story, actually, a simple story. One night, just a few months after we were married, Bobby and I, probably in June or July, I remember it was hot, I woke up, and Bobby wasn't beside me." Meg's voice took on a dreamy tone. "I got up and looked through the house and everything was quiet. I didn't turn on the lights because it was a full moon, a blue moon. I remember that because later I told myself that such a thing would happen only once in a blue moon. Did I tell you that, Cassie?"

"No."

"So I walked outside, down the pier. I could hear the cicadas. It was so light, fish scales were shining along the planks, and I started to call, 'Bobby.' And then I saw them at the edge of the water, Bobby and my friend, Georgiana, my dear friend and my husband making love."

"Just like Deborah Kerr and Burt Lancaster in *From Here to Eternity*," Cassie added.

Meg scowled. "Shut up, Cassie."

"But that was, what?" I asked. "Forty years ago? You waited forty years to get even with them?"

"Yes. But all those forty years they knew the reckoning was going to happen some day. It was a dark undercurrent, waiting."

I figured it wasn't the time to point out that Judge Haskins and Georgiana Peach had led busy, happy lives

231

for the last forty years. I obviously wasn't dealing with a rational woman here. I looked over at Cassie, who was propped back on her heels.

"Don't look at me," she said. "He screwed me, too. Literally and figuratively."

"I thought he became your guardian after your parents died."

"He did," Meg interceded, "and, Cassie, don't say it was all bad. You know better than that."

I suddenly felt dizzy. I put my head down against my knees. "You mean," my voice was muffled against my pants legs, "that all that's happened has been about getting even with a man, who looked like a weasel?"

"Of course not," Meg said, "but it sure made it easier. You see, Bobby was a lot of things, but stupid wasn't one of them. He'd figured out who was tampering the records. And we made quite a bit of money while we were setting Georgiana up, didn't we, Cassie? Quite a bit. Heidi Williams is going to be able to live very comfortably somewhere. Maybe Key West. Or Toronto? They say the theater there is spectacular."

"What about Cassie?" I asked.

"Oh, she'll stay here if she likes. Georgiana's responsible for everything, the murders and all the changes that have been made in the lineage charts. And for stealing and destroying records. That's what Cassie's making sure of now. Yesterday when we thought Georgiana was going to die, we didn't think we would have to be so careful." Meg grinned. "She's had that ulcer for forty years. My 'help me' message did a number on it, didn't it?"

"You just walked in and shot him?" I mumbled against my legs.

The dreamy voice again. "I almost didn't. He thought I was a woman named, I understand, Jenny Louise. He came into the living room wearing a robe, and he smiled when he saw me. I said, 'Where have you been, Bobby?' and he said, 'A long way, Meg.' And I asked him to take off his robe."

"Why?" Cassie asked. "There couldn't have been any surprises."

"But there were. Bobby wasn't a big man, but he had a strong body, a barrel chest, and short legs. Good Irish stock. And the man standing before me looked as if his bones were trying to break through his skin."

"A Rose for Emily," Cassie said.

"Shut up," I told Cassie.

Meg smiled at me. "He was beautiful," she said. "Old and beautiful. I could see the veins crisscrossing on his chest." She paused as if remembering details of his body, and then in a moment, continued. "He said, 'Meg, you're going to kill me, aren't you?' and I said, 'I think so, Bobby.' So he said, 'Okay,' and I shot him in the head." Another pause. "I thought I would feel better."

"I'm sorry," I said. I really was. I was sorry for this woman, for the many threads of her life that had brought her to this violence.

"Thank-you." Meg drank the last of her coffee and put the cup down.

And now the big question. What were they going to do about me? I might be sorry for Meg, but she certainly wasn't rational. Throw Castine Murphy in for good measure and the answer was clear.

Meg stood up. "Cassie, you through? Why don't you put those boxes in the car and be thinking about what we can do with Patricia Anne. I swear I hate this."

"So do I," I said into my knees. I tried to think. Trinity knew I was here at the office, but she would be at the hospital all day. No one else knew I was here. Yes, they

233

did. I had left word on Sister's phone. But she wouldn't be looking for me. If anyone called, they would just assume I was out for a while and leave a message. Even Sister. Even Fred. Fred. A few tears slid down onto my pants legs. At my funeral, he would tell the kids, "I told her to stay out of that mess." He tombstone. He would certainly marry one of the girls from Atlanta within six months. "Oh, Fred," I whispered, sniffling.might even have those words put on my

"Here. Use a Kleenex." Meg pressed one into my hand. I heard the front door open and close.

"Bobby did look a little like a weasel, didn't he?" Meg said. I watched her shoes as she went around the coffee table and sat down again. "Amazing how the women adored him."

I rose up and wiped my face with the Kleenex. "There's no accounting."

"True." Meg leaned forward. "You know, Patricia Anne, I really hate to shoot you. It makes an awful mess. I was startled when I shot Bobby."

I thought of Sister's story of the blood blooming like anemones on the white canvas Keds. "I hate the idea, too."

"We'll see if Cassie can come up with something. She said something about giving Georgiana snake venom when she found out she had an ulcer. I thought that was a clever idea. It'll get into your blood stream that way. But I decided I'd rather have Georgiana found guilty. Get what she deserves."

"That Cassie is a clever girl," I said.

"Oh, good. Sarcasm. You're feeling better, aren't you?"

I wouldn't say that, I thought.

Cassie took the last box out. When she came back in, Meg said she had to go to the "little girls' room," and then we would talk.

"She's crazy, you know," I whispered to Cassie as soon

234

as the door closed.

"Aren't we all."

"Possibly. But are you so crazy you think she's going to let you stay here while she takes off as Heidi Williams?"

"Shut up, Mrs. Hollowell."

"This whole thing is so Gothic. Imagine spending a lifetime waiting to get even with some man who hurt you."

"At least she's not sleeping with his dead body."

"What?"

"Like in that Faulkner story you had us read where there was long gray hair on the pillow by the skeleton. I hated that story. This whole thing keeps reminding me of it somehow."

" 'A Rose for Emily'? That's why you said it awhile ago?"

"Yuck."

"Cassie?" I was going to try to reason with her, but just then we heard the toilet flush, and in a moment, Meg bounced out of the bathroom. "Well, girls," she said, looking bright and cheerful. "What are we going to do about our little problem?"

CHAPTER 18

MY SUGGESTION WAS THAT THEY LET ME GO, that they had my scout's honor, so help me God, that I would not tell anyone what they had done or were about to do in the future, that it was none of my business who they wanted to throw out of windows or shoot in the head or blackmail or which family records they wanted to change or steal and, as far as I was concerned, they could just take off for wherever they wanted to go or even stay in

235

Birmingham, I would stay out of their way, cross my heart and hope to die.

Meg smiled benignly at me. "You do tend to babble, don't you?"

"She always did, even in class," Cassie said, a remark that hurt.

"Which isn't solving our problem," Meg turned to me. "You know, Patricia Anne, I hate to kill you. I've got nothing against you. In fact, I like you."

"Thanks," I said. God! Nutty as a fruitcake. I looked at Cassie, but she was busy studying her nails. Just as crazy, I decided. There wouldn't be any help there.

"Take her with you," Cassie said. "Company on your trip."

"No, I couldn't tolerate that babbling as far as the Mississippi state line. I'd lose my mind."

"Then, what's your choice?" Cassie asked.

Meg Bryan shook her head pityingly. "Patricia Anne, I'm real sorry about this." She reached into the pocket of her skirt, and I was looking at the tiny pistol. I wasn't sure, but I figured tiny pistols were as deadly as big ones. The hole through Judge Haskins's head was proof of that.

"Let's go," she said. "Cassie, you ready?"

"Where are you going to take her?"

"Doesn't your house have a basement?"

"Oh, no you don't. I'm not getting stuck with a body."

The word "body" galvanized me. I grabbed the lamp from the table by the love seat and swung it at Meg's hand, knocking the pistol loose. It skidded across the floor and Cassie and I both lunged for it. She won, hopping up with the pistol in her hand while I lay there wondering if I had broken my hip. My arm. My leg.

"Get up," she commanded.

"In a minute," I said. Tears of frustration, pain, and

236

fear burned my eyes.

"Give me the gun, Cassie," Meg said. "Patricia Anne, I can't believe you did that."

"No," Cassie's voice was firm. "I think I'd better keep it. Mrs. Hollowell's right. There's no way you're going to let me out of this alive."

"Don't be stupid, Cassie." Meg started toward her and I moved my leg, tripping her. For some reason, it had occurred to me that I had a better chance with Cassie than with Meg. After all, she had been naïve enough to be duped by Meg.

Meg's head hit the counter with a crack that didn't sound good. I sat up and looked at her prone figure.

"Is she dead?"

A moan answered me.

"Oh, God," Cassie said. The hand holding the pistol was shaking. "Oh, God, what am I going to do with the two of you?"

Meg's moan was the only answer.

"I can't leave you here. Somebody will be here in a little while."

"Meg killed the judge all by herself, didn't she?" I asked.

"Of course."

"And she pushed Heidi Williams out of the window by herself?"

A slight pause. "Yes."

"Then why don't you call the police and turn her in?"

Cassie wheeled on me. "You bitch. You think I'm that stupid? They might not get me for murder, but they sure as hell would get me for blackmail and record-tampering. Get up!" I struggled to my feet. Pain shot up my right arm in such an intense arc, I thought I would faint. "Now get her up."

"I think my arm's broken."

"Get her up anyway."

I struggled to get the half-conscious. Meg propped into a sitting position against the counter. "She can't walk," I said. "She could have a fractured skull."

"Then you and I'll drag her out. People will just think she's had one-day surgery since we're so close to the medical center. If they pay any attention."

"Where are you taking us?"

"I don't know. I've got to have time to think."

It was at that point that I got the Brer Rabbit idea. The caves under Vulcan. Bo Mitchell had said hiding someone there would be like putting them on Highway 280.

"Just don't put us in the caves under Vulcan," I pleaded. "Please, for God's sake, I don't think I could take it. The snakes, the dark."

"I think my basement will do for the time being," Cassie said. "Now, get on Meg's right side and help me pull her up. Don't think this gun isn't still on you, though."

Meg was a dead weight, and, frail as she might appear, that dead weight was a considerable amount.

"I can't do it," I said.

Cassie aimed the gun at my head. "Put your shoulder under her arm." It worked. I pulled Meg's right arm around my shoulder and held on with my left. My own right arm felt paralyzed.

"Now, walk."

We started toward the door, dragging Meg between us. If anyone coming down the street thought this woman had just had one-day surgery, it would scare them away from the procedure for life.

The trip across the room seemed to take an hour, an hour of agonizing pain, nausea, and the fear that I was going to faint before we could get to the door. I had no doubt that my keeling over and dropping Meg would make up Cassie's mind and she would kill us both. So I concentrated on the brass doorknob, willing each step toward it.

And then we were there. Cassie reached over and opened the door and there stood Sister, holding a pot of pink gloxinias.

"Hi!" she said cheerfully. "I got these for Georgiana, but—" I saw the expression change on her face. "What's going on?"

I'm not exactly sure what happened in the next few minutes, but this is the way Sister related the series of events. I fainted and fell to the left, and Meg fell on me. Cassie, caught off balance, tried to jump over both of us and get by Sister, who was filling the doorway. Sister reached out and tripped her and Cassie sailed over the two steps to the sidewalk, where she landed on her hands and knees. The gun went sailing through the air, and Sister had the presence of mind to jump down the steps and sit on Cassie, thumping her soundly on the head with the pot of gloxinias. There was no way anybody would think this strange sight was one-day surgery, so the 911 switchboard was lit up by passing motorists reporting women fighting or up to some kind of no good.

By the time the police arrived, I had regained consciousness but still had Meg on top of me. Cassie still had Sister on top of her, a position Sister refused to abdicate until two policemen were holding Cassie. This took some doing, since the reason for the altercation wasn't clear, and the policemen had to remove Meg from me so I could explain.

"It was so exciting," Sister explained that night at Henry and Debbie's. "There were ambulances and police cars and traffic stopped like you wouldn't believe."

I was full of pain pills with my arm in a cast. I looked lovingly at everyone and smiled. Philip and Haley. How sweet. I forgive you, Philip, for being twenty years too old. Sister, Henry, Debbie, Fred. My beloved Fred.

"Your eyes are crossed, honey," he said.

"What do you think they'll do to Cassie?" Philip asked Debbie.

"Throw the book at her. Blackmail, changing and stealing federal records, accessory to murder, if not murder. I don't think we'll be seeing much of Miss Murphy for a while."

"How about Meg?" Sister asked.

"They'll plead insanity. Rightfully so." Debbie reached over and took Henry's hand. "I don't think they can make it stand, though. I think she'll be found competent to stand trial."

Haley spoke up, "They'll have to monitor her for a few days in the hospital. Apparently, she took quite a blow to her head. She's got a hairline fracture, but the main thing is the brain swelling." She smiled at her Aunt Sister. "Cassie's head must be harder."

Henry turned to Debbie. "Can you believe that? You've been married to me for less than a week, and a homicidal maniac has already fallen out of my family tree."

Debbie leaned over and kissed him. "Wait until you see what shows up on mine."

"We're all nice people," I said. "There's nobody in our family who's not nice. Fred's nice, Haley's nice, Sister's nice, Woofer—"

Fred patted my cast. "We're all very nice, honey."

"You know, I love Trinity," Haley said. "She wasn't involved, was she?"

"Not at all. Nor Georgiana Peach, either," Mary Alice

240

explained.

I wanted to tell the whole story, but my tongue wasn't working quite right. "Meg," I said carefully, "was sitting on Georgiana because of Burt Lancaster."

Everyone smiled, so I knew I had gotten my point across. "Was that why she called with the 'help me' message?" Haley asked.

"Scare her ulcer," I said thickly.

"Incidentally," Sister turned to me, "Georgiana's out of intensive care. Trinity called."

I giggled. "How many Moon Pies did George Peach eat if George Peach did eat pie?" That, they tell me, was the last thing I said before I put my head on Fred's lap and went to sleep

Dear Reader:

I hope you enjoyed reading this Large Print mystery. If you are interested in reading other Beeler Large Print Mystery titles or any other Beeler Large Print titles, ask your librarian or write to me at

Thomas T. Beeler, *Publisher*
Post Office Box 659
Hampton Falls, New Hampshire 03844

You can also call me at 1-800-251-8726 and I will send you my latest catalogue.

Audrey Lesko chooses the titles I publish in Large Print. Our aim is to provide good books by outstanding authors—books we both enjoyed reading and liked well enough to want to share. We warmly welcome any suggestions for new titles and authors.

Sincerely,